Amos Pinkn...
viselike grip...

"Enough of this nonsense," he snarled. "That farmer wronged me, cowboy, and he was made to pay the price.

"But his offense, grievous as it was, was nothing compared to what you have done. You have laughed at me and made mock of me behind my back and perhaps put my plans in some jeopardy."

"Major, I—"

"Listen to me. Your end, when it comes—and it will come soon—will take much longer than the farmer's and be even more terrible. You will die a thousand times in shrieking agony before merciful death at last takes you.

"Now go, cowboy. And think on this: We will meet again, you and I, by and by.

"And Mister Gentle, here, will keep his blade honed sharp until we do."

Me and
Johnny Blue

❯═❯═◦═❮═❮

JOSEPH A. WEST

A SIGNET BOOK

SIGNET
Published by New American Library, a division of
Penguin Putnam Inc., 375 Hudson Street,
New York, New York 10014, U.S.A.
Penguin Books Ltd, 27 Wrights Lane,
London W8 5TZ, England
Penguin Books Australia Ltd,
Ringwood, Victoria, Australia
Penguin Books Canada Ltd, 10 Alcorn Avenue,
Toronto, Ontario, Canada M4V 3B2
Penguin Books (N.Z.) Ltd, 182–190 Wairau Road,
Auckland 10, New Zealand

Penguin Books Ltd, Registered Offices:
Harmondsworth, Middlesex, England

First published by Signet, an imprint of New American Library,
a division of Penguin Putnam Inc.

First Printing, May 2000
10 9 8 7 6 5 4 3 2 1

PUBLISHER'S NOTE
This is a work of fiction. Names, characters, places and incidents are either
the product of the author's imagination or are used fictitiously, and any
resemblance to actual persons, living or dead, business establishments,
events, or locales is entirely coincidental.

ONE

Well boys, you've asked me to write down the story of me and Johnny Blue Dupree and how we bested the vicious outlaw Amos Pinkney and his woman Cottontail, and in so doing saved our great Republic for democracy, freedom and decency. Fact is, me and Johnny Blue was just a couple of poor, out-of-work cowboys, but we changed the course of history and saved our blessed nation from the horrors of a second Civil War.

An' I hear tell there's them as says they want to know more about the Boston Mauler and the five hunnerd dollars me and Johnny Blue won from him and then lost and then won again, though that's not exactly how it happened. And you want to hear the story of how Johnny Blue and me left Montana for-ever to find that reckless rider's long-lost little sister, who was sold into slavery when she were just a younker.

Boys, it's a story that will take a heap of telling. But I got a stub of pencil here and a stack of brown wrapping paper from Jack Ryan's hardware store, and I'll write it down plain and simple just the way I recollect it.

Of course, time changes things for a man. It softens the edges of places once familiar and deepens the shadows, so that memory can lose its way and stumble this way and that, like a rider in a mist. And time has a way of blurring faces: some loved, some hated, some feared, so they come to mind like faded tintypes hanging on memory's wall.

But the winter of '86 and '87, and what happened afterward, is burned deep into my mind like a brand on the rump of a yearling steer.

Some things a man never forgets.

Some things a man wishes he could forget.

Me, I was 23 years old in the fall of 1887, when ol' Granville Stuart of the DHS ranch up in the Judith Basin country of the Montana Territory paid off me and Johnny Blue Dupree. It was a bad time to be unemployed, with winter coming on hard and not another cowboying job in sight.

But I didn't blame Granville Stuart none. Like many an owner, he was now flat broke and getting out of the ranching business forever.

The great blizzard that had blown in October of '86 and lasted through till the end of February the next year had all but destroyed the cattle business in the territory.

The DHS herds, which had once been counted in the thousands, were long gone, piled up dead by the tens of hundreds in the draws and canyons like cordwood, carrion for the wolves and the vultures.

Me and Johnny Blue didn't realize it then, but ranches would never again operate on the same scale. The days of the free-roaming cowboy and the great cattle baron were gone forever. The time of fences was at hand. An' we all know now what that meant for the poor cowboy.

It was a death.

It was the death of how he'd lived for thousands of years since man first herded cows. It was the death of the freedom the cowboy had known, and the death of everything he'd once stood for, like decency, honor and stalwart courage.

After the winter of '86, the future belonged to the fence and the farmer.

Boys, the strange thing was, the summer before had been hot and dry.

Johnny Blue said the chickens around the cook house were plucking themselves to stay cool, and the days were so scorching, us punchers rode the range dressed in just our drawers, hats and boots.

Hell, boys, I recollect one time I seen a big ol' diamondback rattler crawl into my campfire, looking for shade under the coffeepot.

But as summer turned to early fall, there was some strange omens in the air. Me and Johnny Blue were watering a herd near the west bank of the Judith when Johnny Blue pointed up at the sky.

"Geese," Johnny Blue said.

I followed his pointing finger and saw three Vs of geese heading south. They were high up, so they obviously wasn't in a mind to drop by anywhere close.

"They're early," Johnny Blue said. "Way too early."

"By at least four, five weeks," I said.

"I seen the beaver last week, up higher on the Judith, and they're cutting twice as much willow for winter than they done last year," Johnny Blue said, studying my face closely, trying to see if I was worried.

"Seen the muskrats too, an' their fur is thicker'n the cape on an old bull buffalo."

"What you tryin' to tell me, Johnny Blue?" I asked.

"I'm telling you we're in for one hell of a winter."

"Nah, it's been too hot. Hot summer, mild winter. That's how it always goes in the territory."

"Could be," Johnny Blue allowed. "Only you ain't any smarter than them beaver."

As things turned out, he was right.

The temperature dove all the way down to zero and below during the October roundup, with men and cattle scattered all over the basin. Me and Johnny Blue, we dug out our mackinaws and sheepskin gloves, and we was still like to die from cold.

"I was talking to a hand from the OH outfit who chews," Johnny Blue said one night in the bunkhouse. "An' all the time we talked, he jest stood there spittin' brown ice cubes."

The snows started in late November and the northern ranges became hell without the heat. Then, on January 9, 1887, things got a lot worse.

It snowed steadily for 16 hours that day, and the thermometer on the bunkhouse wall dropped to 22 degrees below zero.

Me and Johnny Blue were out every day and most of the night trying to look after the cattle as best we could.

We worked from dark to dark. Up before dawn, collapsing exhausted into bed long after nightfall.

And all the time we were frozen stiff, the ice turning our mustaches gray so we looked like tired old men. Our ponies were suffering too, their ribs showing like slat fences, and their backs covered with running saddle sores.

Every one of the DHS hands, even the cook, was out with the cattle, keeping them back from the rivers and out of air holes and open channels in the ice.

We roped and pulled cows out of drifts, then drove them into what little shelter we could find in the cut banks and ravines.

We knew then, all of us, that we had a disaster on our hands.

Then, on the night of January 15, the mercury in the thermometer sank to 46 below, and there was 16 inches of snow on the level.

Drifts as high as a tall man on a horse were filling the cut banks and gulches. No sooner had one blizzard spent itself than it was followed by another.

And through it all, the cows drifted like white ghosts, steam rising from their nostrils, icicles hanging from their ears and eyes and muzzles.

A thick sheet of ice covered the snow like a boilerplate and stopped the cattle from getting to the grass locked below.

Without food and shelter, the cows were now dying by the thousands.

Me and Johnny Blue were out one day in late January when another killer storm blew in with winds that reached 60 miles an hour.

We'd just pulled a yearling steer out of a snow drift when the storm hit, and Johnny Blue yelled above the howling wind to head for a nearby shallow ravine overhung by a number of huge fallen pines.

"I seen that ravine on the way in," Johnny Blue

called. "The fallen trees have kept most of the snow away and there's shelter from the wind."

I yanked my pony's head around and kicked him forward, but he was floundering in the drift.

"Get off and lead him in!" Johnny Blue yelled.

I jumped off the little paint, sinking in snow to my thighs, and tried to pull him toward the ravine. But he was spooked by the wind and the snow, and he yanked the reins out of my hands, his rump skidding under him into the drift.

I fell into the drift hard, and somehow got a bunch of icy snow in both eyes and I could only open them a crack. Now I was half blind as well as being half dead from the cold.

"Let's go!" Johnny Blue hollered. "Let's go!"

I could see well enough to catch glimpses of him through the driving curtain of the blizzard, leading his own pony toward the ravine.

Then I lost him.

It didn't take me long to realize that I could die out there. The snow was falling thicker now, and I couldn't see more than a couple of feet in front of me. The wind was howling like a Comanche on the war path, driving the snow against my face in a hundred icy, stinging darts.

"Johnny Blue!" I yelled. But the wind viciously ripped the words from my lips and tossed them into the storm, unheard.

The paint was floundering through the drift, her rump toward me, and I knew she was my only chance at survival.

I stumbled after her and managed to grab the trailing reins. I pulled on the pony's head with all my strength and the little paint's rump kicked free of the snow. But I didn't know where the ravine was. I could only see my pony's head and nothing else beyond her on all sides.

I bent my head and stumbled toward where I hoped the ravine lay. I was getting almighty tired and the buckskin was pulling my arms out of their sockets as she tried to shy away from me.

My burning eyes could see only a solid wall of white and I felt that spike of fear a man gets when he knows he's in mortal danger.

I tried calling out for Johnny Blue again. But the wind stifled my voice and mocked my fear.

Boys, I was in a bad way right about then, and I thought about saying a last prayer, to ask forgiveness for all the whoring and drinking and cussin' I'd done in my life.

That's when I felt myself grabbed by the collar of my mackinaw and dragged backward.

"Hold on to your horse, you derned fool, you're headin' the wrong way!" a voice roared in my ear.

It was Johnny Blue.

He half-carried, half-drug me through the blizzard to the ravine, which had only been about fifty feet away, and soon both me and my pony were in its welcome shelter, out of the driving wind and snow.

After a few minutes I was able to open my eyes again, and I saw Johnny Blue's concerned face close to mine.

"You okay?" he asked.

I nodded.

"You almost got yourself killed out there," Johnny

Blue said. "I swear, sometimes you don't have a brain in your head."

"I couldn't leave the pony," I said.

"The pony would have found her own way in, if'n you'd let her," Johnny Blue said. "You know that paint's a heap smarter than you. I've told you that often enough."

Now, boys, Johnny Blue had just saved my life, but I wasn't about to thank him for it. You know what he's like—he'd have cashed in on that right quick an' then charged me interest for the rest of my life.

That Johnny Blue Dupree, he was nobody's fool.

He'd been born into slavery in Davidson County, Tennessee, and it was ol' Nat Love, who'd also been raised down there in a slave cabin, who taught him to rope, ride, shoot, and all the other many and varied skills of the cowboy's trade. I met them both when we were all working for the Pete Gallinge Company along the Gila River country of southern Arizona.

It didn't take me long to realize that Johnny Blue was a top hand. One time I seen him rope, throw, tie, bridle, saddle, mount, and ride an untamed bronco in nine minutes flat.

There's never been a cowboy, then or now, who's ever done it faster.

Johnny Blue wasn't much with the Colt's revolver, but I seen him kill a running mule deer at two hundred yards with his Henry rifle. Now it seems to me if a man can do that, he can hit pretty much anything he shoots at.

Me and Johnny Blue hit it off right from the start.

Maybe that's because we were both raised with no momma or daddy and had learned cowboying on the trail when we were younkers. There was, and I guess still is, a kind of bond between us that was hard to explain, though Nat Love saw it.

"You're the black and white," he said, "the two opposite sides of the same coin. You're both wild sons of the plains, and your home is in the saddle and your couch is Mother Earth, with the sky for a covering."

He drew his bowie knife from his belt and said, "I've got to be moving on, got things to do, places to see. But I want you two to stay together and you"—he pointed the knife at my chest—"you will carry on with Johnny Blue the lessons I've begun."

Don't ask me why, boys, but I felt like that was a real solemn moment. It was like standing at the graveside of some poor cowboy who'd done broke his neck, listening to the foreman say the words from the Book.

Ol' Nat took the point of his knife and pricked my forearm till the blood came, and then he did the same with Johnny Blue. Then he pressed our arms together.

"Blood brothers," he announced. "The Cheyenne taught me that. You are kin under the skin. Black and white. Two sides of the same coin."

Nat rode out the next day. And me and Johnny Blue, well, we've been brothers ever since.

But I still wasn't about to thank him for saving my life.

I could feel the temperature dropping fast in the ravine, and as my eyes cleared I walked back into the gloom to see how far it cut into the hillside, thinking it might be warmer there.

Boys, you can imagine my surprise when I saw another hand there, sitting on his gray horse, calm as you please, jest watching us and grinning like a persimmon-eating possum.

"Hell, that's Shorty Stevens," Johnny Blue said over my shoulder as he came up behind me. "I'd know that grin of his anywheres."

Shorty was one of Jesse Phelps's hands from his OH Ranch near Utica, and I recollect thinking that ol' Shorty was way off his range. But he was a good companion when he was sober and a steady hand, and I greeted him cheerfully enough.

But he didn't answer me none, just sat there in his saddle, grinning.

"Well, Shorty," I said, and I guess I felt kinda irritated, what with the storm and nearly getting killed an' all, "you ain't being too neighborly."

But Johnny Blue hushed me up right quick.

Half blinded as I was, I walked up closer to Shorty and he didn't move a muscle or even look in my direction.

Then I saw why.

Ol' Shorty's pony wasn't gray. It was a sorrel under a coat of ice. And Shorty's mackinaw and hat and his face were covered with ice.

He'd froze to death, him and his pony together.

Boys, that's no sight for any Christian man to see.

I looked at Johnny Blue and his face was stunned, like he couldn't believe what his eyes was telling him. Johnny Blue's hat was tied to his head with a woolen scarf that knotted under his chin. But he took off the scarf and then the hat and bowed his head.

Me, I did the same thing.

Then me and Johnny Blue said a prayer for Shorty Stevens, a man we hardly knew. But he was a poor cowhand, just like us, though now the worst of his trail was behind him and he was riding a range on a sky blue pony where there is no sickness or sorrow.

Amen.

A few days later, after the storm had blown itself out, me and Johnny Blue took Shorty's body back to the OH, where the folks there thanked us most kindly. Of course, there was no way of burying Shorty until the spring thaw softened the earth, so we sewed him in a blanket and laid him in the ice house till then.

We was in the bunkhouse later, drinking coffee spiked with good, three-dollar-a-gallon whiskey, watching Jesse Phelps struggle with a letter he was writing to his friend Louie Kaufman in Helena.

"I got to tell him how bad things is up here," Phelps said. "He's got a right to know. But I jest can't get the words right."

"Mister Phelps, there just ain't enough words to tell it," Johnny Blue said. "And there's the truth."

Well, I couldn't argue with that.

Boys, do you recollect Kid Russell, the artist feller? Charlie Russell warn't much of a hand in them days, but he'd always buy you a drink when you was broke, and he could draw and paint a picture like the dern thing was real.

One time he gave me a little carved buffalo he whittled one evening while we was both at the big Utica roundup. I kept that little buffalo for years, till an Apache took it from me. But that's another story.

Well, I quit watching Jesse Phelps trying to write his letter and walked over to where Charlie was sitting, and looked over his shoulder.

He had this little flat box of paints and he was

rapidly making a picture of a starving cow circled in the snow by wolves.

"That's right on, Kid," I said. "We seen that happen more than once, me and Johnny Blue over there."

Charlie looked up at me, but he didn't say nothing. He jest shook his head, kinda sad like, and kept on painting.

Then, when the picture was finished to his satisfaction, he took a brush, dipped it in paint and lettered these words:

Waiting for a Chinook

Then he walked over and gave the picture to Jesse Phelps.

"Put that in your letter," the Kid said.

Jesse looked at the picture for a long time. Then he put his hand up to his eye and it looked to me like he was brushing away a tear.

"Kaufman don't need no letter now, Kid," he said. "Your picture is gonna tell him all he needs to know."

Later I was told that when Louie Kaufman got the picture and saw that the dying cow was wearing his own Bar-R brand he knew how things was on the range. He showed that picture to his fellow ranchers and anybody else who cared to look at it.

Then he got drunk.

Well, we was all waiting for a chinook, and it finally blew in on February 27, 1887.

Me and Johnny Blue were out in the melting snows every day. We often rode for miles without seeing a single living cow.

"How much you reckon we've lost, boys?"

Granville Stuart asked me and Johnny Blue one day early in the thaw.

"It's bad, Mr. Stuart," I said.

He sat there on that big black thoroughbred of his'n, studying my face like he was trying to read what was written there.

"How bad?"

I looked up at the sky, then down to the ground, and I had a lump in my throat as big as an apple. I couldn't say the words.

"Nine out of ten, Mr. Stuart," Johnny Blue said.

"Ninety percent? Are you sure?"

"As sure as we're settin' on our horses right here."

Granville Stuart's chin slumped on his chest and he didn't look up again for a long spell.

Then he slowly raised his tired, red-rimmed eyes to mine and said: "Boys, it's all over.

"A business that captivated and fascinated me most of my life has suddenly become distasteful. I never again want to own an animal I cannot feed and shelter."

He swung his horse away from us.

Then he stopped and said over his shoulder, "Let's pick up the pieces. Save what we can. Then we'll make an end to it."

Come fall, the DHS was no more and me and Johnny Blue were out of work.

When we rode out of Granville Stuart's ranch for the last time we each had five dollars in our ragged Levis. An uncertain future lay ahead of us.

Mr. Stuart had tried to be a good loser, but anyone could see he was bleeding real bad inside.

"I wish you the best, boys," he'd told us as we said

our goodbyes. "This territory has a great future and you can grow with it. But the life we knew is gone, and nothing will ever be as it was before."

Then he totaled up our wages and began deducting for this and that. He charged Johnny Blue forty dollars for the DHS buckskin pony he was riding, on account of how Johnny Blue's own bay had broke a leg the summer before.

That buckskin wasn't worth more than ten, but I didn't feel this was the time to mention it.

And he took fifty cents for the box of .44–.40 cartridges he gave us, though I know it pained him to have to do it. But Granville Stuart had his partners to answer to, and between them they'd lost more than 100,000 dollars in five months.

Well, boys, the good days was gone, and anyone could see that me and Johnny Blue had fallen on hard times.

And any fool could tell they was about to get harder.

Me and Johnny Blue, we headed east toward the ranches along the Musselshell looking for work.

Ice still clung to the edges of the creek bottoms and flurries of sleet and hail slashed across the trail, driven by a numbing wind from the high peaks of the Rockies.

Most of the ranches that bordered the Musselshell were already closed, their hands out on the trails, riding the grub line like us.

And the few that were still in business all had the same answer.

"Sorry, boys, we're paying off hands, not hiring 'em."

Then we heard tell that even the big Swan Land and Cattle Company had quit the ranching business, and in Nebraska the Niobrara Cattle Company had gone belly up.

"Things don't look too good for us, do they?" Johnny Blue said as we made camp in a stand of willow near the Judith Gap.

It was now late October and we were still broke and riding the grub line, tired, dirty and missing our last six meals.

One by one, all the cowboying friends we knew had drifted away.

Those hands who had not become ranch owners or foremen or saloon keepers, or who hadn't been shot or had their necks broke, had already moved south, some of them all the way to the Brazos.

Others had become outlaws and rustlers and were riding lonely trails where the nighttime owl hoots and a man steps careful.

Even Charlie Russell was gone. The Kid told us he was moving up into Canada for a spell, to live with the Bloods, on account of how they were kin to the Blackfeet and he'd always got along well with them Indians. The Bloods even give him a name, Ah-wah-cous, which means antelope in Injun.

"I want to paint the Indians before they're all gone," Charlie said, "like the beaver and the buffalo before them. Now the land belongs to sober men who turn over the sod grass side down. Ain't no room for wild Indians in that world."

Then he turned his pony and packhorse north. We would see him again . . . but that's another story.

The range was emptying fast. First the cows died. Now the people were gone.

"Johnny Blue," I said, "I've been thinking."

"Never knowed you was a man much into thinking," Johnny Blue said.

"Well, I never much needed to till now."

We sat by a sizzling, sleet-spattered fire, sharing our last sourdough biscuit, drinking watery coffee made with our last fistful of Arbuckle.

I split the biscuit with my knife right down the middle, then separated the crumbs into two equal little piles.

"What you been thinking?" Johnny Blue asked without curiosity.

"I been thinking we need a job, and a warm place to hole up for winter."

Johnny Blue looked at me, chewing on the stale biscuit.

"That's not for me," he said. "I've got something to do back in Arizona."

I couldn't believe my ears. "What's so all-fired important in Arizona?" I asked. "Not that you can get there without money, so it really don't matter much."

Johnny Blue opened his mackinaw and fished in his shirt pocket. He came out with a crumpled piece of paper that he passed to me.

"Nat Love sent me this," he said. "He's got news of my sister."

I took the letter, but didn't read it just yet. "I didn't know you had a sister."

Johnny Blue nodded.

"My daddy was a field hand and my mama was a cook on a plantation in Davidson County. My daddy died, then my mama and little sister was sold down the river a few months before the war ended. I stayed on at the plantation, then when the bluecoat Yankee soldiers come, they gave me to Nat's folks to raise. I was about three years old, I guess. "

"Tell on," I said.

"Well, Nat's father died, and Nat became head of the household. At fourteen, he was supporting me, his mother and widowed sister and her two children, all from what he made as a sharecropper and the dollar and a half a month he made breaking horses.

"Nat Love's a good man, and because he's a good man, he sent me that letter."

I opened the letter and read:

Dear Johnny Blue,

I hope this finds you as well as it leaves me, though I do have a touch of the rheumatisms as I write.

I am breaking horses here in S. Dakota and writing my autobiography, *The Life and Adventures of Nat Love: Better Known in the Cattle Country as Deadwood Dick,* and it is coming along as well as can be expected.

I have some news for you. A rider was passing through the other day and says he heard from a bluecoat horse soldier that ol' Geronimo has surrendered at last to General Miles at Skeleton Canyon. Seeing I was a man of color, this rider said the soldier told him that after the surrender he'd talked to a colored woman at Fort Bowie who'd took up with one of Geronimo's young bucks. The woman said her name was Mattie Dupree.

This Mattie Dupree said she'd been born a slave in Tennessee and sold down the river as a baby and that her parents were dead.

Johnny Blue, I don't want to hold out false hope, but could this Mattie be your little sister? I don't know.

I wish you well.

And the letter was signed, Nat Love, known as Deadwood Dick.

I folded up the piece of paper and handed it back to Johnny Blue.

"You don't even know if it's her," I said. "There could be a lot of women of color named Mattie Dupree."

Even I could hear how hollow that sounded, and Johnny Blue chose to ignore it.

"It's her," he said. "And I'm going to find her."

Two

Me and Johnny Blue rode into the town of Utica the next day, down in the Judith Basin country.

I don't know if you've ever been there, boys, but Utica's a stage station on the road from Billings up into Canada, and it was a lively enough place at one time when the punchers came in on Saturday nights. But now it ain't much, and ain't likely to be much again.

When me and Johnny Blue rode in, there was the stage station and its corral, four saloons and two livery stables and some log cabins, the whole shebang tied together by a corded mud road.

Before the Great Blizzard, Utica had a prosperous air, because the hands from the surrounding ranches spent freely and there was always a sprinkling of bluecoat soldiers from up Fort Benton way with wages burning a hole in their pockets.

But now the place looked seedy and threadbare and down on its luck. To tell the truth, it looked a lot like me and Johnny Blue. I'd no way of knowing it then, but the town would get to look a lot worse—and so would we.

We tied our horses up outside James Shelton's saloon and walked inside and ordered a nickel beer.

"I can see you boys are the last of the big spenders," Shelton said as he put the stein in front of us.

"Hard times, Jim," I said.

There was one of Kid Russell's paintings hanging behind the bar, and me and Johnny Blue studied it closely as we stood there and shared the beer.

It was a piece of canvas about two feet wide by four feet long, and Charlie had painted the whole town of Utica with a roundup going on in the foreground.

I could identify every cowboy in that picture by name, and his horse and his saddlemaker. It even showed ol' Jim Shelton sitting outside his saloon, waiting for business.

Well, all those cowboys in the picture were long gone, and some of them, like poor Shorty Stevens, had died in the storm.

"Any work around, Jim?" I asked Shelton by way of conversation after I'd seen enough of the picture.

"What kind of work?"

"Any kind."

"There's no cowboying work. None a-tall."

"I know that."

"You boys riding the grub line?"

"Looks that way, don't it?"

Shelton wiped the bar with a rag.

"You've left it too late to head south. Winter's taking off."

"I know that too, though my pard here don't believe it."

Johnny Blue shot me a resentful glance, which I ignored.

"Anyhow," I said, "there's no work south. Maybe there's no work all the way to the Brazos."

"I feel bad for you boys. But there's no work of any kind to be had in Utica. The herds and the cowboys have gone. I can see the town dying around me day by day."

I said, "The herds will come back, and the hands, you'll see. They always did after the big snows."

Jim Shelton shook his head sadly and looked at me like I was crazy.

"You're living in the past, son. Them days are gone. They went out with the big snow and died with the cows."

He took our beer glass, which was half empty, and filled it up.

"This one's on me."

I watched ol' Jim's face closely, trying to see if he really meant what he was saying about Utica and the cowboys.

He must have read my mind because he said: "Last year about this time, a hunnerd people lived in town. Now there's maybe fifty. That ought to tell you something."

I looked around the bar and there was a poker foursome going on at one of the tables. And that gave me an idea. I dug in my jeans and came up with two crumpled dollar bills and fifteen cents in change.

"How much money you got, Johnny Blue?" I asked.

"Who wants to know?"

"I do. I got an idea."

"What kind of an idea?"

"Hell, a good idea."

Johnny Blue dug deep and came up with his own two dollars and fifty cents.

Now I had four dollars and sixty-five cents.

It was enough.

"What you gonna do?" Johnny Blue asked.

"I'm maybe gonna make us enough money to last us the winter," I said. "Then we can head south and find our sister."

"You have no call to do that," Johnny Blue said. "She's my kin."

I said, "You and me, we're blood brothers, ain't we? Ol' Nat Love made us brothers. 'Black and white,' he said, 'two sides of the same coin.'"

Johnny Blue nodded.

"Then she's my sister too."

Johnny Blue smiled. "Some folks would find that hard to believe."

"That's their problem," I said. "Not mine."

I cracked my knuckles on each hand, which I always do for luck before playing poker, and wiggled my fingers, which I'd seen a gambling man do one time. "Now to make us some money," I said.

Johnny Blue groaned.

Two shaggy old geezers, fur trappers by the look of them, a soldier I didn't know, and a pasty-faced pilgrim in a neat mustache and an expensive gray frock coat were sitting at the poker table.

"Mind if I sit in, gents?" I asked.

"If you got the money, cowboy, we got a chair," one of the geezers said.

"The game is five card stud for table stakes," the pilgrim said. "That set all right with you?"

I allowed that it did.

"I'm primed to buck this tiger," I said sociably.

The pilgrim smiled, but it never reached his eyes.

"Let's play poker," he said.

Fifteen minutes later me and Johnny Blue were flat broke.

Now, I'm not saying the game was crooked, exactly, but it pretty soon dawned on me that the careful-eyed dude in the frock coat was no pilgrim.

As soon as I saw him shuffle, cut and deal the cards, I pegged him as a professional gambler, a member of that restless breed who traveled all over the west supporting themselves by the pasteboards.

What he was doing in Utica, I didn't know. I figgered he was just killing time waiting for the stage south to Virginia City, or maybe he was on the run from the law.

But I did know that, given the uncertain nature of his profession, gents like him had to be more than proficient with the revolver.

And that pale-faced pilgrim had a bulge in his beautiful gray coat right under his arm, about the size and shape of a handy, short-barreled Colt's gun.

Maybe that's why I figgered it would be a bad idea to brace him.

Over four dollars and sixty-five cents, anyway.

"Well, now what are we gonna do?" Johnny Blue asked as we stood outside Shelton's saloon, the collars of our mackinaws turned up against the keening wind.

Day by day it was getting colder and I could smell snow in the air, and at night frost painted the pines and willows so they looked like slender, trembling pillars of steel.

I shook my head at Johnny Blue and allowed I'd run out of ideas.

"Playing poker," Johnny Blue said. "Now that was a bad idea."

"It seemed a good one at the time," I replied mildly.

"There's more to plowing a field than just turning it over in your head," Johnny Blue said.

I didn't quite get his drift, but it seemed a bad time to say so.

But then Jim Shelton came out and said we could put our horses up in his livery stable and bed down there.

"I guess I owe you that much," he said. "For old times' sake."

The livery barn was dry and sheltered from the wind, but it wasn't warm, there being only a few horses there. Me and Johnny Blue both sat in the hay, saying nothing, thinking of better times.

My empty stomach was growling something fierce, and I especially recollected the crock of brown beans, swimming in hog fat, that always hung over the fire in the DHS cookhouse.

I could never get my fill of those beans, and with fried salt pork and cornbread they were a meal fit for a king.

Boys, let me tell you, I could have eaten a mess of them beans that night.

I was about to reminisce with Johnny Blue about the DHS beans, but he had taken a little tally notebook out of his pocket and was chewing thoughtfully on a stub of pencil.

"What you doing, Johnny Blue?" I asked.

"Nothing much."

"You got paper and pencil. You must be doing something."

"If you really want to know, I'm making a list of your faults, which are many."

"How many have you wrote down?"

"Just one so far. I only just got started."

"What does it say?"

"Stupidity," said Johnny Blue.

THREE

Come morning, I woke up stiff and sore all over. Johnny Blue was already awake.

I lay there in the hay watching him as he fed a handful of oats to my paint and his buckskin, then forked the ponies some hay.

"Those oats any good to eat?" I asked.

Johnny Blue shook his head.

"I wouldn't know. I only found enough for the horses."

I got to my feet and I swear my body crackled as the frost thawed out of my joints.

"Didn't sleep worth a damn," I said to no one in particular.

"Now what are we gonna do?" Johnny Blue asked.

"You asked me that last night, and I still don't know," I said. "Give me some time to think, then maybe by and by I'll come up with somethin'."

Johnny Blue shrugged.

"Thought you might have had another one of them bright ideas of your'n. One of them schemes to make us all rich."

I was about to say something right sharp when Jim

Shelton walked into the barn. He was carrying two cups of coffee and a pint of whiskey.

"Morning, boys," he said. "I brung you something to drink."

He handed me and Johnny Blue each a cup and sweetened the coffee with a good belt of the whiskey.

Jim studied us both for a few minutes as we gratefully sipped the hot coffee, then he said: "Boys, I know times are bad and you're down on your luck. But you can't stay here all winter. You got to be moving on."

"We was planning to, Jim," I lied, because I didn't have a plan of any kind.

"Maybe I got something for you," he said. "I know it ain't much, but it's something."

"We're listening," I said.

"Do you recollect that gambler feller you was playing poker with last night?"

I said that I got burned real bad and that I wasn't likely to forget him anytime soon.

"Well, he tells me there's a feller in Great Falls who's offering a purse of five hunnerd dollars American to any man who can last fifteen rounds with his bare knuckle champeen boxer.

"It seems this champeen came to scratch thirty-six times against John L. Sullivan in Boston in '84, and might have beat him too, if'n ol' John L. hadn't been helped by his seconds to toe the line in the final round."

"Five hunnerd dollars, you say?" I asked.

"That's what I'm told. Five hunnerd dollars American."

I was finally starting to get an idea.

27

"Johnny Blue," I said, "how would you like to make enough money to keep us on easy street all winter and still have enough to go looking for our little sister come spring?"

He shook his head. "You're crazy."

"Now don't be hasty," I said. "All we have to do is last fifteen rounds against some broken down prizefighter, pick up our five hunnerd bucks, and we're warm and cozy all winter long."

"No way," Johnny Blue said.

"I've seen you fight, Johnny Blue. You're right handy with your dukes. As good as anybody I've seen. Well, locally at least."

"You're loco."

"It's only fifteen rounds! You went longer than that when you fought ol' Tube Wilson at the Rafter-Y over on the Musselshell three years ago after he said you was an uppity lowdown nigger. A lot of folks said you almost beat him. They tole me that straight."

Well, me and Johnny Blue stood there looking hard at each other over the rims of our coffee cups. And it became pretty obvious to me he wasn't about to agree to anything I said.

Now, I'm not one to argue principle with a man, especially when we're enjoying the "convivial cup" together, but desperate times call for desperate measures.

"Johnny Blue," I said, "do you recollect that time when you was swept off your horse and liked to drown after all that rain swelled the south fork of the Judith?"

"No," he replied.

"Let me see," I said, "it was in June, no July, of '84.

As I recall, I was the one that dived in and saved your skin, on account of the fact that you couldn't swim."

"I don't remember that a-tall."

"Then there was that time I shot the grizzly off'n you when we was hunting down in the Pig-Eye Basin country."

"Nope," Johnny Blue said. "Don't recollect that neither."

"That was . . . let me see . . . the fall of '85. Must have been, because I still have that mad ol' bear's tooth marks on my right leg, and that's something a man doesn't forget. Still pains me tolerably bad in the winter sometimes. But I'm grateful that I'm still alive, an' grateful that them as I saved is still walking the earth an' gettin' a chance to be all-fired *un*-grateful.

"Then there was that time—"

"Enough!" Johnny Blue exclaimed. "I'll fight this champeen of your'n, but if I'm hurtin' real bad you ain't gonna carry me to no line. I'm only doing this because I want to find my sister, no other reason."

"I understand that, and I won't let him hurt you," I said. "I'll shoot him off'n you, jest like I shot that big ol' grizzly bear off your back."

"Do I have your promise on that?" Johnny Blue asked. "Let me hear a solemn oath on that."

"Trust me."

Johnny Blue's eyes rolled in his head.

"Yup, that there's what I was afraid of."

Jim Shelton coughed politely.

"Boys, I don't want to rain on your family picnic, but Great Falls is a three-day ride from here. Have you given any thought to how you're gonna get there without supplies of any kind?"

"Well, we could kill our chuck along the trail," I said.

"I ain't dependin' on that," Johnny Blue said. "I seen you shoot a rifle, an' a man could starve to death."

I had to admit I was stumped.

For the first time in my life I began to realize that being flat broke has a way of creating some unforeseen problems for a man.

"Well, boys," Jim Shelton said, "I'll supply you with some coffee and bacon and a mess of sourdough biscuits and two dollars cash money. You ain't gonna be living high on the hog by any means, but at least it will keep your bellies full."

"How we gonna pay you, Jim?" I asked.

"What have you got?"

In the end I had to part with my Model 1873, .44–.40 Winchester that had cost me two months' wages in Billings just a couple of years before.

But as they say, you have to speculate to accumulate, and I considered the loss of my rifle an investment for the future. A five-hunnerd-dollar investment.

Later that morning Jim Shelton sacked us up some grub, which I tied to my saddle horn.

"You ready to ride?" Johnny Blue asked. He was kinda slumped in his saddle and looked almighty sulky on account of having to fight the bare knuckle champeen an' all.

Mounting up, I kneed my pony beside his. "You're gonna do good, Johnny Blue," I said. "This plan jest feels right to me."

"You ain't the one doing the fighting," he said.

FOUR

Our first day and night on the trail to Great Falls passed without incident.

But on the second night, after we'd eaten and lay shivering in our blankets by the thin heat of a fire made with damp wood, Johnny Blue raised up on one elbow and whispered: "Do you smell something?"

I sniffed into the wind.

"I don't smell nothing," I said.

"Wolf," Johnny Blue said.

"Hell, wolves never been known to attack humans." I pulled my blanket over my head. "Go back to sleep."

"Dead wolf," Johnny Blue said.

And now I smelled it too, rank and gamey, the smell of old deaths.

There was four of them that I could see, and they were coming at us through the timber, staying well away from the dim circle of firelight.

Wolfers.

Wild animals in human form who trapped wolves for the two-dollar bounty on their pelts. I'd once been warned by a lawman who spent the night at the DHS that these men would rob and kill a poor cowboy or soldier only for his horse and saddle and guns.

31

I no longer had my rifle, but I slid my Colt from its scabbard beside my head and held it to my side under the blanket.

Johnny Blue had his .44–.40 Henry to hand, and I heard him crank a round into the chamber.

"Hello the camp," a man called from the woods.

Johnny Blue rose and stepped outside the circle of firelight.

"What do you want?" he asked.

"Smelled your coffee," the same voice said. "We sure could use some. Been out of Arbuckle for more'n a week now."

Like Johnny Blue, I'd stepped out of the firelight and held my Colt ready.

"Come on in, and keep your hands where I can see 'em," I said.

"Sure thing," the voice said.

The four men came toward us leading their horses, and pretty soon we could see two more behind them.

As they came closer to the firelight, I saw that the wolfers were huge yellow- and red-haired men, shaggy and unkempt with long beards and bearskin coats to their ankles. Their hats were made out of the skull and pelts of prime wolves.

The four carried Winchester rifles and strapped around their waists were cartridge belts, bowie knives and Colt revolvers.

Behind them were the two others, leading heavily laden pack horses. But as they got closer I saw they were handsome Indian women. They were dressed like the men, save for the wolf caps, and by the look of their braids I took them to be Flatheads.

Boys, I was feeling a might uneasy right about then.

Me, I'll offer coffee and a share of what food I have to any honest man who rides into my camp friendly and open, dishonest ones, too, if they behave themselves, but I draw the line at wolfers. They're a lowdown, shiftless breed who would cut your throat for your last dollar and steal a widow woman's only milk cow. I've never really cottoned to men who hunt and kill animals for a living, even the buffalo hunters I'd met, and the men who had come into our camp were the worst of the breed. Like I said, I draw the line at wolfers, and I was about to draw that line now.

"Smelled your coffee way back in the woods," the biggest of the four men said. He was enormous, with shoulders as wide as two hickory ax handles and a head that sat on his neck like a beer barrel. He smiled, showing blackened teeth, and even those were few and far between. Above his matted red beard his eyes were small and hard, and he looked mean and sneaky and ready to kill. "Figger we could trade for some Arbuckle?"

"We only got enough," Johnny Blue said. He was still holding his Henry at the ready.

"Too bad," the wolfer said.

He studied me and Johnny Blue closely, then he looked at our saddles and tethered horses.

"Drovers?"

I allowed that we were.

"Too bad. Cows are all gone."

He jerked a thumb back toward the pack horses.

"Plenty of wolf, though. My name's Pike," the wolfer said. "Jacob Pike."

He looked at me closely again. "Don't I know you?"

I shook my head. "Never seen you before in my life, mister."

Pike nodded.

"Too bad. About the coffee, I mean."

"Well, like he said. We just got enough and none to spare."

"Where you headed?" Pike asked.

I didn't feel inclined to tell him, but Johnny Blue said: "Great Falls. We got friends there. And we know the law."

Pike nodded again.

"Headin' up that way myself. Maybe I'll see you there."

"Maybe so," Johnny Blue said.

Pike took a long look at my Colt and Johnny Blue's rifle. He was no mental giant, and I could see he was slowly grappling with some kind of decision.

Despite the cold, the palm of my right hand holding the Colt was sweating. If the time came for gunfighting, I sure hoped I could hold on to the rubber handle of the ruddy thing.

But ol' Pike must have figured that what little we had was not worth gunfighting for. And I guess he knowed, as well as me and Johnny Blue did, that he'd be the first man down.

"Well, we got to get goin'," he said. "Pity about the coffee."

"Yeah, it is," I said.

The big wolfer looked over his shoulder at his companions then circled his hand in the air. "Move on out," he said. "There's no hospitality for a man here."

He turned to me one last time. "I'll remember you," he said, and the threat in his voice was plain as the broken nose on his face. "And I'll sure remember about the coffee."

We watched them disappear into the dark of the woods.

It seemed me and Johnny Blue had made ourselves a bad enemy over nothing more than a cup of coffee. An enemy who would remember.

When I lay back in my bedroll I thought some on that, and it took me a long time to get to sleep again.

We saw no more of the wolfers and the rest of our journey passed without incident.

Me and Johnny Blue rode into Great Falls in a driving sleet storm in the early hours of Saturday evening. We were cold and tired and hungry. We saw the horses bedded down and fed at the livery stable, though it put a big hole in the two dollars we'd gotten from Jim Shelton.

"How much do we have left?" Johnny Blue asked.

"Not enough for a hotel room and barely enough for a cheap meal," I said.

We were standing on Central Avenue under the canvas awning of a dress and shoe store that gave us little shelter from the wind and stinging sleet.

Johnny Blue rolled a thin cigarette with the last of his tobacco and flared a match to light it. For a second or two the burning match gave the illusion of warmth. Then it went out in the slashing wind and I was cold again.

"Remember the saloon ol' Charlie Russell told us about?" Johnny Blue asked. He had his mackinaw collar up around his ears and what skin the coat didn't cover, his hat did.

"He said there was always food on a counter for anyone who wanted it. He said all a man had to do was buy a beer and he could fill his belly for free."

"It was called the Sideboard, as I recollect," I said. "I wonder where it is?"

Johnny Blue flicked his cigarette butt, sending it spinning across the street in a shower of sparks. "It's right over there," he said.

This was my first time in Great Falls, and right off I'd seen that it was no cow town.

The blizzard that had destroyed the range had swept over the town and held it hostage to snow and ice for months. But Great Falls had fought back and emerged stronger than ever. They'd even cut the railroad through from Lewistown in the teeth of the worst of the '87 storms.

Granville Stuart told me one time as we sat in his library that Great Falls had been designed and founded by Gibson Paris back in '83. He'd called it "a planned community," and the wide streets were laid out like a grid and just about every house, store and saloon in the place was made out of dressed sandstone and brick.

As the population grew, more stone was always needed, and it was now being dragged from quarries as far away as Butte by the new railroad. To a man like me, born and raised in wooden cow towns, the place looked like one of them big northern cities I'd seen likenesses of in the newspapers, all noise and hustle and bustle.

Cavalry soldiers from as far away as Fort Maginnes and Fort Assiniboine in buffalo fur coats and hats jostled past us, talking big and bragging as soldiers always do, going from saloon to saloon, spending their month's wages on one rip-roaring night in town.

It seemed to me that them who weren't busy taking the soldiers' money were working on the mighty Great Falls silver smelter, which was beginning to take shape at the north edge of town on the other side of the Missouri.

Boys, it seemed to me that everyone connected with the town was making money hand over fist that fall, and spending it just as fast, even the local sod-busting farmers.

Everybody that is, but the poor cowboys.

I heard a babble of voices as Irishmen, Swedes, Germans and even a few Chinamen rubbed shoulders on the streets and crowded into the roaring saloons.

When me and Johnny Blue walked into the Sideboard, the saloon was crowded with soldiers, farmers and construction workers from the smelter.

A couple of exhausted saloon girls lurched around a tiny dance floor with drunk, fur-coated soldiers and somewhere beyond the sea of bodies I could hear a tinkling piano.

Everybody was talking and shouting at once, jostling each other, and the floor was an inch deep in spilled beer. To me, it looked like a scene out of Hades, and thankfully it was just as warm.

Me and Johnny Blue elbowed our way to the bar.

I ordered two beers, and as the bartender pulled them he looked at us curiously. He laid the beers on the bar and said, "You boys here to see the fight?"

I placed my last dollar on the bar.

"What fight?"

"You mean you ain't heard? Why, one of ol' Amos

Pinkney's boys is going up agin the Boston Mauler to-morrow evening. Whole town's gonna be there."

The bartender took my dollar and laid eighty cents back on the bar.

"Expensive beer," I said.

The man shrugged.

"Everything is expensive in Great Falls."

"This Pinkney," I said, "would he be the Amos Pinkney that rode with Jesse and Frank James and them back in Missouri?"

"The very same. He's clean nowadays. They say he and Frank got pardons from the governor."

Someone called for whiskey and the bartender rushed away to serve him.

I sipped my beer thoughtfully. Things were not going quite as I planned.

"Well," Johnny Blue said. "I guess we made this trip for nothing."

"Maybe. Maybe not."

There was a tall, lanky feller standing next to me, a farmer by his long face and the way he was nursing a warm beer, hoping somebody would buy him another one.

"You two come in to see the fight?" he asked.

"Could be," I said. "I was told this Boston Mauler feller was taking on all comers. How come there's talk of only one fight?"

"He done beat everybody else," the farmer replied.

I jerked my thumb in Johnny Blue's direction. "He ain't beat him."

The farmer studied Johnny Blue for a spell, then he said: "Cowboy, I got a woman at home could beat him."

I expected that Johnny Blue wouldn't take too kindly to this, especially coming from a sod buster an' all, but he just shrugged and said: "Known a few women like that myself."

Then he turned to me and said: "Let's go see if we can find those eats Kid Russell told us about."

The farmer directed us to a counter near the bar. "He'p yourself. If there's anything left."

A couple of Irish laborers in laced boots and dungarees were picking through the remains of food that had obviously lain there since lunchtime. They finally gave up and moved away in disgust.

Me and Johnny Blue weren't that choosy.

We each got a dried up slice of rye bread that wasn't too moldy and laid a couple of slices of limp and sweating yellow cheese on it. There were some beans that had long since grown cold in their pot, which we spread over the cheese. We topped that with some dill pickles and salted peanuts and some raisins and crowned the whole thing with another slice of bread.

Then we ate one of the best meals of our lives.

As I chewed, I considered our options.

An obvious one was to get Johnny Blue to fight Amos Pinkney's boy tonight. That way, if Johnny Blue won, he would have a clear shot at the Mauler.

Trouble was, if he was used up too bad, Johnny Blue might be in no condition to fight tomorrow night. That is if he won, and I wasn't too confident about that.

Boys, it seemed to me that Johnny Blue just wasn't showing the right fighting spirit.

There had to be an easier way.

The first thing I had to do was know my enemy.

And that meant Amos Pinkney. I had it in my mind that ol' Pink and me could reach an understanding and make a deal around Johnny Blue and the Boston Mauler.

So, after we'd filled our bellies I sought out the farmer who'd spoken to us earlier. I asked him where ol' Pink and his fighter might be found.

"Well," the farmer said, "he might be found here, but he ain't gonna be."

Well, that was sod buster talk right enough. You can never get a straight answer out of a farmer about anything.

I tried again.

"Well, if he ain't here, mister, where is he?"

The sod buster gazed sorrowfully into his empty glass, but when he saw that I wasn't about to bite at that particular worm he sighed and said, "He's camped outside of town, thattaway." He jerked his thumb north. "You can't miss him. He's got a couple of tipis and a covered wagon."

"Tipis?"

"Yeah, seems he's took up with Injuns."

I thanked the farmer for his help and left him staring morosely into his empty glass.

"Let's go," I said to Johnny Blue.

"What do you have in mind now?" he asked.

"I figger we'll go make talk with ol' Pink. An' by and by maybe even cut a deal."

"What kind of deal you got in mind?" Johnny Blue asked suspiciously.

"Any kind of deal I can get," I said.

We walked outside and headed north on Central Avenue, into the teeth of the sleet storm.

I pulled my hat down over my ears and my mackinaw collar up to meet it. The icy wind found every rip and tear in my coat and teased me with freezing fingers. My teeth were chattering like castanets.

The streets were empty but for the fools, the broke and the cowboys.

Amos Pinkney's encampment was set beside the corral of a livery stable, sheltered from the worst of the wind by a solidly built brick barn.

From where I stood it seemed a downright cozy location.

The two tipis were covered in painted canvas and I could see the glow of fires inside. A lantern cast a warm orange light through the swaybacked canvas of the Conestoga wagon.

Me and Johnny Blue stood outside near the wagon in the wind and cold and I hollered: "Hello the camp!"

I saw the barrel of a Winchester poke out from under the canvas of the wagon and a man said: "What the hell do you want?"

"Excuse me," I said, "but we wish to speak to Mr. Pinkney."

"Who's you?" the voice said.

"Just two cowboys down on our luck," I said. "We want to talk to Mr. Pinkney."

"Go away. You'll get no handouts here."

The flaps of both tipis opened and I saw two large men in their drawers step outside. Both were carrying rifles.

"I knew it," Johnny Blue said. "We're dead."

But, desperate as I was, I had one card left to play. And I hoped it would work.

"Long live Dixie," I said. "Long live Robert E. Lee an' Mrs. Lee. Up the South. Huzzah! Huzzah!"

There was a long silence.

Then I saw women come out of the tipis and put fur coats around the shoulders of the men in the long johns. Then the huge riflemen padded toward us.

"Yup," Johnny Blue said with an air of finality, "we're dead."

But just then a man climbed out of the back of the wagon. He was tall and gaunt and handsome, in his late 40s at a guess, with a shock of gray hair and a mustache and goatee to match.

I knew he could only be Amos Pinkney.

A gray, Johnny Reb cavalry cape was thrown carelessly over his shoulders and under it he wore a frilled white shirt and tan riding breeches tucked into knee-length boots of soft leather.

Two gunbelts crossed his slim hips and each held a pearl-handled Remington .45 in a tooled holster.

Ol' Pink tucked his thumbs into his gunbelts and rocked back on his heels. "I'll speak to any man who invokes the name of General Lee and the Sacred Cause," he said. "What do you want?"

I knew Amos Pinkney by reputation, and he wasn't a man to be trifled with. I heard tell he was a mucho bad hombre and even men of reputation like Frank James stepped lightly around him.

Early on in the Civil War he had rode with Frank and Jesse under Quantrill. He soon showed he was of the right metal to be forged and shaped in the fire of horse raider warfare and came to the attention of Bloody Bill Anderson. After ol' Bill was shot in 1864,

Pinkney ended the war as a major in some wild Texas cavalry outfit.

Some said he'd killed a dozen men and had even gunned women and children during the war. The mere fact that they was Yankees or Yankee sympathizers was enough to guarantee a Pinkney bullet. I'd even heard tell that thirty scalps once hung from his horse's bridle, some of them blond and with ribbons still in the ringlets.

"I'll say it just one more time, cowboy. What do you want?"

I tried to talk but I found my tongue stuck to the roof of my mouth and couldn't utter a sound.

The two enormous riflemen had been joined by another, taller and broader than the others. He came toward me carrying a lantern that he stuck in my face.

"Do you know this fellow?" Pink asked.

The huge man, who reeked like a long-dead goat, studied me closely for a second or two.

Then he hissed: "Well, well, well, if'n it ain't the coffee drinker."

I looked up.

And beheld the scowling, murderous features of Jacob Pike.

FIVE

"You apparently know this man," Amos Pinkney said to Pike.

"I don't know him real good," the wolfer growled. "But I do know he don't like to share his coffee."

Pink shook his head at me. "Any man who won't share the warmth of his fire and offer a fellow traveler the comforting cup is lowdown."

I finally found my tongue and stammered, "It was a misunderstanding, Mr. Pinkney. Mister Pike approached our camp in the dark and our coffee was all gone."

"I smelled it plain enough," Pike snarled.

"Well, enough of coffee," Pinkney said. "I think I know what sort of men I'm dealing with. Now, I'll ask you one last time. What do you want?"

What had seemed like a good idea in the warmth and safety of the Sideboard, didn't seem so danged great out here in the driving sleet and freezing cold.

Especially when I was circled by rifles and facing a man who was said to have twelve notches on his guns.

"Could we go inside and talk?" I suggested. "Maybe in one of the tipis. It might be easier."

"Talk all you want right here," Pink said. "But make it fast. I'm getting cold and when I get cold I get angry."

"Oh God, we're dead," Johnny Blue whispered in my ear.

I ignored him and plunged ahead, reckless now. I was surrounded by dangerous men and I figured my chances of survival were getting slimmer by the minute.

I might as well say my piece and get it over with.

"Mr. Pinkney," I said, "we rode all the way from Utica so my friend here can fight the Boston Mauler and win the five hunnerd dollars prize money.

"See, we're from way out the Judith Basin way and we just got paid off by Mr. Stuart of the DHS ranch.

"We're broke and we need a warm place to pass the winter. Then we got to head for Arizona and look for our little sister who was taken by the bloodthirsty Apache and return her to the bosom of our family. That's why we came here after the five hunnerd."

Ol' Pink was looking at me with a strange expression on his face, like somebody was holding a rotten fish under his nose.

"Our sister? *Our* sister?" he said. "That's passing strange."

I nodded and kept talking, figgering this was not the time to go into it.

"Now I realize you have your own champeen all primed and ready to take on the Mauler. But I think I can save you a lot of trouble and inconvenience. That's why I'm here. To make a deal."

"What kind of deal?" Pink asked.

Somebody guffawed, probably Pike, but Amos Pinkney waved a hand and silenced him.

"I'm waiting," Pink said.

"It's like this, Mr. Pinkney," I began, as my tongue started to find its way back to the roof of my mouth again.

Fear can do that to a man.

"I suggest that your champeen, whoever he is, drop out of the fight and that Johnny Blue here take his place.

"That way, neither you nor your champeen will be inconvenienced in any way, and after Johnny Blue goes the fifteen rounds, we can split the prize money right down the middle."

I searched ol' Pink's face, trying to figure what the man was thinking, but his hard, handsome features were wary and guarded, revealing nothing.

"And that," I said, "is my proposition. And I believe it to be a good one."

Ol' Pink stood there in silence for a while. And I watched as the space between his eyes knotted in puzzlement.

Then his face slowly cleared.

And he laughed.

And Pike and his wolfers laughed.

And then the Flathead women laughed.

And Johnny Blue, desperately trying to save his own skin I reckon, laughed.

Me, I didn't feel like laughing.

After the laughter went on for a while, ol' Pink wiped his streaming eyes with the back of his hand.

"I like you, cowboy," he said. "I'm probably going

to shoot you down like a mangy car. But I have to admit it, I like your nerve."

This time I tried to laugh with him. But what came from my tightening throat was a high-pitched, girlish shriek.

After a while ol' Pink's mirth subsided and he said to Jacob Pike, "Tell him who's going to fight the Mauler tomorrow night."

"I am," Pike said, beating his chest like a big ol' mad grizzly bear.

Pink looked at me with his cold, hooded blue eyes. He was shivering slightly in the icy wind, and I fervently wished he'd go back into the wagon where it was nice and warm.

"Cowboy, do you honestly think your skinny sidekick there would last even a couple of rounds with the Boston Mauler, the man who almost bested John L. Sullivan? If you do, you are truly out of your mind."

He turned to Johnny Blue. "What do you think, boy?"

"Me, all I wanted was to earn enough money so I could go find my sister," Johnny Blue said. "I never wanted to fight no Boston Mauler."

"Oh, so now she's *your* sister," Pike said.

"He misspoke himself, Mr. Pinkney," I said. "See, me and him, we're brothers."

That started another round of laughter, and after it ended, Pike said, "You sure as hell ain't gonna fight no Mauler, cowboy. I can tell you that."

"Ah, yes, let me just say that Mr. Pike is eagerly looking forward to his appointment with the Mauler,"

Pink said. "Now, you wouldn't want me to deprive him of that little pleasure, would you?"

"I sure as hell would not," Johnny Blue said.

"I'm very glad to hear that," Pink said.

I could see I was stacked up against a cold deck, so I said, "Well, I can believe you're getting chilled out here, Mr. Pinkney, and since our business is done, we'd better be getting on our way. I'd love to talk some more, but it is getting late."

I started to walk away, but Pink's voice stopped me.

"Cowboy, a word of advice. Amos Pinkney doesn't share. He takes. Remember that.

"Just to draw a little picture for you. I have a dozen and more associates arriving in Great Falls by the noon train tomorrow. These are men, like Mr. Pike and his partners, that I must feed, house, supply with ammunition and horses all winter long.

"We have immediate business in the Idaho territory, then come the first blush of spring we will move south where . . . a certain great enterprise awaits us.

"Such a large troop costs money, a great deal of money.

"So you can see that I cannot readily share the five hundred dollars I intend to win from Doctor Silas Fortune's Mauler tomorrow night.

"You do understand that, don't you?"

I gave ol' Pink my undying assurance that I understood every single word and then some, and would understand them forever.

He nodded and smiled, and I'd seen friendlier grins on a lobo wolf.

"One last thing, cowboy. If you ever come bothering me again with your harebrained schemes, I'll shoot you down in the street like a cur. Do you understand?"

Fervently, I assured ol' Pink that I did.

"Very well. I am satisfied.

"Now if I may call on Mr. Pike to see you off the premises?"

Pike grabbed me and Johnny Blue by the collars of our mackinaws and lifted us clean off the ground. He carried us to the street then threw us, sprawling, into the freezing mud.

"You should have shared your coffee with us," he growled.

I picked myself up and watched Jacob Pike's retreating back as he shambled away.

Johnny Blue retrieved his hat from a filthy puddle and rammed it on his head. "Congratulations," he said. "That was quite a deal you cut."

I did cut one deal that night, though.

The owner of the livery stable, a taciturn Scotsman named Blackerby who wore a tam-o'-shanter hat, took the rest of my money and allowed us to spend the night in the barn.

There were maybe two dozen horses in the barn, most of them enormous, corn-fed cavalry mounts, so the place was warm. Outside, the sleet storm had increased in intensity and I could hear the stinging drops rattle like kettle drums on the tin roof of the stable.

Johnny Blue sat in the hay and fished out his little notebook. Again he studied me from time to time, chewing on the end of his pencil.

"Has your list got any bigger yet?" I asked.

"Nah."

"How come?"

"I just can't seem to get past the first one."

I got up from under the ill-smelling hay I'd covered myself with and walked over to Johnny Blue.

"I need your revolver," I said.

Johnny Blue's eyebrows arched in surprise.

"What do you need a gun for?" he asked.

"I got a plan," I said.

Johnny Blue shook his head at me. Then he sighed long and kinda sad, but he stood and opened his blanket roll and got out his revolver, a self-cocking 1877 Army Model Colt in .44–.40 caliber.

"What y'all gonna do with that?" he asked. "You know you can't hit nothing you aim at."

"We were roughly handled tonight," I said. "I'll let no man do that to me, not even Amos Pinkney.

"I'm gonna use this here gun to get us our five hunnerd dollars and get even with ol' Pink."

Johnny Blue studied my face closely for a long time.

"Now I know what else to write in my book," he said finally.

"And what's that?"

"That you're plumb crazy."

Six

Johnny Blue just sat there and stared at me. And his face . . . well . . . let me see. Boys, do you recollect ol' Dave Ketchum up on T-Bar, him with the one eye and the simple son? Well, one day I seen Dave pull on his boot and there was a rattler inside it. Johnny Blue's face was a match for what Dave's looked like that day. Like he'd just felt a rattler chomp on his toes.

"You're gonna get yourself killed if you go back there on the prod," Johnny Blue said.

I got out my pocketknife and opened it up.

"What we're gonna do is strike tomorrow at midday, when Pinkney meets his Texas gunmen off the noon train."

Johnny Blue shook his head. "You're crazy as a loon."

"Well, maybe so," I said. "Now give me that stub of pencil you keep writin' down my faults with."

"Sure thing. Just make sure you give it back to me. I'll need it to write your epitaph."

I shrugged like I didn't care, then I took Johnny Blue's Colt and unscrewed its walnut handles. Then I got the pencil and began to write.

Early next morning, me and Johnny Blue were out on the street, heading back to the Sideboard saloon.

The sleet had stopped, but the sky was iron gray and it was still cold. I reckon there was about three inches of slick and slippery mud on the street.

The Sideboard was warm and apart from a few drunks sleeping it off at tables and the bar, the place was empty. The bartender I'd spoken to last night was swabbing the floor without much enthusiasm and he looked hungover and surly.

There was a pot of coffee on the stove and some tin cups hanging on hooks, and I asked the man if me and Johnny Blue could partake.

"Help yourself," the bartender said, which was neighborly enough, but then I heard him mutter under his breath, "Damn freeloading . . . no good cowhands . . . sons of bitches . . . don't give a damn . . . lousy job . . . me mother was right . . ."

I poured my coffee, then filled Johnny Blue's cup. The coffee was strong and warm and sweet and it tasted real good.

I let the bartender mutter for a while, then said, "By the way, good mornin' to you."

The man stopped, leaned on his mop and looked me in the eye. "Okay, tell me one thing that's good about it," he said. "Tell me just one damn thing."

"I'm glad you asked me that," I replied, "because this might be a very good mornin' for you." I rapped on the bar with my knuckles. "That sound you hear is opportunity knockin'."

"Go to hell," the bartender said.

Johnny Blue, who'd cruised the free lunch counter, sidled up to me. "Picked clean," he said. "But I got these. Open your hand."

I stuck out my hand and he poured six salted

peanuts into my palm. I tossed them into my mouth, and it was like chewing on rock salt.

"Better than nothing," Johnny Blue said when I made a face.

The bartender got tired of mopping the floor and moved back behind the bar. "Are you two gonna order a drink or are you just gonna chug down free coffee all morning?"

"Hard times, my friend," I said. "But our misfortune can be your gain."

I pulled the .44–.40 out of my mackinaw pocket, and right away the bartender clawed for the ceiling.

"Oh God, mister, don't shoot!" he gasped. "I got a wife and kids and a sick old mother. Oh, please don't kill me."

Boys, I was more surprised than that bartender. I looked around the bar, hoping none of the sleeping drunks had woke up. Then I waved my hands and said: "Shhh . . . now just you shhh."

I reckon my waving the gun around made the guy's nerves even worse, because he opened his mouth and shrieked: "Murder! Bloody murder! Police! Police!"

Johnny Blue walked quickly up to the bar, grabbed the man by the scruff of his neck and shook him like a mangy dog.

"Listen, my friend," he said, "jest relax. He's not gonna shoot you. His gun ain't even loaded. Show him."

I thumbed open the loading gate, turned the muzzle of the gun up and spun the cylinder.

The bartender's gray cheeks slowly started to get some color back and he lowered his hands. "Not loaded? Cowboy, you shouldn't go scaring honest folks like that."

"No offense intended," I said. "The fact of the matter is, I wanted to sell you this fine weapon."

The bartender shook his head angrily.

"I got all the guns I need."

"I can't abide a surly bartender," I said. "Maybe I'll change my mind and not sell it to you."

"Go to hell."

"Mister, I'm offering you this fine Colt's self-cocker for just three gallons of Anderson's rye whiskey. It seems to me, you'd jump at the chance."

"Hey, that's my—" Johnny Blue began, but I cut him off.

"Ah well, it's probably all for the best," I sighed. "Seems to me, you ain't man enough to own this here gun."

I turned to Johnny Blue.

"Let's go try somewhere else," I said. Then I added in a whisper loud enough for the bartender to hear, "It's not every day a man passes on the chance to own the gun that kilt ol' Jesse."

Well boys, that did the trick.

The man stepped out from behind the counter and said: "Now just hold up there, cowboy. Are you saying this is the gun that killed Jesse James?"

"The very same."

"Aw, you're full of horse crap."

"Suit yourself."

I moved toward the door, but the bartender's voice stopped me.

"How do you know this is the piece that killed Jesse?"

I sighed, and said slowly, like I was talking to a

farmer, "Mister, Bob Ford hisself gave me this here Colt when we was ridin' the grub line together back in Missouri. Didn't he, Johnny Blue boy?"

"That's my—"

"Damn right he did," I said. "Put it right in my hand, Bob Ford did. Said it was a memento, for old times' sake."

I knew I had my fish. Now all I had to do was reel him in.

"Lookee here," I said.

I took out my knife and unscrewed the handles. Then I turned them over and showed them to the bartender.

"Ol' Bob wrote them words hisself," I said. "I seen him write them with a stub o' pencil and a salt tear o' sadness in his eye."

On one handle were the words:

I
KILT
POOR
JESSE WITH
THIS .44–.40

and on the other:

IN
HOPE
OF LIFE
ETERNAL
—Bob Ford

I wiped my sleeve across my eyes.

"Amen and hallelujah," I said. "It makes me sad to

recollect it. Them words are straight from ol' Bob's noble soul and would melt a heart of stone."

"I'll give you five dollars for it," the bartender said.

"Nah," I said, "I've changed my mind about sellin' it."

"Okay. Suit yourself."

I heard a train whistle in the distance. The bartender took out his watch and glanced at it.

"It's still an hour till noon," he noted. "She's early for a change."

Boys, let me tell you that just about then I was starting to feel kinda desperate, so I baited my hook with another worm and threw it back into the pond.

"Mister, this here gun, the gun that shot ol' Jesse in the back, can be yours for just three gallons of Anderson's pure rye whiskey."

"I'll give you two," the bartender said.

"Done," I said.

As the bartender left to get the whiskey I replied, "These is hard times, Johnny Blue. Don't think about it as losing a gun. Think of it as findin' a warm place to spend the winter."

Johnny Blue shook his head. "I jest don't feel right about what you just done."

"Well, I reckon it feels jest fine to me," I said.

Me and Johnny Blue, we almost ran out of the saloon with the whiskey before that surly bartender got to thinking about things too much and changed his mind.

Once we got outside I hurried toward Amos Pinkney's encampment, Johnny Blue tagging along at my heels. I carried the whiskey, he carried nothing but a worried expression.

It had grown even colder as we got closer to the noon hour and a few flakes of snow were being tossed around by a north wind so strong I seen a chicken lay the same egg three times. Boys, that wind was a warning of a terrible winter to come and I knew me and Johnny Blue was fast running out of options.

Johnny Blue shivered, from the cold or something else I do not know. "Will you please tell me what we're doing?" he asked. "And when are we gonna drink our whiskey that I gave up my gun for?"

"This whiskey," I said, "is Anderson's pure rye. It ain't for the likes of you."

"Then who's it for?"

"It's for our mutual friend, Mister Jacob Pike."

Johnny Blue stopped dead in his tracks.

"Now what's the problem?" I asked.

Johnny Blue swallowed hard."If Amos Pinkney catches us anywhere near his place, we're dead men."

"He won't catch us," I said. "He's busy meetin' them gunmen of his'n off the noon train."

"Yeah, but suppose they come right back here?"

I shook my head. "Listen, if them boys have come all the way up from Texas, they've worked up a two-bottle thirst by this time. They're headed for the nearest saloon right now."

"Maybe Pike's with them," Johnny Blue said.

"I thought about that," I told him, "but I don't reckon Amos Pinkney would want ol' Pike as part of any welcoming committee. He ain't exactly genteel folks."

"I reckon not."

"Good. Now let's get this thing over with."

"What thing?" Johnny Blue asked suspiciously.

"Trust me," I said.

Johnny Blue just groaned.

When we got to Pink's camp the place looked deserted, which suited me just fine so long as Jacob Pike was there.

I cupped my hands to my mouth and hollered: "Hello the camp!"

"Nobody here," Johnny Blue said. "Let's go."

I tried again.

"Hallooooo the camp!"

This time the sides of the largest tipi bulged here and there and I heard the almightiest cursing come from inside. The flap flew open and Jacob Pike stepped outside, pulling a suspender over his naked shoulder. He had a Winchester in his right fist and his face wore a wicked scowl.

"Dead," Johnny Blue said. "This time, both of us. Stone dead."

"What the hell do you two want?" Pike demanded.

Behind him I saw one of the comely Indian women. She was smoothing her dress around her shapely knees and she was looking at me with murder in her eyes.

"Speak, damn your hides," Pike snarled. "You interrupted me when I was fixin to get laid. I'm gonna put a bullet into both of you, just see if I don't."

"Mister Pike," I said quickly. "We come in peace."

"What do you want, curse you?"

"Jacob, Jacob, Jacob. We . . . I mean me and him . . . we got to thinkin' about the coffee an' all an' we feel real bad about it. That's why"—I held up the jugs of whiskey—"we figgered to make it all up to you."

Pike's rifle muzzle dropped a little, and above his

open mouth his little piggy eyes were screwed up tight as he tried to figger this out.

I guess he threw a pretty wide loop over his brain because he managed to rope a thought. "Major's gone to meet them Texicans of his'n," he said. "Left me here."

"Well, that's just too bad," I said. "Isn't it, Johnny Blue?"

"Sure is," Johnny Blue said.

"Major says I don't have . . . the necessary social graces to make a favorable first impression on the gentlemen from Texas. What do you suppose he meaned by that?"

"Well, all the Major is saying is that you are such a noble, kind and generous soul that those Texans wouldn't appreciate you, Jacob.

"I know them boys, an' they all think they're Texans by divine right. It's been my experience that you can always tell a Texan, but you can't tell him much."

This time the big wolfer grabbed on to that thought and hogtied it.

"Yeah," he said, his face brightening. "That's me alright. A noble, kind an' . . . what was it you said, tramp?"

"A noble, kind and generous soul," I repeated.

"Yeah, that's it. That's what the Major must have meaned."

"Oh yes, that's what he meaned, Jacob." I held up the jugs of whiskey. "Now, will we let bygones be bygones?"

The big man shook his head. "The Major says I can't drink today on account of how I got a big fight tonight. Major says I got to kill that man. Beat him to death with these." He showed me his huge fists. "So there's no mistaking who won. An' then I'm gonna get the five hunnerd dollars for the Major."

"That's very generous of you, Jacob," I said. "But the Major didn't mean for you to have no whiskey a-tall. He doesn't mind you having a drink with friends. He just says you should use moderation."

"Is that what he meaned?" Pike asked.

"That's what he meaned," I said. "Didn't he, Johnny Blue?"

Johnny Blue looked warily over his shoulder, then said: "He sure did."

Pike's face brightened. "Well, then it's okay. We can go into my tipi."

The wolfer slapped the Indian woman on the rump.

"You get lost. But come back later."

The woman tossed her head and stalked away, hips swaying.

"Handsome woman," I said, as we bent and went through the flap of the tipi. The place was warm and cozy with soft wolf skins scattered on the floor. Something smelling of meat bubbled in an iron pot suspended over a small fire in the middle of the floor.

"She's a good woman," Pike said. "I don't have to beat her no more'n three or four times a month."

"What's her name?" Johnny Blue asked. I knew he wasn't really interested, but he was nervous and needed to hear himself talk.

"Who cares?" Pike said.

"Oh, not me," Johnny Blue said hastily. "I jest wondered what you called her."

"Cowboy, that's her name," Pike growled. "Her daddy was an old brave with three wives an' eight daughters an' no sons. When I bought her, I asked what she was called an' he said, 'Who cares?' So that's her name as far as I'm concerned."

"And a right purty name it is, too," I said, shooting Johnny Blue a look that could have killed. I held out a jug. "Here, Jacob, try a swig of this."

The big man took the jug and drank mightily. Then he wiped his mouth on a hairy forearm and passed it to Johnny Blue. Johnny Blue put the jug to his lips, but he caught my warning shake of the head and that canny cowboy, he only pretended to drink.

Then he passed the jug to me and I did the same.

Pike took the jug and cradled it on top of his massive belly. "I just wanna say to you two tramps that you're just a couple of worthless, no good saddle bums. But this is real American of you."

He shifted his hips, cocked one cheek toward me and let rip with a tremendous fart.

"The pleasure's all ours," I said.

Johnny Blue sniffed the simmering cauldron and asked: "What's for lunch?"

"Prime wolf meat with some rattlesnake for flavor," Pike said. He hunted around where he sat, then pulled out a wooden bowl from under him and a horn spoon. These he tossed over to Johnny Blue. "Help yourself."

I watched Johnny Blue spoon a huge helping of stew into his bowl. He attacked the food like a starving man.

The six salted peanuts I'd eaten for breakfast were rolling around in my empty stomach like buckshot.

I was missing a whole passel of meals, but I decided to pass on this one. I reckon there's just some vittles you don't feed to a hog, unless you want a dead hog.

Pike took a swig from the jug and shoved it between his knees, apparently deciding that Anderson's pure rye wasn't for the likes of me and Johnny Blue.

"Boys, let me tell you about my life on the plains," he said.

"We'd love to hear it, wouldn't we, Johnny Blue?" I said.

Speaking through a mouthful of stew, Johnny Blue said, "Oh yeah, sure we would."

"Well," said Pike, "it all began when I was borned in Illinois an' raised an orphan. I was taken in by a farmer, a hard, God-fearing man who beat me every single day of my life till I was twelve years old. That was the year I got big enough to kill him. I killed him with these." Again he held up those massive, hairy paws.

"Well, I took all the money that was there an' a horse an' headed west . . ."

Boys, Pike's tale went on and on, and I calculate the wolfer had killed as many men as you got fingers and toes, most of them with his bare hands. This was not a man to be trifled with, let me tell you.

As Pike talked, Johnny Blue kept peeking out the flap of the tipi, his eyes big as all hell. He knew as well as I did that if Amos Pinkney came back with those Texans, we were as good as dead.

It was also taking ol' Pike a long time to get drunk. I began to wonder if I should have got cheaper whiskey, the stuff that comes out of the bottle blue and makes a jackrabbit spit in a coyote's eye.

"An' then I met the Major, God bless him," Pike

was saying. "I kilt this United States marshal for him one time, and he's rewarded me with nothing but sweet an' gentle kindness ever since."

There was a definite slur in Pike's voice. The man was finally getting drunk.

"The Major is an offisher . . . an offticer . . . an offisher an' a gen'leman," Pike said. "He's a blue blood . . . the Rose of Tralee . . . he's . . ."

The man's huge head slumped onto his chest and he began to snore.

"Let's get out of here," Johnny Blue said.

I held up the jugs and shook them. The few last drops struggled out of the necks and hissed into the fire. "We just made it," I said. "It took both jugs."

Pike all at once stopped snoring and Johnny Blue gently pushed him with the toe of his boot. "Oh God," he said, "we didn't kill him, did we?"

"Nah," I replied, "he'll sleep like a baby till midnight."

"He's not gonna fight the Mauler tonight," Johnny Blue said.

"No, he's not," I said. "But you are."

We looked out of the tipi, saw the coast was clear, and quickly walked down the street. I pulled the threadbare collar of my mackinaw around my ears and saw Johnny Blue do the same.

"I don't like this," he said. "I don't like this one bit."

"You worry too much," I said. "There's nothing to it. We fight the Mauler, pick up our five hunnerd and we're out of here and on the trail to Billings before Amos Pinkney knows what's happening.

"Then it's you an' me in a nice hotel living warm and cozy as chipmunks all winter."

Johnny Blue shook his head.

"We'll make it," I said. "Now all we got to do is find this Doc Fortune feller and tell him there's been a change in tonight's bill."

"If we live long enough," Johnny Blue said.

SEVEN

There were few people on the street because of the icy wind and snow flurries, but I stopped a man who was bundled up in a gray overcoat and fur hat.

"Hey, mister, where can I find this Doc Fortune feller?" I asked.

The stranger, a drummer by the look of him, didn't show much inclination to stop until Johnny Blue stepped in front of him.

"Who are you looking for?" the man asked irritably.

"Fortune," I said, "Doc Fortune."

"Never heard of him."

The drummer moved to step around us.

"He owns the Boston Mauler," I said.

"Well why the hell didn't you say so?" It seemed like the little man didn't want to take his hands out of his coat pockets, because he motioned with his chin. "On t'other side of town. The Masons set up a marquee tent for the fights beside their temple. You can't miss it."

The tent was as large as a good-sized saloon, green colored, and it flapped in the breeze like a wet flag.

Me and Johnny Blue walked through the wide entrance. It was warmer now that we were inside and sheltered from the biting wind and sleet flurries.

It seemed that the entire tent was filled with rows of tiered seats, all facing toward a cleared area in the center where a small, gray-haired man stood by as an enormous and battered pug skipped rope.

This could only be the Mauler, and he was the biggest man I'd ever seen in my life, before or since.

Boys, do you recollect ol' Gut Johnson, the Swan hand who rode in a buckboard because he couldn't find a pony that could carry him?

Well, the Mauler was bigger than him.

You know me, I'm five foot eight in my boots, and I always reckoned that the size of a man's got nothing to do with his height, but boys, I got to tell you that the Mauler was enormous. He topped me by a good nine or ten inches, his arms were as big as my waist and his huge belly hung between his massive thighs like a sack of grain. His neck, as thick as a steer's, held up a shaved head that looked as round and as hard as a cannonball. I reckoned even his shadow must've gone three hunnerd pounds or more.

I looked at Johnny Blue and saw that he was just standing there staring right at the Mauler, his eyes bugging out of his head.

"We gotta talk, you and me," he said. "I mean, we got to talk right *now*."

Johnny Blue turned on his heel and was about to walk out of the tent, when a booming voice stopped him in his tracks.

"Hold on there, young feller," Doc Fortune said, "and state your business."

I grabbed Johnny Blue by the arm and pushed him forward. "Are you Doctor Fortune?" I asked, knowing full well he was.

"I am Silas Fortune, yes."

I introduced me and Johnny Blue and then said, "We've brung you a message."

"Indeed?"

The Mauler, sweating like a hog, stopped his rope jumping to study us and the Doc turned on him right sharp, "Bartholomew, I don't recall telling you to stop."

The big man looked sheepishly at the Doc, then at us, and started to skip again.

"And what is this intelligence you have brought me?" he asked.

"Well, Doc, we're friends of ol' Jacob Pike, and we're here to tell you he's feelin' right poorly and can't fight the Mauler tonight."

Doc's face fell. "This is most distressing. What ails the man, for heaven's sake? He looked strong as an ox when I saw him last."

"Strong drink and low company," I said. "He's not to be trusted."

Doc considered this new turn of events for a few moments, then waved his arm at the Mauler. "You may stop now, Bartholomew." To me and Johnny Blue he said, "This really is too bad. This was to be Bartholomew's last fight in Great Falls and we were expecting a large crowd. Were we not, Bartholomew?"

"Indeed we were, Doctor," the Mauler said.

His voice surprised me. It was soft and light, almost like a woman's, and I remember puzzling over how such a small voice could come out of that huge body.

Doc shook his head.

"Well, there seems to be nothing for it but to pack up and move on. There will be no Doctor Fortune's

Elixir of Life sold in Great Falls tonight. There's no profit in no-shows."

"Ah, well, see," I began, "I believe we have the solution, Doc. You see, my friend here is quite willin' to take Mister Pike's place. He is fully qualified."

Johnny Blue, who had not once taken his eyes off the Mauler, said, "I'm no longer so sure about that."

"Your friend seems suddenly less than willing," Doc said.

"He's just a bit shy, is all," I told him.

"The hell I am!" Johnny Blue protested. "I could get myself killed."

Doc Fortune shrugged. "Well, it is late. But maybe I could find someone else, a pugilist the Mauler has not yet beaten. Though he's already beaten a round dozen or more."

"Good idea," said Johnny Blue.

I could see things were not going well, so I made an excuse to the Doc and took Johnny Blue aside out of earshot.

"Are you crazy?" I asked him. "We got five hunnerd dollars riding on this fight. Do you want maybe we should starve or freeze to death this winter and never be able to find our sister?

"Do you want to just walk away from here and leave her with Geronimo? Is that what you want?"

Johnny Blue's face was troubled and I could see he was struggling with his own fear and his desire to be reunited with his kin.

"Do you see the size of the Mauler?" he asked. "I know he'll kill me for sure."

"Put your mind at ease," I told him. "I've got a plan."

Johnny Blue put his head in his hands and groaned, but I ignored his dramatics and said, "Listen, it can't fail. I'm gonna arrange with Doc Fortune for the Mauler to carry you for fourteen rounds. I'll tell him we've got a big side bet that you can last that long so we don't really care about the five-hunnerd-dollar purse.

"I'll say to the Doc that you'll toe the line for the fourteenth time, then take a dive for the dirt as soon as the Mauler lays a knuckle on you."

Johnny Blue eyed me suspiciously.

"Why would Doc Fortune go along with that?"

"Think. As far as Doc's concerned, the crowd gets a good show, he sells a lot of that snake oil of his, and he doesn't need to risk his five hunnerd.

"It's perfect. Or so he thinks."

"I don't get it," Johnny Blue said. "What's in it for us?"

"What's in it for us?" I said, like an echo. "Hell, we pull the ol' double cross and walk away with a cool five hunnerd dollars. That's what's in it for us."

"I still don't get it."

"It's so easy," I said. "You take your dive in the fourteenth, just like I've arranged it, and I drag you back to your corner. But to everybody's surprise, especially the Doc's, you get up and toe the line again.

"See? It's the fifteenth round and we've won our money. All you got to do is take another dive and we're out of there.

"The Doc knows he's been had. The Mauler knows he's been had. But in front of the crowd, there's nothing they can do about it but pay us."

"Do you think it will work?" Johnny Blue asked. "I'm not so sure I want to go through with this."

"It can't fail," I said. "Trust me."

I told Johnny Blue to stay where he was and went over to speak to Doc Fortune and the Mauler. I knew my whole scheme to get the five hunnerd hinged on what happened next. If Johnny Blue refused to fight, it was all over.

Of course, I knew they wouldn't go for a hare-brained scheme like the one I'd just outlined to Johnny Blue, but I had to make it look as though they were, so I told them he was eager as a beaver to go through with the fight.

"See him standing over there, Doc?" I said. "Look how confident he is. He says now he's thought about it, he'll kick the Mauler's ass till his nose bleeds."

The Doc looked over at Johnny Blue and that irresolute rider waggled his fingers at him and smiled. The Doc smiled back.

"Now Johnny Blue is like a brother to me, and I set great store by him," I said, "but I just thought I should mention that he did say the Mauler is just a big, empty tub of lard, all gurgle and no guts. When I heard that, I told him maybe that he was going a little too far and that the Mauler might settle his hash for him."

The Mauler looked over at Johnny Blue, who smiled and waggled his fingers again.

The Mauler smiled back.

Like a wolf, I thought.

I walked over to Johnny Blue.

"It's all settled," I told him.

"Are you sure?"

"Hell, yes, didn't you see the way they smiled at you? That means everything is just fine."

Then I called over to the Mauler: "I told him the fight was all settled and that you know what you have to do."

The Mauler grinned and crashed a huge fist into his open palm.

"I'm primed," he said. "I'll take care of your dusky friend there. I'll take care of him reeeal good."

Johnny Blue's eyes bugged out of his head again. "Are you sure—" he began warily.

But I cut him off.

"Trust me."

EIGHT

The afternoon passed without incident, though I must have made a hundred trips to the livery stable door, each time dreading what I might see come walking down the street.

Early that evening when me and Johnny Blue walked to the tent a light snow was falling and the wind had dropped. It felt ten degrees warmer, I reckoned.

Doc Fortune stood outside the entrance to the marquee on a box, brandishing a bottle of his patent medicine. He was haranguing a growing crowd of bundled-up men, women and children eager to see the coming battle.

"Roll up, roll up, my lords, ladies and gentlemen," Doc said in the booming voice of one of them Washington-bound politicians.

"Your purchase of just one bottle of Doctor Fortune's Elixir of Life will not only cure impotence, lumbago, lethargy, constipation, cancer, piles, pimples, toothache, tinnitus and nervous disability brought on by the indiscretions of youth, but it will also gain for you admittance to the fight of this or any other century.

"I will present to you the one, the only, the original Boston Mauler, lately returned from Europe where he thrilled the crowned heads of twenty nations with his fantastic feats of pugilistic prowess.

"This is the man who made the great John L. himself cry uncle. And I assure you, each and every man will get a chance to shake the Mauler's hand after the contest is over.

"You will shake the hand that shook the world.

"And for tonight and tonight only, you will see this behemoth of the bare knuckle toe the line against that battling blue blood from faraway Ethiopia, that dusky demon of the desert, that master of a hundred wives, Prince Ali Ben Hassan!"

"Hey, Perfesser!" a man in the crowd yelled. "I thought we was gonna see that big wolfer feller fight the Mauler."

"Alas, the gentleman is indisposed," the Doc said. "But fear not, sir, his loss is your gain, let me assure you."

Another man in a fur coat and plug hat studied the elixir bottle and asked the Doc, "Will this stuff grow hair?"

"Why, it is guaranteed, my good man, or your money back," the Doc said. "I saw it grow hair on a man who'd once been scalped alive by the savage Comanche."

The man removed his hat, revealing a shiny, completely bald head. "Will it grow hair on this, Perfesser?" he asked.

"Miracles do happen, my friend," the Doc replied and the man and the crowd laughed.

Me and Johnny Blue walked into the tent, catching

a nod from Doc Fortune, who seemed to be in fine form this evening.

Inside, the seats were already filling up. The atmosphere was gloomy and smoky, the tent lit by a dozen or so kerosene lamps.

The Mauler was already sitting on a stool in the cleared area in the middle of the tent. About twenty feet and a line of whitewash as wide as my hand on the browned grass separated him from the opposite stool. I sat Johnny Blue on this stool and helped him off with his hat and mackinaw.

"I don't like the way he's looking at me," Johnny Blue whispered. "I don't like it a-tall."

The Mauler was grinning and nodding his head at Johnny Blue, pounding his fist into his open palm. I'm not a nervous man, but it looked to me like the Mauler could fight a buzz saw and give it a three turn start.

I tried not to let Johnny Blue see the shudder that shook me as I said, "You've got nothing to worry about, Johnny Blue boy." I kneaded his shoulders. "It's all been taken care of. He won't lay a knuckle on you."

"You're sure about that?" Johnny Blue asked. "He looks as mean as an ol' mossy-horned bull and madder'n all hell."

"Sure I'm sure," I said soothingly. "Now let's get your shirt off."

"My shirt? Why should I take my shirt off?" Johnny Blue asked, a rising note of panic in his voice.

"Well, you don't want it covered in bloo—"

I realized my mistake and stopped, but it was too late.

"Blood! You was gonna say blood!" Johnny Blue whispered urgently. "I heard it plain. Who's blood are we talking about?"

I had to think fast.

"Black, I was gonna say," I told him. "Your shirt will get black from all that oily stuff they're rubbing on the Mauler's chest."

Boys, I know that sounds lame, but it was all I could come up with at short notice.

I helped Johnny Blue unbutton his shirt and then pulled his vest over his head.

Now, a lot of people were gathered around the Mauler, shaking his hand and telling him how great he was an' stuff, but one left him and strolled over to where Johnny Blue sat. It was the farmer we'd seen in the Sideboard the previous evening and he was sucking on a bottle of beer somebody else must have bought for him.

"Evenin'," I said.

The sodbuster nodded without answering me, all the time studying Johnny Blue's naked chest.

Then he shook his head, said something under his breath like, "Tut-tut-tut," and walked away.

"The farmer don't give much for my chances, does he?" asked Johnny Blue, a worried expression on his face.

"Well, he don't know the fix is in, do he?" I said.

Johnny Blue shook his head.

"I'm not so sure about this. It seems a might thin to me."

"Listen," I said, "you just got to toe that white-washed line fifteen times, no matter what happens.

That's all you have to do, then we can go look for our sister. It's easy."

"If'n it's so easy, how come you're not doing it?" Johnny Blue asked.

"Bad back," I said.

Johnny Blue was about to say more when a tow-headed boy in blue-checked homespun came up and kicked me on the side of my leg.

"Hey, what was that for? You little—"

"There's a man outside wants to talk to you," the boy said, ignoring my outburst. "Done give me a nickel to tell you that."

I rubbed my leg. "What's his name?"

"He didn't give it."

"What's he want?"

"He didn't give that either."

The boy stuck his hand out.

"Get lost," I said.

He stuck his tongue out.

I swiped at his head, but he ducked, and with a mocking laugh was gone.

"Must be Doc," I told Johnny Blue. "Jest you stay here and set tight till I get back."

"I ain't going nowhere," Johnny Blue said mournfully.

Outside the snow had stopped and there was still a small crowd of people clustered around Doc Fortune.

He caught sight of me and said, "Ah, my cowboy friend. We're doing very well tonight, as you can see."

I nodded. "Did you want to see me, Doc?"

The little man shook his head at me as he exchanged his elixir for dollars.

"Not I (thank you ma'am). Is your boy ready?

(Thank you sir, drink it in health.) Fight time soon, y'know."

"He's ready. Says he's primed to whup his weight in wildcats."

"That's the spirit. I'll see you inside real soon."

I nodded to the Doc again and looked around. The last few stragglers were entering the tent and none paid me the slightest attention.

This was strange. Who wanted to talk to me?

I pulled the collar of my mackinaw up around my ears and walked around the side of the marquee, away from the lamp-lit entrance, and peered into the gloom.

"Anyone there?" I asked.

That's when the cold muzzle of a long-barreled Colt poked out of the darkness and came to rest right between my eyes.

NINE

"**D**on't say a word, " a harsh voice commanded. "Jest step over this way real relaxed and easy."

I walked into the gloom, the muzzle of the revolver, unwavering, on the bridge of my nose.

"There's been some mistake—" I began.

"No mistake, cowboy."

I heard the scratch of a match to my left and watched in horror as the flaring light illuminated the cruel face of Amos Pinkney as he lit a long, thin cheroot.

"Nice to see you again, cowboy," Pink said from behind a cloud of blue smoke.

As my eyes adjusted to the gloom I saw the man who was holding the Colt to my head. He was tall and broad with a savage scar angling across his bearded right cheek.

"Evening, Major," I said, surprised that my voice was almost steady. "I didn't expect to see you here."

Pink nodded.

"No doubt you didn't. Especially since poor Mister Pike can't be with us tonight. He's somewhat indisposed, you know. All at sixes and sevens, as the English say."

"That's too bad," I said, my voice quivering like an aspen leaf in the wind.

"Yes indeed," Pink said. "It is just too bad. It seems that Mister Pike partook too much of the festive bowl after falling in with rough companions. Goodness knows, I've warned him about low company many times in the past."

"Bad whiskey and bad company," I croaked. "They've been the ruin of many a good man."

Pink nodded again.

"Yes, haven't they though."

He stood there studying my face for a while then said, "But enough of this small talk. Let's cut to the heart of the matter."

Pinkney's hand shot out and grabbed me around the jaw in a steel vise. I felt my lips pouting out, like I was about to kiss a pretty gal.

He slammed my head against the tough, wet canvas of the tent and pushed his face so close to mine I could smell the sharp cheroot smoke on his breath.

"Cowboy," he said, "I'm going to tell you a story. Do you like stories?"

I couldn't move my jaw to talk, but I did my best to nod my head.

"Good," ol' Pink said. "That's very good.

"Now this story is about a man I once knew. Now this man was a farmer, a big, strapping chap and a hard worker from all accounts. After I returned from the war, this farmer sold me and young Jesse and Frank and some others a hunting dog.

"He told me this dog would point quail and never break, even if he fell over from hunger and exhaustion.

79

"I was so happy! And the dog did point wonderfully well. But I soon learned that all it would point was turtles. Turtles!

"So I took my gun and shot that dog dead."

I struggled against Pink's hand and managed to squeak: "Major, maybe we can reach some kind of accommodation, you and me. I—"

"No, sssh, listen," Pink said. "For here is wisdom.

"Now that farmer made mock of me behind my back. He told his family and his friends, which were many, how he'd made a fool of the stupid Johnny Reb.

"He laughed at me. And his family laughed at me. And this hurt me so deeply." He shook his head at me sadly. "So very deeply.

"Well," Pink sighed, "I paid that farmer a visit, me and this gentleman here, Mister Jericho Gentle, who had just recently come into my employ.

"Mister Gentle had once been a man of the cloth, an ordained minister, till he got a taste o' hell at Chickamauga and discovered that he savored slaughter more than scripture.

"So I turned that laughing farmer over to Mister Gentle's tender mercies. Now tell the cowboy what you did to that farmer, Mister Gentle."

"I skun him," the man called Gentle told me. "I skun him to the white marrow bone."

Boys, if you think I was scared about then, think again. I was terrified.

"Major," I gasped, "we can still split the money. We can—"

"No, no, no, cowboy," Pink said. "It's very important that you listen to the story.

"See, after Mister Gentle had finished his work with

the skinning knife, he took what was left of that farmer and crucified him to the door of his barn. But Mister Gentle, pious soul that he is, forebore to crucify the man in the manner of our Blessed Savior, but rather, nailed him to the rough boards head down.

"Now, cowboy, have you paid attention thus far?"

I swore up and down that I had.

"That's good," Pink said. "That's very nice.

"Let us go on. Now, that farmer was a strong man, and he screamed for three days and two nights because he so very much wanted to die, but could not.

"And, lo, his womenfolk came to that terrible place amid great lamentation and gazed upon him and tore out their hair and rent their garments and begged me to deliver the merciful ball. Yet I did not.

"You see, that man had wronged me and laughed at me and made mock of me, and his screams of mortal agony were a soothing balm to my soul.

"Then, as dusk fell on the third day, the farmer died and Mister Gentle and I bowed our heads in prayer for his immortal soul, though we both feared that he was now among the damned.

"And thus ends my story. What do you think of it, cowboy?"

"See," I babbled, "ol' Pike asked for coffee and then we had the whiskey and the gun that shot poor Jesse and we meant no harm and ol' Pike wanted to get laid and he gave Johnny Blue this stew and—"

Amos Pinkney tightened his vise-like grip on my jaw.

"Enough of this nonsense," he snarled. "That farmer wronged me, cowboy, and he was made to pay the price.

"But his offense, grievous as it was, was nothing compared to what you have done. You have laughed at me and made mock of me behind my back and perhaps put my plans in some jeopardy."

"Major, I—"

"Listen to me. Your end, when it comes—and it will come soon—will take much longer than the farmer's and be even more terrible. You will die a thousand times in shrieking agony before merciful death at last takes you.

"Now go, cowboy. And think on this: We will meet again you and I, by and by.

"And Mister Gentle, here, will keep his blade honed sharp until we do."

TEN

Pink released me, then he and Gentle faded into the night.

I stood there for a while, trying to calm down, and took stock of my situation, which wasn't too good. As I saw it, I had two choices and one of them wasn't hardly a choice at all.

If me and Johnny Blue beat the Mauler and won our five hunnerd, we could stay and fight it out with Pinkney and his gang. Boys, you all know that in them days me and Johnny Blue weren't gunfighters, though some said in later years that I was, so that idea was just buckin' a losing game.

The more I thought about it, the more I figgered the best plan was to get our money, then light a shuck out of Great Falls and hole up for the winter someplace as far from Pink as we could get.

I guess it all boiled down to living or dying. And me and Johnny Blue had to live if we were ever going to find our little sister.

Now that I'd made my mind up, I went back into the tent and made my way through the crowd to Johnny Blue's side.

As soon as he saw me, Doc Fortune left the Mauler

and came hustling over. "Where have you been?" he asked. "We got to get this fight started."

"Don't hurry on my account," Johnny Blue said.

"I was jest talking to some well-wishers, Doc," I said. "We're ready when you are. Johnny Blue's joshing you, he's as keen as mustard. Ain't you, Johnny Blue boy?"

"No, I ain't. I—"

"See, Doc?" I said. "He's got that ol' chamber of commerce spirit. He's rarin' to go."

Now Doc, he looked kinda doubtful about Johnny Blue's eagerness an' all, but he said: "Well, let's get the show on the road before this crowd starts tearing the place apart. They're getting a might restless."

The crowd cheered as Doc walked into the center of the tent and straddled the white line. Doc held up his hands for silence.

"My lords, ladies and gentlemen, tonight I bring you a battle that is destined go down in pugilistic history. For a purse of five hundred dollars American, the Boston Mauler, the man who brought the great John L. himself to his knees, the man who is the cherished champeen and favorite of the crowned heads of Europe, the man who has fought three hundred times and lost but once, and that to the aforesaid Mister Sullivan, has been challenged by that sable sultan of the Ethiope sands, that gory gladiator of the Gobi, Prince Ali Ben Hassan!"

The crowd cheered the Mauler and booed the Prince.

"Listen to them cheer for you, Johnny Blue," I lied.

"Yeah, right," quoth the sable sultan. "What the hell does 'gory' mean?"

"Brave," I said. "Brave as a bigamist."

"You sure?"

"Would I lie to you?"

Boys, whatever Johnny Blue was about to say is lost to posterity, because Doc ordered the Mauler and the Prince to toe the line.

Now, me and Johnny Blue hadn't been eating too good of late, and standing there beside the Mauler, Johnny Blue looked downright puny.

Boys, you recollect Johnny Blue. He always had a good breadth to his shoulders and them big arms of his, but the Mauler was enormous, like somebody had carved him out of a living oak, and for the first time I began to have serious doubts about the outcome of this scrap.

You know me, boys. If I could, I would have changed places with Johnny Blue right there and then. But on account of the cold weather, my bad back was playing up and I had a touch of the rheumatisms to boot. In days of yore when the cattle still roamed free on the range, both these ailments were the poor cowboy's lot. And I can tell you, all things considered, they'd laid me pretty low. So all I could do was whisper a few words of encouragement to my stalwart brother and hope for the best.

I watched the Mauler and Johnny Blue shake hands, then Doc said, "Get to fighting, lads."

And the battle was on.

Except it wasn't a battle.

The Mauler shoved out a big fist and pushed Johnny Blue away, giving himself some room.

That's when Johnny Blue took a dive for the dirt.

And I don't mean he took a dive and made it look

good. I mean he dived like a frog into a pond and then lay there hugging the sawdust.

"He's done for me at last," Johnny Blue gasped.

The crowd roared in disappointed rage and the Mauler stood there shaking his massive bald head in bafflement.

"I didn't touch him," the Mauler yelled to the crowd.

The crowd jeered and catcalled and some of them were already demanding their money back.

Doc came over to me and whispered urgently: "Get him to the line or you won't see a penny of that five hundred."

I kneeled down beside Johnny Blue.

"You gotta get back to scratch," I told him.

Johnny Blue, who could be an obstinate man when he was sober, shook his head. "I'm done for," he said.

The crowd was really getting worked up by this time, and I heard one rooster crow about "getting a rope."

"Johnny Blue," I whispered, "we're facing a necktie party for sure. You gotta get back to scratch."

"Can't. I've had it."

"Dammit," I said, "he didn't lay a finger on you."

"Oh, yes, he did," Johnny Blue said. He pointed to his chest just under his left collarbone. "He hit me right here. I'm gonna be as bruised as all hell tomorrow."

I quickly saw that this tack was getting me nowhere, so I came at it from another direction.

"Johnny Blue," I said, "if we don't win the five hunnerd we can't go looking for our little sister. Is that what you want? Do you want her to starve to death on some reservation in Arizona?"

"No," Johnny Blue said. "I don't want that."

"Right, then," I said. "You know what you have to do. A shy dog don't get any biscuits."

Johnny Blue nodded, determined now.

"I'll do it," he said. "I'll do it for my sister."

Johnny Blue, his homely face set and determined, toed the line.

The crowd cheered.

Then came one of those wonderful moments in the history of pugilism that me and every mother's son in that tent were privileged to witness.

Boys, if I live to be a hundred years old, I'll never forget it. It is something I will tell my children, and their children, and their children's children. It is truly the stuff of legend.

The Mauler snapped a straight left to Johnny Blue's chin. Then another. And another. The way Johnny Blue's head kept bouncing backward, I reckon the Mauler must have hit him six, seven, maybe eight times in the space of two seconds. The Mauler's fist moved so fast it was a white blur, like a streak of lightning.

It was devastating.

It was magnificent.

The crowd gave a mighty Huzzah! Then another. And I, swept up in the moment, could not help but join my voice to the general uproar.

Even when Johnny Blue crashed onto his back at my feet, I found myself joining in yet another loud Huzzah!

You may talk of John L. Sullivan all you want, boys.

But pound for pound, the Mauler was the greatest bare knuckle fighter I have ever seen.

An example of his handiwork now lay in the sawdust at my feet.

I didn't see any blood on Johnny Blue, but his face looked badly swollen already. Snot was running out of his nose and his left leg was twitching, but at least he was almost conscious.

"Wha . . . wha . . ." he whispered.

"He sucker punched you, Johnny Blue," I said. "Before that you was doing real good."

"Before that . . . real good . . . before . . . real good . . ."

As I helped Johnny Blue to his feet, my conscience was bothering me real bad. I had cheered the Mauler while my blood brother was getting battered to a pulp. I felt sick at heart and lowdown.

Boys, the way Johnny Blue staggered to the line again would have jerked tears from a glass eye. Of course, the Mauler immediately flattened him, but—I gotta say it—this time Johnny Blue went down with dignity.

Johnny Blue gamely toed the line again.

And got flattened.

He came to scratch again.

And got flattened.

Boys, I won't bore you with the details, but this fight was becoming painful to watch.

Then, I guess it was about Johnny Blue's ninth time to the line, a miracle happened.

By this time he was cut up real good and he had yet to lay a fist on the Mauler as far as I or anyone else could see.

But he was as angry as I'd ever seen him, like a randy rooster in an empty henhouse.

And he was loaded for bear.

Johnny Blue swung a wild right at the Mauler's head, which landed smack on that fearful fistologist's left ear.

The Mauler let loose with a bellow of pain and Johnny Blue followed up with a straight left to the point of the champ's chin.

The big man's eyes rolled up in his head and he crashed to the sawdust like a poleaxed colossus.

Boys, thus the mighty Goliath of Gath—as my momma used to tell me—must have fallen to the sands of Israel after that fateful stone from the shepherd boy's sling laid him low.

Amid the boos from the crowd, Johnny Blue heard a few cheers and, thus emboldened, he raised his fists above his head and strutted like a peacock.

But pride goeth before a fall.

The Mauler brushed away the attentions of Doc Fortune, shook his head once, then sprang to his feet. Johnny Blue's hands were still above his head when the Mauler hit him hard on the jaw.

Now it was Johnny Blue's turn to hit the sawdust.

And so it went.

After he was flattened for the twelfth time, Johnny Blue thought I was his daddy.

After his thirteenth trip to the sawdust he thought I was his momma.

"How am I doing, Momma?" he asked.

"Real good," I said. "Now get up there and toe the line."

"I can't, Momma," Johnny Blue said. "I'm hurtin', Momma, I'm hurtin' real bad."

Doc Fortune came over and looked down at my stricken gladiator.

"I don't think there's any fight left in him," Doc said. "He looks like he was chewed up by a coyote and dumped over a cliff."

"The hell you say," I replied. "Ol' Johnny Blue here ain't even begun to fight."

"Tell me a story, Momma," Johnny Blue said. I manhandled him to his feet and whispered into his ear: "Johnny Blue, you only got to toe the line two more times and we got our five hunnerd dollars and can go find our little sister. You can do that much."

"Will you come with me, Momma?" he asked.

"I'll be right here," I said.

Boys, that brave soul staggered to the line for the fourteenth time and lifted his fists. The crowd cheered wildly and I never felt so proud of him as I did in that moment.

I looked at the Mauler and the gentle giant had a stricken, disbelieving look on his face.

"Kid," the Mauler said, "you gotta stay down this time. I don't want to kill you."

Johnny Blue made no reply but swung at the Mauler and missed by a mile.

The Mauler cut loose with a lightning-fast right-and-left combination to Johnny Blue's head, and once again that valiant rider crashed to the sawdust.

Even I could see that it was all over.

Johnny Blue had done his best. I couldn't fault him for that. All I could do was stand there and kiss our five hunnerd bucks good-bye.

"Did I whup him, Momma?" Johnny Blue whispered. He was lying flat on his back, his face all beaten and bloody.

"No, you—"

Then I had an idea.

Boys, you know in the Good Book how Judas betrayed our Savior for thirty pieces of silver? Well I was about to up that ante and betray my blood brother for five hunnerd silver dollars.

Even after all these years, I still feel the shame of it. But understand, these was desperate times and we badly needed that money.

"Is he finished?" Doc called out to me.

"Not by a long shot," I said.

"It's your funeral," Doc said.

"Momma, I don't want to fight no more," Johnny Blue whined.

Me, I pitched my voice as high as I could—oh, the black, burning shame I feel!—and I squeaked: "Son, do you know what that bad man over there said to me?"

"What did he say to you, Momma?" Johnny Blue asked anxiously.

I squeaked again. "He said I was nothing but a dollar whore and lowdown."

"He said *what*?" Johnny Blue roared.

I knew I had him.

"He said," I squeaked, but then my tortured throat broke down and I had to finish in my normal voice. "He said your poor momma is a dollar whore and lowdown."

Now, Johnny Blue was so badly beaten I could have mopped up what was left of him with a sponge. But he slowly and painfully staggered to his feet and snarled, "I'm gonna kill him!"

Boys, that reckless rider staggered to the line, then, arms windmilling, flailed into the startled Mauler.

"What did you call my momma?" he yelled. "I'm gonna kick your ass so hard it's gonna take you two and a half days to get your breath back!"

The Mauler was so taken aback, he staggered into Doc, who pushed him toward the raving Johnny Blue.

"I didn't call your momma nothing," the Mauler gasped, defending himself from Johnny Blue's wild swings. "I don't even know your mother."

The crowd cheered itself hoarse and I heard voices yell: "Give him the money! He's won it fair and square. He done toed the line fifteen times. Huzzah! Huzzah!"

The Mauler stepped aside to let one of Johnny Blue's fists sail past his head, and Johnny Blue followed it and pitched forward, unconscious, onto his face.

I ran over and straddled Johnny Blue's body and stuck out my hand. "Give me our money, Doc," I said.

By way of reply, Doc turned to the Mauler.

"Bartholomew," he said, "this was ill done."

The Mauler hung his huge head. "Sorry, Doc," he muttered. "The kid had more guts than sense."

"We will talk more of this later," Doc said.

"Doc," I said, "I hate to be buttin' in at a time like this, but I want our five hunnerd."

That melancholy medicine man turned to me as if seeing me for the first time.

"Cowboy," he said, "I don't carry that kind of

money on my person. Get your friend cleaned up and then come over to my hotel. I'll pay you there."

Some of the crowd had come over to stare at the fallen Johnny Blue and to shake the Mauler's hand. But now they were drifting toward the exit.

Doc hurried after them.

"Gentlemen, gentlemen! I still have a supply of Doctor Fortune's Elixir of Life. Yours for the never-to-be-repeated, giveaway price of just fifty cents a bottle. Gentlemen, please . . ."

The Doc vanished through the tent flap on the heels of the departing crowd.

The Mauler pulled a shirt over his head and then buttoned himself into a jacket that looked to be at least two sizes too small for him.

He nodded to Johnny Blue's still body.

"When he wakes up, tell him . . ."

I could see the Mauler frown as his slow brain worked to find the proper words.

"Tell him he done good," he said at last.

"I sure will," I said.

He turned on his heel and hurried after the Doc.

The tent was empty now and me and Johnny Blue were alone. I cradled his head on my lap and lightly slapped his cheeks.

To my relief, his eyes fluttered open.

"Momma," he said.

"Yeah, right," I said. "Now get to your feet, we got five hunnerd dollars to collect."

"Did I do good, Momma?" Johnny Blue asked. "Did I lick him for you?"

"Yeah," I said. "You done real good."

I helped Johnny Blue to his feet, and, I'm the first to admit it, he looked terrible.

Boys, do you recollect ol' Silent Sam Bodene, him with the chewed off ear and the Bible thumping wife, that was kicked in the face by an army mule on the Fort Peck Indian Reservation in the summer of '81?

Well, I seen Sam the day after it happened in Joe Mulrey's saloon. His nose was broke and his eyes and lips were so swollen the only way we could get whiskey in him was by pouring it into his good ear.

Well, Johnny Blue looked like that.

Only worse.

Boys, let me tell you—me and him, we was doing our share of suffering for that five hunnerd.

Like I already said, the tent was empty, and the only sound was the wet canvas flapping in the wind. Most of the oil lamps had gone out, and dark shadows hung in every corner and cranny, like black spiderwebs.

Then I felt it, a prickling at the back of my neck as the hairs there stood on end.

Somebody was watching us. Watching us real close.

ELEVEN

I had my Colt tucked into the waistband of my pants, so I pulled it, then got my arm around Johnny Blue. I half dragged him out of the tent and into the street outside.

It was bitter cold, the wind driving a stinging sleet into my eyes.

"Are we going home, Momma?" Johnny Blue asked.

"Yeah, " I said. "We're going home."

I had to get to the livery stable and get Johnny Blue on his horse. Then to the hotel and collect our money. After that . . . well, my only plan was to light a shuck out of Great Falls and put as much ground between us and Amos Pinkney as possible.

It was close to midnight, and there was nobody on the street except us poor cowboys, the cold having driven everyone else indoors.

Johnny Blue was raving now about his momma and his home and his baby sister. And he kept saying how he'd just beaten up on Tube Wilson, a fight that everybody knows had happened years before.

"You was gonna put a bullet in ol' Tube, wasn't you, baby brother?" Johnny Blue said. "On account of how you said you'd shoot him right off'n me if he was startin' in to win that fight? Didn't you say that?"

"Yeah," I said. "I sure enough said that."

I kept turning my head this way and that like a barn owl with a case of nerves, expecting at any minute to see Pinkney and his boys emerge from the shadows.

But the street was still empty.

The livery stable came into view on my right and I dragged Johnny Blue toward it. One of the doors was open a few feet and beyond that, the place was dark.

The hairs on my neck were prickling again and I heard a jangling in my head like when an ornery cook beats the triangle with a ladle, calling the hands to supper.

I dragged Johnny Blue to the boardwalk and got him under the wooden awning of a cake and cookie store where I sat him down.

"Stay there," I told him.

He looked up at me, squinting through his half-closed eyes. "I ain't goin' anywhere," he said.

Johnny Blue was still half a bubble out of plumb, but he was starting to sound like his old surly and disagreeable self again, and right then I knew there was hope for him.

I stepped off the boardwalk into the street and started cautiously toward the barn, my Colt held high alongside my head like I'd seen a Texas Ranger do one time in El Paso just before he shot a feller.

I reached the open door of the barn, then stopped, wondering what to do next.

A quick look up and down the dark street told me that there was still no one around. But I had that uneasy feeling again that someone was watching me. A bat flitted past close to my head, swift and noiseless, but it made me start, and somewhere out there toward Pinkney's encampment I heard a dog bark.

Now, a blue Colt's gun can give a man a heap of confidence in dark places, and I hear tell there are some, most of them dead, who even believe it makes them bulletproof. But given the odds I was facing that night, even good ol' Sam's wheelgun brought me little by way of comfort.

But one thing was sure—I was all through being stampeded by Amos Pinkney. Even a worm will turn. And, boys, I was turning.

I thought: "The hell with it!" and kicked open the barn door and charged inside. I had my gun ready, the hammer under my thumb, but the barn remained dark and silent.

I moved cautiously inside and let my eyes get accustomed to the gloom. Something scuttled to my right and I threw down on it, but it was only a big ol' barn rat.

Outside, I heard Johnny Blue singing. He was making such a racket I knew it was time to move quickly.

I saddled my pony and Johnny Blue's buckskin, then went outside and got Johnny Blue to his feet.

"Where are we going, Momma?" he asked.

"Shhh." I held a warning finger to my lips. "We're going to get our money and then we're outta here."

Johnny Blue was crazy as a loon again and fought me so I couldn't get him into the saddle.

"If'n I was you boys, I'd light a shuck out of here."

I turned, bringing the Colt up real fast, and made

out the tall, skinny form of a man standing in the doorway.

"No cause for gunplay, cowboy," the man said. "I mean you no harm."

"Come closer so I can see you plain," I told him, my Colt cocked and ready.

The tall figure detached itself from the doorway and strolled toward me. Now that I could see him close I recognized the long-faced hayseed I'd met in the Sideboard. He still looked so down-in-the-mouth he could've eaten oats out of a butter churn.

"You been watchin' me for quite a spell," I said. "Now state your business."

"Jest thought you'd like to know, Amos Pinkney and his boys are looking for you all over town. I reckon they'll be here mighty soon."

Now, I had a lot on my mind right then, but I couldn't help but notice that the farmer was still carrying his empty beer glass.

"Tell me something, mister," I said, "was you born with that glass in your hand?"

"Seems like," the hick said.

Like I told you before, you never can get a lick of sense out of a farmer, so I changed tack and asked him to help me get Johnny Blue on his pony.

Now, that raving rider was heavy, maybe as heavy as an elephant tusk with the elephant still attached. But between me and the farmer, we managed to get him into the leather.

I mounted my own pony and grabbed the reins of Johnny Blue's buckskin.

Time was pressing and terrible danger lurked just around the corner, but my dang curiosity got the better of me again. You know me, boys. If'n a sign says DON'T TOUCH, I'll touch, just to see what happens.

It was like that spring up in the Judith Basin country when I put Johnny Blue up on Hallelujah Harmon's big thoroughbred stud and told him it could jump a four-bar fence, when I knowed full well it could only jump a three. But I was curious and wanted to see what would happen.

Do you recollect how the big stud pulled up right quick and Johnny Blue flew through the air, flapping his arms, trying to fly, before he landed in that big pile of cow shit? Johnny Blue was a mite upset and wasn't in a mind to listen to any talk of curiosity that day. He chased me for ten miles, taking pot shots at me with his Henry, before he cooled down and went back to the bunkhouse.

Well, just to bobtail this story, curiosity has been one of my lifelong failings, and it also has a habit of killing the cat.

But now I had to hold up and ask that farmer feller why he'd helped me the way he'd done.

"Amos Pinkney killed my brother," the rube said.

"Was he a gunfighter?" I asked.

"Nah, just a farmer, like me."

"Then how come ol' Pink killed him?"

The farmer sighed.

"It was right after First Bull Run. Amos Pinkney, who was with Jubal Early then, was given a newfangled Adams revolver by an English officer an' he wanted to try it out. So he pulled a prisoner out of the ranks and shot him down.

"The prisoner was my brother. He'd just turned sixteen that summer."

"I'm mighty sorry," I said. "That was a poignant and tragic end, even for a sod buster."

"Yeah, well, you'd better light a shuck out of here or you'll soon be joining him."

I nodded, and thanked that farmer most kindly, then I kneed my horse out of the barn, pulling Johnny Blue's pony after me.

Boys, before I continue with my story with all its many woes, trials and tribulations still to come, let me pause and talk once more about that farmer.

I didn't hear until months later that he'd been found hanging in the very barn where I'd left him. It seems Amos Pinkney found out that he'd aided in me and Johnny Blue's escape and arranged a little necktie party. There are them as say the poor rube was still clutching an empty beer glass when they cut him down all blue and dead.

Now, someday when we meet again in the sweet by and by, I'm gonna slap that farmer on the back and fill his empty glass with Heaven's own brew and it won't cost him a nickel. Until then, let him plow the fields of glory and sow the seeds of righteousness.

For ever and ever.

Amen.

But as I left the barn that night my immediate concern was with the living—the desperate and dangerous men who were outside, and who would do their best to kill me.

TWELVE

I kept to the shadows as best I could, glancing behind me constantly, hoping against hope that I wouldn't see Pink and his boys in the deserted street.

I guess the Good Lord was on my side, because as it happened I reached Doc's hotel without incident. I left Johnny Blue outside, slumped unconscious in his saddle, and walked up to the front desk. The clerk, a bald man in a checked vest with sideburns hanging down to his chest, looked up briefly, then ignored me while he delved into a book by Mr. Dickens.

Truth to tell, my nerves were stretched pretty tight. My belly felt like it was full of bed springs and I had a crick in my neck from looking over my shoulder.

I wasn't in any mood to deal with an uppity hotel clerk. He had this little bell thing on his desk and I slapped down on it pretty hard.

The man didn't even look up.

"Hold your horses, cowboy," he said.

Well, that done it.

Grabbing hold of the clerk's fancy vest, I hauled him to his feet. At the same time I pulled my Colt and stuck it right under his nose.

"I got one question for you, mister," I said.

"Ask away," the clerk wailed. I reckoned just about then his heart was missing more beats than a drummer with the hiccups.

"Where's Doc Fortune's room?"

"Doc ain't here."

"The hell he ain't."

"I'm telling you the truth, mister. He ain't here. He never came back after the fight. An' he owes me nineteen dollars and thirty-six cents."

I stood there feeling kind of numb all over.

"Seems like you've been had, mister," the clerk said.

I let him go and stomped outside.

As I stepped into the saddle I tried to think this thing through.

I figgered Doc wouldn't head north toward Fort Benton, not with winter coming on. Besides, there was no direct freight road between there and Great Falls, and Doc had a wagon.

East lay the Judith Basin country, lonely miles of emptiness with ruined ranches and a few half-starved Indians. To the west was the Rockies, the first snows of winter already threatening to block the passes. Only a desperate and daring man would take that route, and then only if he had to.

Thus there was only one way open to Doc, and that was to take the freight road south toward Helena. From there he could go on to Butte or maybe even hole up in Virginia City.

If I was going to catch him and get my money, I had to head south. Trouble was, Doc had a full hour's start on me. Sure the wagon would slow him some, but I was dragging along a bull-headed buckskin pony with a looney on his back, to say nothing of Pink and his boys, who were after my hide.

Boys, I had a tail hold on a grizzly bear that night and things didn't look like they was about to get better any time soon.

Then they got a whole bunch worse.

I heard the *bang!* of a rifle and a bullet zipped past my ear like an angry hornet.

Through the driving sleet I saw three or four of Pink's men running toward me, rifles at the ready. I still had my Colt in my hand and I thumbed off two quick shots. I didn't know if I hit anybody. In fact I kinda doubted it, but I had the satisfaction of seeing the gunmen scatter for cover.

Kicking my paint on, I trotted quickly away from the hotel hitching post and into the darkness some distance away from the oil lamps on either side of the door that lit up the front of the building and splashed yellow light into the street.

Johnny Blue's buckskin was spooked by the shooting and he balked a little at first, but then he settled down and followed willingly enough.

I saw orange flame spurt from a rifle muzzle in the darkness and again a bullet whizzed just past my head. Like most I've met, those Texans were good with the Winchester and they were finding the range.

The only advantage I had was that Pink's men weren't mounted as yet, and it would take them time to saddle up.

Thumbing off another couple of shots at a shadowy figure hugging the wall of a store across the street, I didn't wait to see if I'd hit him but turned my paint into the alleyway between the hotel and what looked like a restaurant next door. The alley was narrow and very dark and I didn't know where it would come out, but I dug my spurs in hard. Anything was better than lingering in that dangerous street.

My pony started forward, but the buckskin almost tore my arm off as he balked again, tossing his head before he broke into a shambling trot. Johnny Blue bounced in the saddle like a sack of grain. If he fell off we were done for. But I had no choice. I had to get us out of Great Falls in a hurry.

The half-formed plan I had in my mind was to head east out of town, then loop wide to the south and maybe join up with the freight road just north of Cascade, which was about thirty miles away.

Urging my pony forward, I rode through the alley, then turned at the rear of the hotel. I reined up and studied the dark, sleet-swept country beyond the edge of town. And right then I knew I'd never make it.

Even in the dark I saw enough to tell me that it was rough, treacherous country, cut by shallow hills and brush-covered gullies. There were few trees and little cover for even one man on a fast horse. Burdened as I was with Johnny Blue and his buckskin, I'd be a slow moving, easy target out there. Even if they took a leisurely time to get mounted, Pinkney and his Texans could ride me down before I'd covered a mile.

Kneeing my pony into a walk, dragging the reluctant buckskin with me, I turned along the south wall of the hotel. The street was just ahead, and I heard the voices of men calling out to each other in the darkness.

I knew then there was only one way out of Great

Falls that night. And that was to charge right through the center of town, past the Texans, and get directly onto the freight road.

Even dragging the buckskin, I could make fairly good time on the road, and maybe even put a fair piece between myself and Pink and his Texans. But would it be enough of a distance to lose them in the darkness?

I didn't know. The only thing I knew for sure was that it was a long shot. And it was the only shot I had.

THIRTEEN

I reloaded my Colt, which wasn't easy on account of how my fingers were numb with cold and I was chewing on a mouthful of my own heart at the same time. But I got it done and only dropped three or four cartridges that I had no time to pick up.

I took my gun in the right hand, my own reins and the buckskin's leathers in the left. So far there wasn't any sign of Pink and his boys coming up this far, and I figured they were busy with their horses.

Turning to Johnny Blue, I told him to hold on tight. I don't know if he understood me or not, but he leaned forward on his saddle and grabbed his pony's neck, so I figured he was sane enough to realize the fix we were in.

Then I swallowed hard and dug my spurs into my pony's side and rounded into the street.

To my surprise, the buckskin broke into a shambling lope, so maybe he also knew the fix we were in.

Boys, I can't say we charged through the center of town. I don't reckon we could've outrun a newborn calf, but what we lacked in speed, I made up for in noise.

I yelled, "Yeehaw!" and "God bless honest Abe!"

and the like, figgering Pink and his Texas would be so surprised they'd forget to shoot.

Yeah, I know, I was either an optimist or a dang fool. Take your choice.

As we hammered past Garnett's livery stable through the fast-falling sleet I noticed two men run through the open door. I fired once at the man on the right and he immediately dove for the dirt then came up to a crouch real fast, a Colt bucking orange flame in his hand.

I fired at him again, and this time he gave a startled yelp of pain and his hands went up and he staggered backward through the open door of the livery stable.

The other man's hands had flashed to his holstered guns and I knew this had to be ol' Pink himself. I fired and he dove behind a horse trough. But as he fell, his Remingtons came up quick as lightning and began to spit lead. Pink was fast with his guns—quicker than anybody I've seen before or since. But, like most revolver fighters, I reckon he didn't practice with his Remingtons at a distance of more than seven yards. In this kind of running fight across almost the whole width of the street in the dark, he was at a real disadvantage. Pink thumbed off maybe six or seven shots, and all of them went wild.

I fired again and kicked up a fountain of icy water in the trough, which gave ol' Pink a shower bath.

As I loped past, I heard him curse as his guns opened up again. But we were now well beyond revolver range and the sleet was falling like a lace curtain between us, so he was shooting blind.

I spurred my pony again and he broke into a fast gallop. The buckskin came alongside, his neck stretched out like a racehorse. I saw blood on his left flank. He'd been stung by a bullet and now, his orneriness forgotten, he wanted away from all that flying lead as badly as I did.

As we hit the freight trail, I gave the ponies their heads and let them gallop flat out for a couple of miles. Then I eased them back into a steady lope.

Johnny Blue was still slumped over in his saddle, and after an hour I stopped and checked on him. I didn't dare dismount because I knew Pink must be following hard.

Both Johnny Blue's eyes were swollen shut and his head looked about twice its usual size. His lips were split and his mustache was caked with blood.

"How you doing, Blue boy?" I asked, kindly enough.

"I'm fine, Momma," he whispered. "Are we going to get our little sister? Are we, Momma? Are we?"

Boys, all things considered, I wished Johnny Blue was his old surly self again, mean as a bulldog on a gunpowder diet. Today, long after he became a legend, there are them as say he was born so mean his poor momma had to feed him with a slingshot.

Well, maybe there's some truth to that. But that night the battered man on the buckskin was just a looney shadow of the old Johnny Blue, and believe me, boys, that pained me tolerably.

I buttoned Johnny Blue's mackinaw tight around his neck and pushed the collar up around his ears. Then I told him to stay put and not wander off. I eased his Henry from its scabbard and backtracked our trail for half a mile. It was bitter cold, and the sleet was now mixed with a heavy, freezing rain.

I sat my horse and my eyes tried to penetrate the gray wall of misty rain and sleet, but the trail beyond was lost in the gloom. There was no sound but for the hissing downpour, and for the second or third time that night I wondered how far Pink and his boys were behind us.

One of the Texans was down thanks to my bullet, and ol' Pink wouldn't take that lightly, and naturally wouldn't let it go unavenged. Forgiveness wasn't in his nature. But where were they now?

The question bothered me, and the quiet emptiness of the night was making me more than a mite uneasy.

Of course, what I didn't know then was that Pink had stopped to hang that poor farmer feller for the warning he'd given me. And that had allowed me some precious breathing room.

But with time running out fast, I had to find the Doc real quick, get my money, then hole up in a place where I could nurse Johnny Blue back to health.

Me, I was a good nurse in them days. I'd nursed a lot of cows through a whole heap of ailments and I figgered Johnny Blue wasn't a whole lot different from a sickly bull calf. I reckoned I could get him well enough again, unless he felt real poorly and asked me to shoot him, which of course an ailing calf can't do on account of how it can't talk.

I rode back down the trail and found that wandered waddie right where I'd left him. Both my pony and Johnny Blue's buckskin was played out, but I kicked my paint's ribs and he broke into a shambling trot, and the buckskin half-heartedly followed.

When I looked over my shoulder, which was often, what I could see of the sleet-lashed trail behind told me no one was following. But I knew that Amos Pinkney would chase an enemy to the gates of hell if need be.

Maybe he was out there right now in the darkness, just watching. And waiting.

The hairs on the back of my neck lifted at that thought, and I tried to concentrate on something more pleasant, like what I was going to do to Doc Fortune when I caught up with him.

But then good ol' Johnny Blue, with his usual unhappy timing, decided that now was a good time to add to my troubles.

He began softly enough, then he started to bawl like one of them sick bull calves I just told you about.

He was singing, and I reckoned anyone within ten miles of us could hear him.

"I'm dreaming now of Hallie,
sweet Hallie, sweet Hallie,
I'm dreaming now of Hallie,
For the thought of her never dies.
She's sleeping in the valley,
the valley, the valley,
She's sleeping in the valley,
And the mockingbird is singing where she
    lies."

He finished this verse and then lapsed into silence for a moment or two, and I began to think the worst was over. But then I'll be damned if he didn't stand up in the stirrups and lean out of the saddle with a foolish grin on his face, a hand cupped behind his ear.

"Listen to the mockingbird,
Listen to the mockingbird,
The mockingbird is singing o'er her grave;
Listen to the mockingbird,
Listen to the mockingbird,
Still singing where the weeping willows
    wave."

Boys, the racket that raucous rider was making was enough to alert the whole territory, Amos Pinkney included.

I recollect I yelled something real profound like, "Oh shit!" and clapped spurs to my pony.

Now we had to put distance between us and Pink real fast.

My mount took off in a startled gallop and I dragged the buckskin along with us. Johnny Blue fell over onto his pony's neck and he grabbed on for dear life, though he was still singing jerkily, grinning like a demented possum, and he kept trying to cup a hand behind his ear.

Our full tilt gallop through the blinding sleet ended in disaster—because we charged smack into the back of Doc Fortune's wagon.

FOURTEEN

My paint saw the danger and pulled up short, but the buckskin, following so close behind, rammed his head right into my butt. I was thrown over the saddle horn and I shot out of the leather and through the open back of the wagon like a ball from a cannon.

I ended up on the bed of the wagon in a heap of bottles, cans and other assorted junk. My head hit something solid on the way in, and for a second or two I saw stars. Somewhere in my flight, I'd dropped the Henry rifle.

"Mother of God, it's wild Injuns!" I heard Doc holler. "Bartholomew, to arms!"

I tried to talk but my head was spinning and my tongue wouldn't move.

Doc stopped the wagon and turned in his seat.

"Avant, feathered fiend," he yelled. "There's armed and desperate federal marshals here!"

I found my voice at last and yelled: "Doc, you son-of-a-bitch, I'm gonna kill you!"

"Is it, Bartholomew? Can it be?" Doc asked the Mauler. "Is it our young drover friend who has dropped in so unexpectedly for a visit?"

"Damn right it is, Doc!" I yelled. "And I'm gonna rid the ground of your shadow because you're a cheating skunk and lowdown."

I rolled out of the wagon and searched the muddy ground for the Henry. I found it just as Doc came around the side of the wagon.

"Give me my five hunnerd or I'll shoot you down like the mangy cur you are!" I yelled.

The hulking form of the Mauler appeared out of the gloom and he stood at Doc's shoulder.

I swung my rifle toward him and said, "Mauler, I've got nothing agin' you, but I'm in a mind to burn powder so don't give me no reason to kill you."

The Mauler stood right where he was as Doc said in a wheedling tone, "My dear young friend, this has all been a simple misunderstanding."

"Then give me my money, you skunk," I replied. "That will go a long way toward clearing things up."

Doc hung his head.

"I don't have it," he said. "I did have it, but five card stud and bourbon whiskey have been my undoing, though I must admit, I had a good mother."

"Doc," I said softly, a chunk of ice forming in my belly, "now I'm gonna punch your ticket with this here widow maker."

"Wait!" Doc squawked. He reached into his pocket and pulled out a fistful of bills and coin. "There's a hundred and thirty dollars and fifteen cents here. It's all yours, cowboy."

I reached out my left hand and took the money, keeping a firm grip on the Henry. I stuffed the cash in my pocket, a cold, killing anger still seething inside me.

"Doc, you're a skunk, and you're two hunn . . . three . . . you're a heap short," I said. "There's dangerous men on my trail and I needed that whole five hunnerd. You cheated me and my partner, and for that I'm gonna snuff out your candle."

"No!" Doc wailed.

"Have a care, this man is unarmed!" cried the Mauler.

But the time for pleas had long since passed. I was hot and my trigger finger was tighter than two hitches on the plowline.

Well, boys, as it happened, two things saved Doc Fortune's life that night.

The first was the eighth of an inch of slack I had to take up on the Henry's trigger.

The second was that Johnny Blue chose that instant to utter a dreadful cry and fall off his pony in a stone-cold swoon.

The ice in my belly melted instantly as I heard Johnny Blue thump to the ground. I ran to that prostrate puncher's still body and cradled his head in my lap.

"Blue boy," I cried, "can you hear me?"

But he was out like a dead cat.

"Bartholomew," Doc said, "get him into the wagon."

"Right, Doc," the Mauler said.

He picked up Johnny Blue like he was a child and laid him gently in the back of the wagon. Doc climbed in after him.

I saw Doc put his ear to Johnny Blue's chest and when he turned to me after a minute or so, his face was grim.

"If he is to survive, this man needs care and rest," Doc said. "More care and rest than I can give him here."

The sleet storm had increased in intensity and I shivered in my mackinaw, more from fear for Johnny Blue than from the bitter cold.

"Can we make it to Cascade?" I asked.

Doc shook his head at me.

"Son, that's twenty, maybe thirty miles away. After a couple of days in this wagon, in this weather, your friend would be dead."

"Dammit, Doc!" I said. "Isn't there anything you can do for him?"

Now, boys, at this point I reckon there are some of you who wonder why I didn't go ahead and shoot Doc like I planned. I've pondered that some myself, but I reckon a man can hardly say: "Well, thanks for helping my partner, Doc. Now jest stand over there while I plug you." The moment had passed and you can't kill a man in cold blood without your dander up and your hat set at a fighting angle.

Leastways, that's the way I see it.

As it happened, I was glad I didn't shoot some daylight into ol' Doc, because he was about to save Johnny Blue's life.

"There's a sporting house off the trail about a mile or so back," Doc said. "It's run by Miss Georgia Morgan, an old friend of mine. We can take your partner there."

"Doc," I said, "there are dangerous and desperate men on my trail and they could be here at any minute and I'll have to make a fight. If we backtrack a mile, we'll run right into them."

Doc smiled. "You're talking about Amos Pinkney and them Texans and wolfers of his, ain't you?"

"The very same."

"Son, only fools are out in a night like this, and from what I know of him, Amos Pinkney is no fool. If I was a betting man . . . which I am, but we needn't go into that again . . . I'd bet that Pinkney and his boys are all tucked up in bed, snug as bugs."

"Don't count on it, Doc," I said. "That man is a killer and he don't forgive too easy."

"Unlike you," Doc said.

I made no answer to that, on account of how I couldn't think of one right quick. Doc went on, "Pink knows he can kill you later, at his leisure so to speak, so I wouldn't worry too much about him. For now."

"Doc, I know them's meant to be words of comfort," I said, "but with a man like Amos Pinkney, you just never know where his loop will land. My pardner is hurt bad and my own axle's dragging in the dirt, but we need a place to rest. So lead on to Miss Georgia Morgan's establishment."

It seemed that Doc didn't trust ol' Pink to be abed as much as he said he did, because after a quarter mile we left the trail and struck out for the cathouse across rough country.

It took an hour, riding into the fangs of the sleet storm, before we pulled up outside the porch of a two-story frame house with a sagging roof and some slanted timbers supporting one gable-topped end wall of the building.

I guessed it had to be four in the morning, but every window was lit up, and I supposed the place was doing a booming business.

I dismounted and we climbed onto the porch as Doc tried the door. It was locked.

Doc looked at me and shrugged. He rapped loudly on the door and hollered: "Georgia! It is I, Doc!"

After a few moments, the door opened and a huge and handsome woman of color stood there. I figured her to be in her mid-twenties.

"Georgia!" Doc exclaimed. He tilted his head to one side and spread his arms wide. "My precious. My love. Come to me!"

Miss Georgia Morgan slammed the door in his face.

FIFTEEN

Doc turned to me and shrugged again. "Women!" he said. He walked close to the door, stuck his mouth against the crack between door and jamb and hollered, "That was droll, Georgia. Very droll."

The Mauler climbed the stairs to the porch with the unconscious Johnny Blue in his arms. He elbowed Doc aside and kicked the door angrily.

"Let us in!" the Mauler yelled.

"Go away!" said a voice from within the house.

The Mauler kicked at the door again.

"We've got an injured man here."

A few moments passed before the door opened a crack, just enough to admit the sawed-off, double barrels of a 10-gauge Remington shotgun.

"Get off my porch or I'll cut you in half," snarled Miss Georgia Morgan.

Boys, I got to hand it to the Mauler, he'd a heap more sand than sense.

"I have a cowboy here who has one foot in the pine box," he said. "He needs rest and a woman's care."

"Go away," Georgia said. "There's only working gals here. We're not doctors."

The big pugilist's shoulders slumped and he had already turned away when Georgia's voice stopped him.

"Wait," she said, "let me have a look at that cowboy."

Georgia came out onto the porch, her shotgun in one hand, a lamp held aloft in the other. She studied Johnny Blue closely for a moment, then exclaimed, "Why, this cowboy is a man of color!"

"Astute as ever, Georgia," Doc said.

"Doc," Georgia said, "I thought I'd shot you dead back in Texas."

Doc sighed. "It seems that everybody I meet tonight wants to kill me or has killed me before."

"That's because you're a lowdown skunk," Georgia said.

"It seems that everybody I meet tonight tells me that too," Doc said.

Georgia turned to the Mauler and tilted her head toward the door. "Bring that poor colored boy inside."

The Mauler carried Johnny Blue through the door as the rest of us followed.

As sporting houses go, this one wasn't much, but it was warm and dry and I was thankful enough for that.

Some packed carpetbags lay at the foot of the stairs and I remember thinking that someone was planning a trip.

Boys, if I'd only realized then what those bags signified, I could have saved myself the whole mountain of grief, misery and danger that was about to descend on me in the days to come.

But I didn't, so talking any more about them bags is as useless as a milk bucket under a bull.

Georgia told the Mauler to lay Johnny Blue on an overstuffed couch in the parlor. She pulled off his mackinaw and shirt, then studied his bruised body.

"This boy has been beaten to within an inch of his life," she said.

"I know," I replied as I jerked a thumb over my shoulder at the Mauler. "He did it."

Georgia rose and confronted that confused pugilist, her hands on her massive hips.

"What's a huge hulk like you doing, beating up on a poor colored boy?" she demanded angrily. "Do you got something against Negroes?"

The Mauler drew himself up to his full height and bristled like an ol' mossy-horned steer.

"Madam," he said, "I beat the Boston Tar Baby and Jem Jackson of Liverpool, England, much worse than that cowboy lying there. Please be aware that both these pugilists are gentlemen of color, and today I'm proud to call them my friends."

"If this is what you do to your friends," Georgia said, "I'd hate to see what you do to your enemies."

"Madam—" the Mauler spluttered, but Georgia turned to me.

"And you, cowboy, are you also this boy's friend?"

"We're brothers," I said.

Georgia rolled her eyes. "That's it! It's high time I got back to Texas and sanity."

"About Texas, Georgia dear—" Doc began.

"Doc," Georgia said, "if I'd found you that day in Fort Worth I would've shot you down in the street. You got the sheriff to lock up that polecat Dave Mather in the juzgado."

"I was only saving Mysterious Dave from your

wrath," Doc said. "You had a bowie knife and you were going to cut off his cojones. I didn't want you to end up in the calaboose, my precious."

"He stole the necklace and ring you'd given me for my birthday!" Georgia yelled. "That was lowdown."

"Dave was always somewhat foolish in drink, Georgia. You know that."

"The sheriff ran me out of town a week later, closed down the Long Branch Sporting House from right under me, where you was a regular customer, I might add," Georgia said.

"Ah, well," Doc said, "that's all water under the bridge. I'm glad there's no hard feelings."

"Don't count on it," Georgia spat.

She turned to me. "Let's get this boy into my bed."

The Mauler moved to pick up Johnny Blue, but Georgia stopped him. "I'll do it. You've done enough damage already."

She picked up Johnny Blue in her massive arms as easily as a mother picks up a baby and carried him to the foot of the stairs where she stopped and nodded toward a small, weasel-faced man in a dirty white apron.

"Luke here will see to your horses and get you all something to eat in the kitchen. There's whiskey, and I'll send the girls down."

As we followed Luke into the kitchen, I reckoned I was wrong about the house being busy. It seemed to me we had interrupted something, maybe something to do with all those packed bags. But I was too tired to think it all through and gratefully sank into a chair at the kitchen table.

Boys, Luke was a homely enough little feller, but he

sure set a fine table. After he stabled and fed the horses, he pretty quick put a plate of stewed jackrabbit in front of each of us, swimming in gravy, onions and potatoes, and a big slab of yellow cornbread. He poured buttermilk from a stone crock then said, "Dig in."

I enjoyed the first square meal I'd eaten in weeks and finished it off with a wedge of apple pie and a quart of sweet, scalding hot coffee.

The women hadn't yet appeared, so I left Doc and the Mauler sitting at the table and went upstairs to check on Johnny Blue.

A brunette gal, wearing practically nothing, directed me to Georgia's room, then said, "See you later, cowboy."

"Sure enough," I replied. I hadn't seen a woman, butt naked or otherwise, for many a long month and that gal was sure pleasing to the eye and to some other things, besides.

The door to Georgia's room was open so I went inside.

She had Johnny Blue propped up on a mountain of pillows and she sat on the bed beside him, trying to spoon broth into his mouth.

"How is he, Miss Georgia?" I asked.

"Your . . . brother is going to be just fine," Georgia said. "All he needs is a few days rest and some hot food. How did this happen to him?"

"He was in a fight against the Mauler, the big guy you met downstairs. Johnny Blue there, he won us five hunnerd dollars, which we ain't got yet."

"Us? How come you didn't fight him?"

"Bad back," I said.

"I bet. How come you didn't get the five hunnerd? This boy here won it square."

"Doc lost it in a poker game."

"That sounds just like that skunk."

"Yes he is, ma'am. He gave us all he had left which was a hunnerd and thirty five dollars and fifteen cents."

Georgia tried to spoon broth into Johnny Blue, but most of it ran down his chin. He opened his eyes and whispered, "Is you my momma?"

"I ain't your momma, son," Georgia said, "but mothering's all you got the strength for tonight, which is a mighty waste of what you do got and, boy, you got something special."

She pulled up the blanket and looked again, saying: "Yup, something mighty special."

She turned and looked at me. "Makes you kinda green with envy, don't it, son?"

I shrugged. "I never paid it much mind. It was just something he peed with."

"That's 'cause you ain't a lady, boy. A lady would pay it mind." Georgia sighed and replaced the covers. "That's only in my professional opinion, you understand."

"Yes ma'am, I understand."

Georgia tucked the blanket around Johnny Blue's neck and smoothed his mustache. Then she rose to her feet.

"I been watching you, boy," she said. "You look more over your shoulder than you do to the front. Who's hunting you, boy? The law?"

"It ain't the law," I said. "It's worse than that—a

group of dangerous and desperate men who will stop at nothing to see me dead."

Georgia laughed. "Who are these desperate men, and why would they be chasing a skinny little raggedy-assed cowboy with boots so thin you could stand on a dime and tell if heads or tails was up?"

"The leader of the band is a desperado named Amos Pinkney," I said, "and he means to shoot me on sight."

I saw something cross Georgia Morgan's face then, a flicker of fear, maybe. One thing was certain, she'd heard the name Amos Pinkney before.

"Do you know this hombre?" I asked.

For a moment, Georgia seemed confused. But she recovered herself right quick and said: "No, I've never heard of the man. But you'll be safe here tonight. Luke will keep watch and he has a fine Sharps rifle."

Boys, Georgia had lied about not knowing Amos Pinkney, but somehow I felt I was safe with her, at least for the time being.

"Why don't you go downstairs and find a nice girl?" Georgia said. "Go to bed with her and rest for a while. It's on the house."

I allowed that this was tolerably good advice and walked toward the door. Her voice stopped me. "Hey cowboy, you look all tuckered out. Better watch out one of them wild young fillies of mine doesn't buck you right off, shape you're in. Hang on tight, now."

"I plan to," I said.

Miss Georgia's mocking laughter followed me all the way downstairs and into the parlor where Doc and the Mauler sat drinking whiskey with five women.

"Ah, dear boy," Doc said. "Come and join us while we explore the pleasures of Venus and John Barleycorn."

Me, I was plumb tuckered out and longed for a soft warm bed and for sleep. Even the whiskey Doc thrust into my hand did little to revive me.

One of the women, a beautiful little gal with blond hair and eyes as green as a mountain pasture walked over to me, took my hand and settled me on the couch beside her.

"You look tired, cowboy," she said.

"He's had a busy day," Doc said from somewhere amidst the ample bosom of the brunette I'd met upstairs. "Gunfightin' an' such."

"Ah," the little blonde said, "so you're a dangerous gunfighter."

"I'm no gunfighter, ma'am," I said. "I'm just a poor puncher down on his luck."

She asked me my name. I told her, then asked for hers.

"Cottontail," she said.

"That's it?" I asked.

She nodded. "Yup, that's it, just Cottontail. I'm from down San Antonio way."

"Pleased to meet you," I said.

Boys, let me tell you, that little gal was a sight to see. She had nothing on but her drawers, one of them bodice things women wear, and a big smile.

I thought she was the purtiest thing I'd ever seen in my life.

"I think I'd better get you to bed," Cottontail said.

Doc was still busy with his brunette, with another red-headed gal pouting beside him. The Mauler had disappeared with the other two gals and I didn't expect he'd be back.

"I'm ready for bed anytime you are," I said.

I picked up my gear and Cottontail led me to a room near the parlor where she poured me another drink from a bottle that she kept under the bed. "This is my own stuff," she said. "Not that cheap rotgut that Georgia passes off as whiskey."

I sipped my drink, which was smooth and warm, and watched Cottontail take off her clothes till she was dressed in nothing but black stockings that tied with pink ribbon just above her knees.

"Now I see why they call you Cottontail," I said.

"A man give me that name," Cottontail said. "I didn't choose it for myself. Cottontail pleased him somehow, so I kept it and now it's the name I use professionally."

"What's your real name?" I asked.

"Cowboy," she said, "that don't matter."

She climbed into bed beside me and helped me off with my clothes. Then she took the whiskey glass from my hand and—hell, boys, you've all been in a sporting house and you know what happened next. Let me just say that before I dropped off into a deep, dreamless sleep, a good time was had by all.

I woke slowly to a hard, gray light that angled into the bedroom through the curtainless window. I judged the time to be well past daybreak and struggled to sit up. A wave of pain hit me, a headache so bad I figured I'd have to be dead for a week before the misery stopped.

"Cottontail," I croaked. "Cottontail, it's me. Your one true love is awake."

There was no answer, and no sign of Cottontail.

I hurried into my clothes and stomped into my boots, and only then remembered to check to see that my money was still tucked into my hatband.

It was gone.

So was my gunbelt and my seventeen-dollar Colt's revolver. So was Johnny Blue's Henry rifle.

What I said next I can't print here, on account of how some regular, churchgoing people might read this. But my cussin' was enough to melt the ears right off a Baptist preacher, as you boys might expect.

Last night's whiskey bottle was still standing on the dresser and I sniffed at it. It smelled like whiskey all right, but mixed up with something else I couldn't put a handle on.

I knew I'd been drugged, which went a long way to explaining why my head felt like an anvil being pounded by a hundred smiths.

I charged out of my room, hollering "Georgia! Georgia Morgan!"

But there was no answer.

I passed a door to my left and saw Doc sitting on the edge of the bed, his head in his hands.

"Doc," I yelled, "we've been robbed!"

Ol' Doc looked at me with eyes like pee holes in the snow. "My dear boy, who cares?" he said. "Go away and let me die in peace."

I ran upstairs to Johnny Blue's room and, my heart pounding, burst through the door.

Johnny Blue was still in bed and he looked like he was fast asleep. I walked over and shook his shoulder. His eyes fluttered open and I saw they had lost that glazed look. He didn't seem to be looney anymore.

I shook his shoulder again.

"Johnny Blue," I said, "wake up. We're in a heap o' trouble."

"Oh God," he said, "it's you."

"We're in trouble," I said. "And I mean *big* trouble."

"Go away," Johnny Blue said.

"We've lost everything, me and you. And Amos Pinkney could be here any minute. It's trouble, Johnny Blue. Heap big trouble."

Sixteen

Johnny Blue tried to sit up. But he couldn't make it and his head flopped back on the pillow.

"Oh, God," he groaned, "why don't you just shoot me an' get it over with?"

"That's what I've been trying to tell you," I said. "I got nothing to shoot you with. Them gals took everything."

"What gals? Where am I?"

"Them sportin' gals. You're in a bawdy house."

Johnny Blue looked as sullen as a mule in a mud bog.

"You mean you was sparkin' a sporting gal while I was in this bed dying?"

I shrugged. "I had to do somethin' to pass the time."

Johnny Blue struggled to sit up again and this time his head cleared the pillow. He looked around the room kinda wild like.

"Where's my Henry?" he asked.

"Why?"

"Because I'm gonna shoot you with it."

I shook my head at him. "The Henry's gone. The sportin' gals took it."

Johnny Blue flopped back onto the pillows.

"Did you check the horses?" he asked.

"The horses?"

"Yeah," he said, "they're big hairy things with tails. Cowboys ride 'em."

The horses!

I ran downstairs and out of the house. I paused briefly and looked around for any sign of Pink and his boys, but the surrounding country was empty of life, the trees bare of leaves and the grass covered in a thick hoar frost.

My boots crunched through ice as I ran to the barn and charged inside.

Doc's broken-down nags were in their stalls contentedly munching on hay. But my pony and Johnny Blue's buckskin were gone.

So were our saddles.

I stood there and commenced to cuss another blue streak, but a voice from the barn door stopped me in mid-stream.

"Cussin' ain't gonna bring them ponies back, boy."

I turned and saw Luke standing there like a little weasel all shriveled up with the cold.

"The ladies took 'em," he said.

Boys, my great loss had turned me mean as a cornered cottonmouth and I was as fired up as a hell and brimstone preacher on Sunday.

"What ladies took 'em?" I asked.

Luke smiled. "Why, Miss Georgia and Miss Cottontail, of course. They lit out just afore dawn. The other ladies left too, figgered they'd winter in Great Falls."

It took a while for all this to sink in, but when it did I said, "Where did they go? I mean Georgia and Cottontail."

Luke smiled again, a thin little slit of a smile and I knew I wasn't gonna like the words that was about to come out of it.

"Boy," he said, "do you know who that little gal you was makin' whoopee with last night is?"

"I know who she is, alright," I said. "She's a low-down, two-bit—"

"Apart from all that," Luke said.

"You're itching to tell me," I said. "So spit it out. And don't say she's the Queen of England."

"Close, cowboy," Luke said, "but no cigar. She's Amos Pinkney's woman."

My jaw dropped and I tried to speak but my tongue couldn't form the words.

Cottontail was Amos Pinkney's personal and private sporting gal—and I'd lain with her, like it says in the Good Book.

"Seems to me," Luke said, enjoying my discomfort, "that ol' Pink's just found another reason to kill you."

I discovered my voice at last and said, "He don't need another reason."

Luke shrugged. "Well, knowing ol' Pink, he'll probably just go ahead an' kill you twice anyhow."

My head was pounding and I felt like I was thinking in a fog. But I wasn't finished questioning Luke just yet.

"Where does Georgia Morgan fit in all this?" I asked him.

"Boy," Luke said, "I'm giving you an education here. I should be charging you money."

"Mister, I feel like I've been through a wringer an' hung out to dry," I said. "I ain't in any kind of mood for bullcrap. Now you jest answer my question or I'm gonna tie your ears up in a bow knot."

I guess ol' Luke saw the handwriting on the wall because his attitude changed for the better right quick.

"Miss Georgia has what you might call a special relationship with Amos Pinkney," he said. "Now as to what that relationship is, cowboy, I have no idea. But she's beholdin' to him, that's fer damn sure." Luke hawked up and spat. "Beats me how a lady like her could get mixed up with an outlaw like Amos Pinkney."

"Beats me too," I said. "Where are she and Cottontail heading?"

"West," Luke said, "into the Idaho territory to join up with Pink. Word came the other day by rider telling Cottontail and Miss Georgia that Pink has business in a town called Alpine and they should join him there. But that's one trail you'd better not follow, cowboy. That is, if'n you ever want to see your next birthday."

But I did aim to follow that trail. I figgered me and Johnny Blue could ride Doc's plugs and maybe head off the two gals long before they reached Alpine and Pink.

Boys, that hunnerd and thirty-five dollars was all that stood between me and Johnny Blue and starvation that winter, and I wasn't about to let it go so easy.

Some have said that I should've just walked away from it, that it wasn't worth it. That's fine to say when your belly's full of beans and your toes are toasting at the bunkhouse stove.

But a man who ain't got a tailfeather left is desperate enough to try anything. And I was desperate. I wasn't gonna roll over and play dead. Me and Johnny Blue had to survive this winter if we were ever gonna head south and find our little sister. And that's something I wasn't about to forget anytime soon.

Right now, I knew there was no time to be lost. But the big question in my mind was whether or not Johnny Blue had recovered enough of his strength to ride.

As it turned out, Johnny Blue answered that question for me.

As I walked back toward the house, I saw him coming toward me—weak as a day old kittlin' in the Mauler's massive arms. Doc, looking like he already had one foot in the pine box, trailed at their heels.

"I take it the horses are gone?" Johnny Blue said.

"They're gone," I answered. "They left Doc's plugs. Probably figgered they wasn't worth the trouble anyhow."

Johnny Blue looked terrible. His face was bruised and his eyes were almost swollen shut. He just hung there in the Mauler's arms like a bride on her wedding night. Any other man tried to do that to him, Johnny Blue would have shot him through the lungs, but I guess he reckoned the Mauler owed him something.

"Well, what do we do now?" Johnny Blue asked.

"I got a plan," I said.

Johnny Blue groaned, but I plunged right ahead.

"Luke tells me them gals is planning to join up with Pink in a town called Alpine in the Idaho Territory," I said. "I figgered me and you could ride them nags of Doc's and head 'em off before they get there. Then all we have to do is grab our stuff back and then we can bunk up somewheres all snug and warm for the winter."

"Easy as that, huh?" Johnny Blue asked.

"Easy as that."

"Okay," Johnny Blue said, "first, I don't remember too much about last night, but I do recollect a large lady of color who looked like she could whup her weight in bobcats. She'll clean both our clocks, especially the shape I'm in. And she has that handy-dandy Henry rifle of mine you gave her."

I tried to object, but Johnny Blue talked right over me.

"And second, how you gonna track them?"

"Track 'em?"

"Yeah, track them. Read sign and sich to see which way they went or which way they didn't went."

"Hell, I can read sign," I said.

"Yeah, right," Johnny Blue said. "Remember that time during the spring roundup of '85 you got us lost up on the Judith and it took us five days to find our way back to camp? I recollect the work was stalled for days because there was search parties out looking for us all over the territory. Tube Wilson was top hand then and he was gonna hang you, 'cept I talked him out of it. Now, why I did a fool thing like that I'll never know."

Boys, I guess you can tell that Johnny Blue was

downright surly that morning, and it's been my experience that there's no reasoning with a man who's surly as a bear waking up after winter. But I was about to give it another try when Doc stepped in.

"When you two get through jawing, maybe I can speak a word or three?"

"Say yore piece, Doc," I said, "and welcome. It's a free country."

"I'll be brief," Doc said, "on account of how I have the worst hangover in the history of mankind and I fear my final hour is nigh."

"You do look a mite peaked, Doc," I said. "Like you'd have to die to get better, if'n you get my meaning."

"I do, and thank you. Now listen, everything I have in the world is tied up in my horses and wagon. Where they go, so do myself and the equally hungover Bartholomew there. I should add that I too have suffered a grievous personal loss and very much desire to recover it."

"What did you lose, Doc?" Johnny Blue asked.

"A little matter of two hundred dollars I had in my shoe," Doc said.

"Doc," I said, "I should have shot you when I had the chance. You held out on me, you skunk."

"It, er, slipped my mind," Doc said.

"What's going on here?" Johnny Blue asked.

I told him about my desperate gunfight in Great Falls and my daring escape, only to find out later that Doc had shortchanged us.

Boys, Johnny Blue, that reeling rider, grew even more surly.

"Why the hell didn't you shoot him?" he yelled.

"Because," I said, "just as I was about to pull the trigger you swooned like a maiden aunt that's jest been propositioned at a church social and fell off yore pony. I thought you was dead."

"Shoot him now!" Johnny Blue hollered.

"Ah, yes, it would be a blessed mercy," Doc said.

"Dammit," I said, "I don't have a gun."

"Which brings you boys right back to where you started," Luke said. That wizened weasel turned to Doc. "How do you know it was Cottontail that made off with yore poke?"

"I don't know," Doc said. "Maybe it was her. Maybe it was Georgia." He got a dreamy look in his eyes. "Ah, yes, Georgia, that doe-eyed houri who took me to her bosom and afforded me a glimpse, brief as it was, through the very gates of paradise." His eyes hardened again. "But either way, I'm down two hunnerd dollars and I mean to get it back."

"Doc," I said, "it could've been Georgia, but I'd bet my last nickel that it was Cottontail. That little gal is slippery."

"Just remember, Doc, that the two hunnerd is ours," Johnny Blue said from the Mauler's arms.

"Let's get our goods and cash returned to our persons and argue about that later," Doc said, which I reckoned was reasonable enough. I could always shoot him when I got my gun back or maybe borrowed one from somebody.

"Have you ever heard of this here Alpine burg, Doc?" I asked.

"It's a mining town," Doc said, "silver mostly. I've never been there, but I hear it has one of the richest banks in the territory, stuffed with cash money from mine profits."

"Maybe that bank is what ol' Pink has in mind," I said.

"That seems more than likely," Doc agreed.

What we didn't know then, but was to find out later to our detriment, was that Pink had more in mind than just robbing a bank.

A whole heap more.

The sleet had stopped sometime during the night, but it was cold enough to freeze the balls off a billiard table. So we all went back to the house where Luke made coffee, spiking the pot with a pint of whiskey. After a few cups of this brew my head cleared some and I began to feel better.

Doc told us that Alpine was in a valley in the Bitterroots right on the Montana border, about forty miles west of Missoula.

"I reckon Cottontail and Georgia headed south for Mullin's Pass and then they'll follow the Mullin freight road west," Doc said.

"The pass will still be open this time of the year on account of how the snows haven't arrived yet. But it's gonna be a long, hard chase, boys. Them horses of mine are better than they look, but even making fifteen miles a day, it will take us two weeks to reach Alpine."

"Don't worry," I said, "we'll catch up on them womenfolk long before Alpine."

"How come," Johnny Blue said, "that every time you say 'don't worry,' I worry?"

"That's just the way you was raised, Johnny Blue," I said. "You're what they call a Doubting Thomas."

"You're right," Johnny Blue said. "I doubt that we're gonna catch them whores."

"Gentlemen, gentlemen!" Doc threw his hands in the air. "Let's not argue among ourselves. I suggest that we now move with all expedition and waste no more valuable time."

As the Mauler hitched the team to the wagon, I tried to get Luke to lend me his Sharps rifle. He refused to part with it, saying it was both wife and child to him.

But he did throw some coffee, bacon and beans into the wagon and he gave Johnny Blue a full sack of Bull Durham, which went a long way toward sweetening that rueful rider's downright disagreeable disposition.

The Mauler carried Johnny Blue to the wagon and placed him in the back, gentle as a nursing mother. He tucked a blanket around Johnny Blue's legs and said: "Comfy?"

Johnny Blue allowed he was, then he said: "Now git the hell away from me."

Boys, you know Johnny Blue, sometimes he could be plumb mean like he'd gravel in his gizzard, so even though the Mauler was eating crow—feathers, beak and all—that ruthless rider wasn't about to forgive and forget.

We reached the trail south just as Johnny Blue built his third smoke of the morning. He fumbled in the pocket of his mackinaw and fished out a match that he thumbed into flame.

"Have any of you," he said through a cloud of blue smoke, "given any thought to where Amos Pinkney and his Texas boys might be?"

"I have," Doc said from the driver's seat. "And my conclusion is this: He's either on the road ahead of us, or behind us. There's no other route to Alpine that I can think of, but for this trail.

"But either way, before or behind, I'd say from now on we're in considerable danger."

SEVENTEEN

"Considerable danger. Yup, that's jest what I thought," Johnny Blue said nodding. "Now, wouldn't it make sense to drop off a reliable man to backtrack our trail some and keep his eyes peeled for Pink and his boys? Then, if that reliable man saw them, he could come a-runnin' and warn us?"

"You're talking about me, right?" I asked.

"Well, you ain't too reliable, but you're all we got," Johnny Blue said. "On account of how I'm too stove up to walk, let alone run."

Doc eased the team to a halt, turned in his seat and nodded his head at Johnny Blue.

"What you say makes perfect sense, my dusky friend. Of course, Bartholomew and I have no quarrel with Mister Pinkney, and have thus little to fear from him, I imagine. But if I was a cattle herding man of somewhat nervous disposition and scrawny appearance who knew that I was the object of that dangerous desperado's wrath, I would surely—shall we say it in a nutshell?—cover my ass."

And boys, that's how, a few minutes later, I found myself picking my way along the frozen ruts in the road, watching the wagon grow smaller in the distance.

I turned up my collar against the icy wind and shoved my frozen hands deep in my pockets. The sleet was gone, but the sky remained a sullen gray and the trees along the road were rimmed with frost like the bare white skeletons of things long dead.

A crow saw me and flapped from a branch, cussing me out noisily for being abroad in this weather. Then he turned and fluttered away, but not before dropping his calling card on my shoulder.

I let the splashy mess stay where it was.

A couple of hours passed and I trudged along in increasing misery. I was cold and hungry and my throbbing head of the morning had returned with a vengeance.

I couldn't see the sun, but guessed it to be gone noon when I felt that familiar prickling at the back of my neck.

The trail behind me was empty as far as I could see, yet I had a sense of doomed foreboding I couldn't shake. In later years, some said I had the gift of second sight and that I'd inherited it from my Irish mother, and I reckon they were right.

I started to run after the wagon, looking behind me now and then to check the trail. But nothing was stirring.

By the time I saw the wagon come into view, I'd been running for close to an hour. My heart felt like it was about to burst and I was gasping for breath, my tongue so far out I was lapping up dirt.

Johnny Blue saw me coming and I heard him holler something to Doc. Doc stopped the wagon and I ran up alongside him.

"Pull off into the trees!" I yelled.

"Is it Pink?" Johnny Blue shouted.

"I dunno! Dammit, just do as I say!"

Doc swung the team right sharply and drove them into the trees. There was little cover among the bare, withered underbrush and I yelled at him to keep on going.

I guess he drove about a hundred yards off the road, the speeding wagon jolting and crashing over fallen trees and crackling over piles of brush, before he pulled the team to a halt under a grove of aspen.

"This is as far as I go. The horses won't take any more of this," Doc said as he jumped down from his seat.

Johnny Blue emerged from under the Mauler, who'd fallen into the back of the wagon during Doc's mad dash for the trees.

"Dammit, Mauler," he said, "you like to broke every bone in my body."

"Sorry," the Mauler said. "Lost me balance."

Johnny Blue said, "Hmph," then turned his wrath on me. "What did you see back there?" he asked.

"Nothing," I said.

"Nothing?"

"Me, I jest felt something. A presence."

"You felt something. A presence?"

"Johnny Blue," I said, "if'n yore gonna repeat everything I say, we ain't gonna get too far with this here conversation."

"Might I suggest, gentlemen, that we end this discussion and observe the road and see if anything *is* there," Doc said.

That sounded like good advice, so we left the Mauler with the horses and snuck back to the road.

We concealed ourselves in a clump of brush near the trail and waited.

And waited.

But soon enough, Doc suddenly stiffened. "Listen," he said.

Johnny Blue listened intently for a few moments then shook his head. "I don't hear nothing."

"Shh," Doc warned. "Listen."

Then I heard it, the soft jingle of bridles and the metallic clang of shod horses on the iron hard road.

Doc put a warning finger to his lips as the riders hovered into view.

Amos Pinkney was in the lead, dressed in his Confederate officer's cape. The man to his right held aloft the old battle flag of the Confederacy, its stars and bars streaming gallantly in the wind. Behind, in column of twos just like the bluecoat soldiers I'd seen ride out of Fort Benton, rode the twelve Texas gunmen, all of them splendidly mounted. The wolfers and their Indian women took up the rear.

I recognized Jacob Pike wrapped to the eyes in his bearskin coat, his Flathead woman riding at his side.

It seemed Pink had abandoned his wagons because the wolfers led three pack horses, each dragging an Indian travois piled high with supplies.

Holding my breath as that proud cavalcade clattered past, I silently gave thanks that they'd not caught us on the open road.

"Jeez," Johnny Blue said as the column vanished into the distance, "that was close."

"I guess now you'll believe me," I said. "I mean it when I say that I can see things before they happen."

Johnny Blue allowed that this was indeed the case.

But he added, "It's because you're crazy, you know. See, crazy people can do weird stuff like that. I knew an ol' boy once in Texas, name of Fartin' Charlie Polk, who could tell when a thunderstorm was coming on, even though the sun was shining and there wasn't a cloud in the sky. But that ol' boy was more than a mite tetched in the head, just like you."

"What happened to him?" I asked.

"Oh, he got struck by lightning, him and his hoss, one summer down on the Canadian."

"I thought he could tell when it was gonna thunder?"

"Oh, he could, but he didn't have enough sense to come in out of the storm when it got there. Just like you."

Doc snorted and shook his head at me and Johnny Blue.

"I swear, you boys have got to be the talkinest drovers I ever crossed trails with," he said. "If you did less talking and more thinking, you'd realize what kind of perilous predicament you're in here."

"What do you mean, Doc?" I asked.

"Boy," Doc said, "you're buckin' a losing game. Now you got Pink's army between you and them whores. You ain't ever gonna get your worldly goods back."

"Then we'll just follow them all the way to Alpine," I said. "Them gals took our money, our horses and our guns—everything we own. Me and Johnny Blue here, we mean to get 'em back. There's surely law in Alpine."

"Suit yourself," Doc said. "But me and Bartholomew are quitting this game right now and heading south."

Doc began to walk back toward his wagon. He turned his head and said over his shoulder. "Good luck to you both."

"Wait, Doc," I hollered. "let's talk this thing through."

Doc waved a hand at me. "Cowboy, I'm all done talking. This thing has gone too far. I don't like the cards I'm holding, so I'm dealing myself out of the game."

I was about to say something else, but Johnny Blue stopped me. "Save your breath," he said. "You're just hollerin' down a rain barrel. He wants out."

Boys, it seemed like me and Johnny Blue was hogtied. We stood there like bumps on a log while Doc turned the wagon and coaxed his team back onto the road.

"*Vaya con Dios,* boys," he said, tipping his plug hat.

But then fate, in the shape of that silent slugger the Mauler, stepped in and saved us.

He reached across, snatched the reins from Doc's hands and pulled the team to a halt.

"Ain't you boys coming with us?" he asked.

"No, we ain't, Mauler," I replied. "We still got business in Idaho."

"And we have business further south," Doc said. He tried to take the lines back from the Mauler, but that pugnacious pugilist would not part with them.

"This ain't right, Doc," he said. "We can't abandon these boys in the middle of nowhere, afoot, and with one of them stove up real bad. That would be a helluva thing."

"Bartholomew, I'm warning you, you're trying my patience," Doc said.

The Mauler turned in his seat and faced Doc squarely.

"Doc, you and me have been together through good times and bad for nigh on ten years. Some of the things we done, like selling that useless snake oil you call medicine, has been lowdown. But I never thought you'd sink so low as to set your hand to this, abandoning friends in need."

"Bartholomew," Doc said, "I must warn you, this is getting mighty close to black, shameful mutiny."

"You cheated these men, Doc," the Mauler said, unfazed. "Now it's time to pay them back. We got to take them to Alpine. We owe it to them."

Doc sighed. "Do any of you dunderheads know what you're getting into? Amos Pinkney is headed to Alpine with a large, well-armed force. Why? To rob the bank there, of course. By the time we reach Alpine, he'll be long gone, and his whores with him.

"But perchance, if we find him still there, we'll be riding into a hornet's nest and I wouldn't give you a plugged nickel for our chance of survival. Now, Bartholomew, you mutinous dog, what do you say to that?"

"I say we take these cowboys to Alpine," said our fearless champion.

Doc sighed again and looked up at the sky like he was seeking heavenly consolation. "Why do I bother?" he asked. "I'm surrounded by idiots."

"What's your call, Doc?" Johnny Blue said.

Doc rolled his eyes like one of them suffering saints

who look like they was raised on nothing but prune juice and Proverbs.

"I suppose, in some minutely small way, Bartholomew is right and it was I who brought you two greenhorns to this perilous pass." Doc let go with one of them sighs again and his chin sank onto his chest. "I believe there is nothing for it but to beat my palpitating breast and say 'mea culpa' and continue on this melancholy path where fickle fate has led me. As Mr. Dickens's immortal Micawber might say, 'In short, let's hit the trail for Alpine.'"

"Huzzah!" I cried.

Johnny Blue reached up and shook the Mauler's hand.

"Mauler, I was planning to plug you first chance I got for what you done to me back in Great Falls. I just want you to know that I'm thinking of reconsidering my decision."

"Thank you most kindly," said the Mauler. "Those are words of deep consolation."

"Climb aboard," Doc said. "Let's get this insane asylum on the road."

EIGHTEEN

Boys, I won't bore you with the full journal of that terrible journey and describe the jolting, back-breaking misery of Doc's wagon. Suffice to say it would take a hundred sheets of this here paper, each stained with salt tears, to do it justice.

We stopped often to explore the icy clay banks of snow-swollen creeks and river narrows to find fords where there were none. And we crossed anyway. Most of the time I was soaking wet, cold to the bone and miserable from hunger.

Our food gave out after five days on the trail and we was reduced to eating 'coons, jackrabbits and anything else we could run down and catch then roast on a fire or boil in a pot.

The only roof above our heads was the canvas cover of Doc's wagon or the green boughs of fir and pine. Frost was our only coverlet, the hard, frozen ground our only couch.

Thankfully, the snow held off, but the weather grew increasingly cold as we cleared Mullin's Pass and headed toward the distant Bitterroots and the Idaho border.

We saw sign that Amos Pinkney and his band had

passed this way before us, but we had no way of telling how far ahead he might be.

Doc, who had once lived with the Cheyenne for a couple of years, reckoned no more than a full day.

"Pink doesn't want to tire out those thoroughbred horses of his on the way in," he said. "He knows he might be forced to tire 'em out on the way back."

One night, as we neared the end of our long journey, Doc came out of the wagon holding a razor and some scissors.

"If you don't mind me saying so, you boys are a mite overgrown," he told me and Johnny Blue. "You look more like a pair of hairy ol' bull buffalo than men. I suggest you make use of these."

Thus it was that, freshly shaved and curried, me and Johnny Blue entered the Idaho Territory a few miles due east of Alpine shortly after dawn.

Doc urged caution, saying that we should leave the wagon and approach the town on foot away from the main trail, for fear that Pink and his boys might still be hanging around.

We drove the wagon into a stand of lodgepole pine and unhitched the team. Doc let the horses loose, saying that they'd stay close to the wagon, and then we hoofed it along the tree line until we saw Alpine in the valley below.

Alpine looked more like a cow town than a mining center. It consisted of one long, wide street, flanked by false-fronted stores and saloons. The town itself was wedged tightly between hills to its north and south.

A shallow creek ran to the west of town, crossed by a wide wooden bridge. Beyond lay some shallow hills that eventually rose to meet the snow-capped peaks of the Bitterroots.

It seemed a pleasant place, this town, a place where a man could put his feet up on the stove and enjoy the quiet.

But that was before Amos Pinkney and his boys rode in.

"There's one hell of a commotion going on down there," Johnny Blue said.

Doc had brought a spyglass and he put it to his right eye.

"There's folks milling around," he said. "They're all gathered in the center of town."

"Looks like ol' Pink done robbed the bank already," I said.

"Maybe," Doc said, "but it may be something else. This is making me a mite uneasy. One of us has got to sneak down there and take a look. I don't want to walk right in if there's any possibility that Pink and his boys are still in town."

"Who's gonna go?" I asked.

Johnny Blue raised an eyebrow like only he can. "You had to ask that question, didn't you? The Mauler's too big. The Doc's too old and I'm too stove up. Who's that leave?"

I thought that over.

"Okay, I'll go take a look see," I said.

"Good boy," said Johnny Blue.

I eased down the hill, taking advantage of what little cover there was, and then sprinted to the rear of a lumberyard at the western end of town.

There was no one around, but a dog saw me and started to raise a ruckus, yanking at the chain that bound him to an upright stake driven into the dirt of the yard.

Knowing I had to get away from the mutt and the fuss he was raising, I made my way to my left, wishing I had a Colt, and came up behind a low shack to the rear of a two-story building that faced the street.

An odor of frying beef made my mouth water and my stomach begin to growl, and I reckoned the larger building was a restaurant of some kind.

There was still a crowd of people milling around on the street, but from my vantage point I couldn't see what was going on. They all seemed to be looking in the same direction, toward the north end of town. There was something happening there that interested them mightily, and I wanted to see what it was.

I decided I had to take a chance.

The back door to the restaurant was open and I sprinted for it and ran inside. I found myself in a kitchen. I guess they had been right in the middle of serving breakfast to the early risers when the commotion happened, because potatoes had boiled over in their pots and maybe half a dozen steaks had burned to a frazzle in the frying pan.

"Is there anybody to home?" I whispered.

No one answered.

I grabbed a potato. It was hot and I juggled it from one hand to another as I left the kitchen and went into the dining room.

It was empty.

All the tables were set with gingham cloths and cutlery gleamed beside unused plates. Someone had left a cigar burning in an ashtray and it still trailed a thin wisp of blue smoke.

Whatever had happened in Alpine had happened in an all-fired hurry.

I ate my potato as I moved to the window. I pulled back the lace curtain and peeked outside. That's when I saw Amos Pinkney.

He stood under a huge, bare-branched oak tree in what I took to be the town square. A noose dangled from one of the tree limbs at his back.

Pink's boys were everywhere, some mounted, some on foot, and it looked like they'd herded the townspeople to this spot. I guessed there were over a hundred and fifty men, women and children in the square, and ol' Pink must have struck fast to take them so unawares. He'd learned how to take a town during the Civil War, and I guess he'd learned that lesson well.

Pink was yelling something at the crowd, but I couldn't hear what it was. I decided to get a better vantage point. So I crossed the dining room and climbed the stairs.

The room to the front was a bedroom, and the window was open, the curtains blowing in the cold breeze.

There must have been twenty floorboards between me and the window and I swear every single one of them screeched as I walked over it. Luckily, there was a lot of noise going on outside, men yelling, women crying, guns going off, so no one heard me.

From the open window I could hear every word that was spoken in the square, and I was close enough to Pink to make out his face and his handsome whiskers.

I looked out the window and saw on the other side

of the square a false-fronted building with a sign that read ALPINE MERCANTILE BANK.

A buckboard was pulled up to the door and Jacob Pike, grinning like a mule eating cactus, watched as the other wolfers carried out bags of cash from the bank and threw them into the back of the wagon.

Pike was sipping coffee from a steaming cup and he had a huge cigar stuck between his teeth. One of the townsmen walked up to him and said something. Pike, still grinning, kicked the man on the butt and the man sprawled his full length on the street.

The wolfers and some of the Texans that were around laughed. They laughed even harder when Pike poured the dregs of his coffee over the fallen man's head.

Me, I made a mental note to put a bullet in ol' Jacob someday. If I lived.

There was a sudden commotion and the crowd in the street parted as a couple of Texans dragged a man with a long brown beard up to where Pink stood. A star gleamed on the bearded man's vest.

This man yelled at Pink and pointed at the noose in the oak tree. "Take that obscenity down. There will be no hanging in Alpine as long as I'm sheriff."

Boys, what happened next really churned me up inside.

Amos Pinkney drew one of his Remingtons and shot the man down. There was no talk, no "excuse me" or "by your leave," just *bang! bang! bang!* an' that poor lawman feller lay dead in the street.

Now I don't hold nothing against a feller who shoots a man fair and square, when both of them are armed and on the prod. But this was cold-blooded murder, and it sickened me to my stomach.

I recollect ol' Pink laughed as he reloaded his gun, and I can still see his face, gloating and evil, as he relished in the taking of a human life. Then I heard him say: "Now bring out that damned Blue Belly mayor."

The crowd stirred and grumbled some after the sheriff was shot, but with the guns of Pink's Texans on them, there was nothing they could do.

I heard later that no one had been allowed to carry firearms on the streets of Alpine for years, by order of the mayor, and that made things so much easier for Pink and his hired killers. Also, the town wasn't ready.

In the olden days, before the Flathead were penned up, the Indians had raided in that area time and again, driving off horses and stock and killing miners. Every man had a gun then and he kept it handy and was primed for trouble. But peace had come to Alpine, and with it came prosperity and law, and the guns were locked away.

But then came Amos Pinkney.

The Texans returned to that cold-hearted desperado with a tall, dignified graybeard in a frockcoat and gold watch chain.

Pink let the man stand there in the street as he walked around him, like he was examining a horse for sale. Then he shoved his face close to the old man's and yelled: "Well, well, well, if it isn't Lieutenant Colonel Thomas St. Claire, all growed up and an honorable mayor."

"Damn you, sir, for an impertinent dog and a rebel traitor," St. Claire replied.

Pink smiled. "You do remember me, Colonel, don't you?"

"Remember you, sir? Yes I remember you. I remember you for a cowardly cur who made war on unarmed men and innocent women and children."

"And I remember you!" Pink screamed. "You shamed me! You shamed me!"

"You shamed yourself," St. Claire said. "After you took Centralia and stripped those unarmed Union recruits naked and shot them down like dogs, you and that black-hearted demon Bloody Bill Anderson.

"And you shamed yourself, sir, when you set your watch and gave your drunken followers three hours to rape and kill and plunder the town."

Ol' Pink ran back to the cottonwood tree and raised his face to the sky. He screamed. And he kept on screaming, a terrible, shrieking caterwauling that made my skin crawl and the hairs on the back of my neck stand on end, till one of his men, I think it was Jericho Gentle, walked over and whispered something in his ear.

Whatever Gentle said quietened ol' Pink down. But he again pointed his finger at St. Claire. "This man," he roared, "stands accused of high treason. The penalty is death! Death! Death!"

Pink walked up to the Colonel and thrust his face close to the old man's steadfast countenance.

"May 10, 1865," he yelled. "Do you remember that day?"

"Yes, damn you," St. Claire replied. "That was the day in Kentucky when I killed that damned murderer William Clarke Quantrill and brought you and your men to military justice."

"You shamed me that day," Pink said. "You made me lay my colors at the feet of your niggers in uniform. Me, Major Amos Pinkney, the hero of Lawrence, Kansas, the soldier with twenty-seven Union scalps hanging from his horse's bridle, made to crawl at the feet of four hundred sniggering niggers."

"You laid down your cursed black flag, sir," St. Claire said. "The colored troops of my regiment knew that flag well enough, for many had suffered greatly because of it."

"Treason!" Pink screamed. "Out of his own mouth, treason!"

Boys, I hope you haven't just et, because what happened next is hard to stomach.

Pink grabbed the Colonel by the gray hair of his noble old head and dragged him to the cottonwood tree where he put the noose around the old man's neck.

Even from where I stood at the window, I could see red foam in Pink's mouth where he had bitten down on his tongue. He was raving terrible oaths and curses that must have been first uttered in the lowest depths of hell.

The rope was choking St. Claire, but I heard him gasp: "Damn you, sir, for a foul-mouthed coyote!"

Pink ran to the other end of the rope, which lay on the ground and yanked on it. The old man's feet lifted in the air and I heard him gasp and clutch at the rope around his neck.

One man with more sand than the rest, a miner by his clothes, ran out of the crowd and put his arms around St. Claire's waist, and lifted him.

"Get this noose off'n him!" the miner yelled at the crowd.

But Jericho Gentle stepped up to the miner's side, put the muzzle of his Colt against the man's temple and blew his brains out. I heard women in the crowd scream and one close to where I watched fainted as the brave miner fell.

Pink yanked on the rope again with the strength of a madman and he ran this way and that under the tree limb, his cape flapping around his ankles, while Colonel St. Claire slowly strangled to death.

As he scrambled here and there with the rope in his hands, Pink was screaming, laughing, and cursing, all at once—and I knew then, as though I needed any reminding, that I had made a truly terrible enemy.

Boys, I wanted to turn and run from that awful place, but something held me rooted to the spot. I felt paralyzed, like a rabbit caught in the gaze of a rattlesnake.

At last it ended. St. Claire hung limp and lifeless and Pink loosed the rope and the old man's body thumped to the ground.

Pink was breathing hard after all the running he'd done, but he wasn't through just yet.

He strode in front of the crowd and screamed: "Ye nest of vipers! You have harbored a serpent to your bosom and ye will feel my wrath!"

Pink took his watch from his pocket and thumbed it open.

"Under the rules of war," he screamed, "when dealing with a traitorous enemy, there are no rules. I hereby surrender this town of Alpine to my soldiers for the next twenty-four hours, to plunder and pillage as they desire."

A great cheer went up from the Texans and Jacob Pike's wolfers. I saw one Texan with a vile, tobacco-stained beard pull a pretty little gal from the crowd and kiss her. The girl screamed and tried to fight him off, but the Texan lifted her off her feet and carried her struggling form across the road to the livery stable.

The Texans standing nearby laughed and cheered.

"Cry havoc," Pink shrieked, "and let slip the dogs of war!"

The people in the square scattered as guns went off and windows shattered all over town. Jacob Pike, his wolfers and the Flathead women ran after the towns-people, throwing them to the ground then stripping them of watches and wedding rings and anything else they could steal.

One young man, a banker by his dress, ran to Pink and tried to reason with him. But ol' Pink, who had an almost dreamy expression on his face, pulled both his Remingtons and shot the man down without ever turning his head to look at him.

I'd seen enough. Amos Pinkney had brought hell to Alpine.

Turning away from the window, I saw the shocked, wide-eyed face of a woman looking right at me. She was a very large lady of color, Miss Georgia Morgan by name, and there was no doubt in my mind that she recognized me.

NINETEEN

Georgia opened her mouth as if to yell something, so I ran out of the bedroom, down the stairs and through the back door of the restaurant.

I ran without stopping through the lumberyard— and then, as it seems to do to me with regularity, disaster struck.

The yard dog, a huge, black brute with sly cunning and recent villainy writ large on his face, had broken free from his stake and had patiently laid there in ambush. As I ran past he sprang at me and sank his fangs into my butt.

I kicked the snarling canine off, and kept running. But then another dog, one of those yappy little terrier beasts, joined in the fray and nipped at my heels. Then came another, and another, till it seemed that every mangy skillet-licker in town was trying to take a piece out of me.

Reaching the hill, I scrambled up the slope, the dog pack barking and snarling at my bootheels, just as a bullet kicked up dirt a few feet to my right.

A quick glance over my shoulder revealed a Texan standing in the street, a Winchester rifle to his shoulder.

The man fired again, and I heard a *piiing!* as the bullet whanged off a rock a few inches from my right toe.

The black dog, obviously a creature of crafty intelligence, figured that the hillside was no place to be and gave up the chase. He bounded down the hill and the others followed, but for the terrier, which took a few more nips at me before also turning and scampering away.

Looking over my shoulder again, I saw the Texan standing there laughing. He'd taken his rifle down from his shoulder, and I figgered he'd mistaken me for one of the townspeople.

I'd left my hat behind and was dressed in my ragged pants and mackinaw, so to that Texan I must have looked like one of the town bums, hardly worth a bullet.

Starting up the hill at a fast run, I heard the report of the rifle again, and this time a bullet burned across the outside of my right thigh. I fell heavily to the ground and rolled maybe ten yards down the slope.

Below me, holding the rifle to his shoulder, was the unmistakable figure of Amos Pinkney, the laughing Texan standing beside him.

Scrambling to my feet, I started to climb the hill again, but a bullet sang past my ear and kicked up a foot-high fountain of dirt just ahead of me.

Amos Pinkney could kill me real easy, and both of us knew it.

There was nothing else for it. I raised my hands above my head, and ol' Pink hollered: "Come down out of there, cowboy."

The terrier had returned, and he nipped at my heels all the way down the hill to where Pink stood. Pink kicked him away and the animal ran off yelping.

"We meet again, cowboy." Pink grinned evilly.

"Major, honest, I didn't get that five hunnerd," I said quickly. "We, I mean Doc, he left town and Johnny Blue was hurt bad an' Doc left town an'—"

"Oh, do stop babbling," Pink said. "I heard the whole sordid little story from a young lady of my acquaintance. You should watch your drinking, cowboy."

Ol' Pink studied me closely. "You don't look well, cowboy. You look kind of peaked." He turned to the Texan. "Don't you think he looks pale, Mister Canton?"

I was surprised to see that the man named Canton, who had a beautiful mustache and who looked as mean as eight acres of snakes, wore a Deputy U.S. Marshal's star pinned to his coat.

"He looks kinda weedy, Major," Canton said. "Kinda weedy and seedy, if you ask me."

Pink nodded. "Yes, that describes this man to a tee. Weedy and seedy, and dishonest to boot."

"Major," I said, "just let me explain."

"What is there to explain? You are here. And the only reason for your being here is that you came to Alpine to kill me, isn't it? You already wounded one of my men, quite painfully I might add, and now you planned to shoot me down in the street as you tried and failed to do in Great Falls."

"No! Hell no!" I wailed. "We come here to get back our money and our horses and our gu—"

I knew right there that I'd thrown a loop over the wrong steer.

"Yes," Pink said, "your guns. And what did you plan to do with those guns once you recovered them?"

"Nothing. Honest, Major, we just planned to ride out of here."

"You keep saying 'we,'" Pink said. "Where are your cohorts?"

I waved an arm. "Up there someplace. In the hills."

Pink nodded. "Ah well, never mind, we'll round them up later." He turned to Canton. "Frank, let's take him over to my headquarters."

There were Texans and wolfers in the street, all of them with whiskey bottles, and some with their arms around the waists of bruised and terrified women. The other townspeople were huddled in their homes, and to appear at a window was to invite an immediate shot from revolver or rifle.

I was limping some on my wounded leg, which had become numb from the thigh down, but Canton's rifle prodded me toward a false-fronted saloon named the Silver Nugget.

Someone had rigged a makeshift flagpole to the front of the building and Pink's Confederate banner fluttered in the breeze.

Pink stopped just as we entered the bar and turned to Frank Canton. He pointed at Colonel St. Claire's body. "String that up till it rots."

Inside, standing at the bar were Jericho Gentle and Jacob Pike. A stack of rifles, revolvers and shotguns were piled in a corner, the guns confiscated from the town.

Pink saw me look at the guns. "Strike just before dawn, order the people into the street, then take the arms," he said. "That is the way of the mounted raider, as Captain Quantrill taught it to me. People without weapons are sheep to be sheared—or slaughtered."

Jacob Pike saw me and laughed, a great roaring guffaw.

"Well, if it ain't my little drinking pardner," he said. "I've been waiting a long time to break your scrawny neck."

He came at me then, murder in his eyes, his hands open wide like the talons of a great, hairy hawk.

Boys, I was in the gravest peril among that den of killers and was fast running out of room on the dance floor. I was sure my time had come.

But ol' Pink stopped the big wolfer in his tracks.

"Leave him be, Jacob," he said. "I have other plans for our drover friend." He waved a hand toward the grinning Jericho Gentle, who was testing the edge of a skinning knife on his thumb. "Do you remember this gentleman and the little chat we had on the night of the prizefight?"

"I'll never forget it," I said.

"Neither will Mister Gentle. Many's the night I've seen him hone that knife of his to razor sharpness, a yearning look in his eye so that I longed to reach out and comfort him. But how could I? Only you could bring him that comfort, cowboy. Only you could end that yearning."

Gentle elbowed himself off the bar. "You want I should peel off his hide now, Major?"

Ol' Pink laughed. "Jericho Gentle, I swear you're like a little boy sometimes. It's always now, now, now, and keep nothing till later." He studied me, then Gentle, then back to me again. "Oh, very well, why not? Just be careful you don't cut yourself."

Gentle walked slowly toward me as Pike moved behind me and pinioned my arms. I heard Pink giggle like a schoolgirl.

I tried to speak, but my tongue wouldn't move. I'd just bought the farm, and I knew it.

Gentle said: "Boy, you'll only scream for a day or two, then it will be over. The Lord is just, but He's also merciful."

"Who knows, you might even be amused," Pink said. "I'm told the pain is quite exquisite."

"Put him down on his back," Gentle told Pike, and the big wolfer kicked away my feet and I slammed to the floor.

"Now get his boots off. I'll start with his feet." He squeezed my big toe. "With theese leetle piggy here . . ."

You know me, boys, I'm only a poor cowboy and I sure as hell ain't much to look at, but I always figgered it's not how a man lives, but how he dies that counts. After this was over, I wanted folks to say about me, "Well, he warn't much, but he couldn't be stampeded an' he died game."

As Gentle leaned over me, his knife ready, I gritted my teeth and vowed that I wouldn't give ol' Pink the satisfaction of hearing me scream.

But then fate, in the shape of a three-hunnerd-pound lady of color, saved my life.

"Stop that!" Miss Georgia Morgan cried from the door of the saloon. "Haven't you chicken rustlers had enough killing for one day?"

For a few long seconds the saloon was as silent as a shadow.

Then Pink said, "Woman, what did you just say?"

"I said there's been enough killing."

"No, there was something else before that. You called us something? What did you call us?"

Georgia's bottom lip was trembling, a strange sight in a woman as big and strong as she was. "I . . . I can't remember," she whispered.

Pink turned to Gentle.

"What did she call us, Jericho?"

Gentle grinned. "It was chicken rustlers. She said it plain enough."

"Yes, that was it," Pink said. "Chicken rustlers. This great enterprise of ours reduced to the dung of the barnyard."

Boys, Georgia's back was to the wall and she was scared and I guess her heart was running right faster than a turkey on Thanksgiving Day, but all of a sudden she seemed to rediscover her courage and she held her head high as she said: "Haven't you had your fill of killing, Major? And you, Jericho, why are you so hell bent to skin this poor little cowboy who don't have enough hide on him to make a throw pillow? I say it's enough. There's been enough innocent blood shed already."

"You say? You say?" I looked into Pink's eyes as they fixed, wild and bloodshot, on Georgia. "What gives you the right to say anything, you pathetic, sub-human ingrate?"

Georgia tried to answer, but I guess her mouth was so dry she couldn't form the words. But she swallowed hard and her voice was steady enough when she finally said: "I was your slave, and you are my father, and both these things give me the right."

"Nothing!" Pink screamed. "They give you nothing! A slave is nothing. A whelp spawned from a slave is nothing! You have no rights, no right to speak, or right to think. The only right you have is to exist and only as long as you're willing to serve and obey those who are better than yourself. And by that I mean the white race."

"If the inhumanity and cruelty I've seen today is an example of the white race, then I'm glad my skin is black," Georgia said. Then she added: "Like my mother's."

Pink just stood there frozen in place for a moment or two, his red eyes staring at Georgia. "You dare say that! You dare say that to me!"

Pink's fist crashed into Georgia's mouth. It takes a lot to drop a three-hunnerd-pound person, and she stayed on her feet. But her head snapped back hard and blood spurted from her smashed lips.

"Get out of here, you black whore!" Pink yelled.

Georgia buried her face in her hands, then turned and ran out the door.

"One day," Pink said to no one but himself, "I'm going to kill that bitch."

I hadn't noticed before, but Frank Canton had come into the saloon. "Major," he said, "that was a helluva thing, I mean hitting her like that."

Pink turned to him, his eyes wild. "If you don't have the stomach for it, Frank, walk on out of here."

Canton thought that one over for a while. "I guess I'll stay," he said.

TWENTY

"Now, cowboy," Gentle whispered in my ear after he watched Georgia leave, "we can get back to our business."

"No, stop," Pink said. "The moment's past and I'm no longer in the mood. Skinning a man is like having sex with a woman. You must have it when you want it, before the urge passes. Now I'm much too upset. That awful woman disturbed me terribly." He put a hand to his right temple and massaged it gently. "She's given me a terrible headache, and I feel all a-dither." He glanced at his skinned knuckles. "And she hurt my hand."

"Aw shoot, Major," Gentle said, disappointment writ all over his face. "I was all primed for the skinnin'."

Pink sighed. "I know how down in the mouth you must feel, Jericho. But don't be so glum. We'll keep this ranny on ice until tomorrow morning. You can have him then, Jericho. It will amuse me over breakfast."

Ol' Pink, his sullen face suddenly lit up. "What a perfectly splendid idea! I've never before skinned a man for breakfast. It will be a wonderful new experence." He glanced over at Jacob Pike, who was standing in the corner grinning. "Jacob, look at me. What do you see?"

Pike blinked stupidly a time or two, his slow mind working. "What do you want me to see, boss?"

"Why, man," Pink said. "I'm all a-tingle with anticipation. Can't you tell?"

Pike nodded. "Sure can, boss. All a . . . a-tingle is what you are fer sure."

"Yes," Pink's face took on that sullen expression again. "That's what I am. What I need now is a bottle, Pike. I'm in the mood to get drunk. Fetch it for me, will you?"

Pike left and Pinkney said: "As for you, Jericho, patience. You'll have your fun tomorrow, I promise." He turned to Canton. "Take this over to the sheriff's office and lock it up. It's your responsibility, Frank, so guard it well."

Canton prodded me with the barrel of his rifle. "On your feet, cowboy."

I pulled on my boots and Canton pushed me into the street. As we walked across to the sheriff's office there were a few flakes of snow tossing around in the wind and the sky was turning a leaden gray. I hoped Johnny Blue and the others had found shelter someplace. It was going to be a cold night.

The sheriff's office was a low one-room shack with a desk and chair out front and a single iron-barred cell to the rear. A rifle rack stood on the wall behind the desk, but it was empty.

Canton threw me into the cell then sat on the chair,

propping his feet up on the desk. He started to build himself a smoke and said, "It's gonna be a long time till mornin', boy, so jest you settle down in there."

"I ain't going nowheres," I said.

"Damn right you ain't. Anyhow, you're better off in here than out there on the street. The Major's getting drunk and he's plumb angry. It's gonna be hell in this town tonight."

I sat on the bunk, my head in my hands, and tried not to think about the morning and Jericho Gentle's knife. That hombre had already scared me out of ten years' growth—if I lived that long.

To clear my mind, I thought of Georgia Morgan and how roughly Pink had handled her. What had Pink meant about a "great enterprise?" It seemed to me he had more on his mind than jest robbing the Alpine bank and hoorawing the town.

"Hey, Canton," I said, "I got a question for you."

Canton thumbed flame to a match and lighted his cigarette. He ignored me.

"It's about Miss Georgia Morgan," I said.

"What's she to ya?" Canton asked.

"Oh, nothing, I'm jest passing time. I don't want to think right now."

"Boy," Canton said, "I don't blame you. Ask away." He stroked his beautiful mustache, teasing the ends into a fine curl.

"Was that right, I mean what she said about Pink being her daddy an' all?"

"Sure. In fact it was the Major who give her the name Georgia. That was when she was his slave, back in the good ol' days."

"But them bluecoat Yankee soldiers set all the slaves free." I said. "Miss Georgia don't owe Pink nothing anymore."

Canton laughed. "Boy, do you have a lot to learn. The Yankees set Georgia's body free, but the Major, he still owns her soul."

"How come?"

"Because Georgia is still the Major's property. He knows it, and she knows it. 'Course, even so, I didn't hold with him hitting her that way. It ain't right to hit a woman, any woman. He should have shot her clean an' proper. That's what I would have done."

Boys, that gave me something to chew on, I can tell you. I wondered how Georgia could've stood by a man like Amos Pinkney all these years.

But who can hope to understand the mind of a woman?

Do you boys recollect ol' Grim Porrey, him with the real bad piles an' the stovepipe hat that lived down on the Musselshell for a spell? Do you recollect his wife, how she had them permanent black eyes and no front teeth? Ol' Grim beat her from hell to breakfast every single day of the week and twice on weekends, but she never left him. I don't believe the thought ever crossed her mind. Yet all the time she had rich kinfolk back East, beggin' her to come home.

Some women are like that. No matter how badly they're treated, they'll always come back for more. I guess that's the way it was with Georgia. Grim's wife, she always said she loved her man. Georgia must surely have loved her daddy.

"Canton," I said, "I'm hungry."

"Tough."

"Don't the condemned man get a last meal?"

"Sure boy, I'll give you something to chew on—if'n you don't shut up, I'll put a bullet in you, Major or no Major."

There was a clock on the wall that I could see from my cell, and it showed a couple of minutes before midnight when the office door opened and Georgia Morgan walked inside.

She was carrying a basket covered in a gingham cloth and a bottle of whiskey.

Canton didn't get up.

"You got no call to be here, Georgia," he said.

Georgia's lips were swollen and cracked wide open and she had a time of it talking. "I brung this for him"—she hefted the basket—"and this bottle for you."

"Does the Major know about this?" Canton asked suspiciously.

"I didn't feel the need to tell him, " Georgia said.

Canton muttered something under his breath. He took the basket from Georgia and rummaged through it, coming up with a fried chicken leg which he chomped down on with his teeth.

"Don't seem right, wasting good food on a dead man," he said, talking around the chicken leg.

"Even a condemned man's got the right to eat, same as everybody else," Georgia said mildly.

Canton took some more of the chicken and a couple of buttermilk biscuits and laid them on his desk. "What's happening outside?" he asked.

"Women screaming, men shooting, people dying," Georgia said.

Canton laughed. "I guess the boys are having a good time."

"You could say that."

There was a big wedge of apple pie in the basket, and Canton took that out and placed it beside his chicken. He peered into the basket.

"Give him what's left."

Georgia took the remains of the meal and wrapped it in the gingham cloth. She passed this through the bars of my cell—and winked.

Me, I didn't know then what that wink meant, but it made me feel a sight better.

Canton had left me with a chicken wing, a scrap of bone from the leg he'd just et and a single biscuit. But I devoured everything in sight and when it was over, I wished there was more.

Meantime ol' Frank was chawing down pretty good and drinking deep from Miss Georgia's whiskey bottle. When he talked his voice was slurred, which surprised me because I took him for a man who could hold his liquor.

"The Major, yore precious daddy, Georgia, is . . . is leadin' us to glory," Canton said. "The South . . . the South . . . will rise again . . . and the Stainless Banner . . . the Stainless Bann . . ."

He rose unsteadily to his feet and I saw him reel backward a few steps. "You bitch," he snarled. "You've done for me . . . I'm gonna . . ."

Canton clawed at his holstered Colt, but Georgia

was faster. She pulled one of them handy-dandy .41 derringer guns from somewhere between her huge bosoms and thumbed back the hammer.

But she didn't need it.

Ol' Frank took a step or two toward her, then sprawled full-length on the floor.

"He'll be out for hours," Georgia said.

"Was that one of Cottontail's bottles?" I asked.

"No," Georgia replied. "That particular tarantula juice was all mine."

She got the cell key from the wall and let me out.

"Cowboy, we don't have a minute to lose," she said. "Do you want to save this town before everyone in it is dead? And do you want to help get me out of the clutches of maybe the most evil man on earth?"

"Well . . . I—"

"Good. Then listen carefully." Quickly Georgia outlined her plan.

She said the buckboard holding the money from the bank, about twenty thousand dollars in notes and coin in all, was in the livery stable. There was no guard, on account of how ol' Pink reckoned the whole town was under guard.

"You've got to pull the Major and his men away from Alpine," she said. "They'll follow the money."

"Which means?" I asked.

Georgia sighed.

"Cowboy, you hitch a team to the wagon and drive it out of town. The Major and the others will follow you. Once they've gone, the townspeople will get to their guns and I got a feeling they won't be buffaloed so easily again."

"That sounds jest fine," I said, "right up until the time ol' Pink catches me up on the trail and then skins me alive."

"I've thought about that," Georgia said. "Three miles west on the trail there's a big rock—"

"I seen that on the way in," I said. "Looks kinda like an animal of some kind."

"Right," Georgia said. "The Flatheads call it Stone of the Bear. If you turn the wagon off the trail at the rock and head north you'll come to an old miner's shack. One of the walls has fallen, so drive the wagon right into the shack and unhitch the team. You can use the horses to head back to Montana."

"How do you know all this?" I asked. "Have you been here before?"

"No," Georgia said. "I had an urgent talk with the sheriff, just before . . . before . . ."

I laid my hand on Georgia's shoulder. "Ol' Pink's gonna be real mad. It'll take him days to find that wagon."

"That's what I'm counting on," Georgia said. "With winter coming on hard, he won't be able to stay around here. He has a place near Virginia City and he'll want to get back there to hole up till spring."

"Why you doing all this, Miss Georgia?" I asked.

Her hand strayed to her smashed lips. "Because what's happening here is sheer madness, and what the Major's planning next is madder still." I saw tears come into her small black eyes. "He hit me, cowboy. He hit me hard and he made me feel like I was nothing, that I wasn't even fit to live. I'll never forgive him for that." She shook her head, her jowls bouncing. "Never."

"It did seem uncalled for," I said. "I mean, what with you two being kin an' all."

Georgia nodded. "We're kin all right. But that's over. I'll never call him my father again. Or my master."

"Tell me what he's planning, Miss Georgia?" I said. "I mean after this, after he gets through with Alpine."

"No time for that right now, cowboy," Georgia said. "We have to move."

I took Frank Canton's gunbelt—he had one of them long-barreled Colts Texans are so partial to—and strapped it around my waist.

Then I rolled ol' Frank over on his back and took that wedge of apple pie and stuffed it into his open mouth, making sure I rubbed plenty of it into his silky mustache.

"That's for being a pig, Frank," I said.

"Cowboy," Georgia said, shaking her head, "you sure are a strange one."

Boys, if I known then what I was to learn years later about what he done to that poor cowboy Nate Champion, I might have plugged Frank Canton right there on the jailhouse floor.

In later years Frank talked hisself into a job as a cattle detective, and he was top gun in the Johnson County War of '92 in Wyoming. That's when he gunned ol' Nate for cattle rustling. As some of you boys can recollect, I knew Nate, even worked with him one time along the Goodnight. He was a steady hand and a good companion when he was sober.

When you come right down to it, he was just a poor cowboy like me and you and he didn't deserve to die for stealing a few cows, especially at the hands of Frank Canton.

But nowadays I console myself with the thought that ol' Nate's up there rustlin' the good Lord's cattle on the range that knows no end and slapping his own iron over that almighty G brand.

Nate, may your calves never suck on the right cow.

Amen.

Miss Georgia stuck her head outside the door and motioned for me to foller. We left the sheriff's office and struck out for the rear of the building, keeping well to the shadows.

Pulling Frank's Colt, I follered Georgia. She stepped lightly enough for a large lady, and she must've had cat's eyes because she picked her way through the shadows like she'd been born to it. A piano tinkled from a house we passed, then it stopped as I heard a man's drunken laugh. A whiskey bottle crashed through a window, sailing into the yard, and that made Georgia freeze. I stopped and brung up the Colt level with the rear door of the house.

But then the piano started again, and I heard the thin, wavering voice of a woman trying to keep up to the piano as the drunken man laughed again.

Georgia was on the move once more, beckoning me to follow her. We kept to the back of the buildings lining the street all the way to the livery stable, midst a gently falling snow that showed no sign of settling to any thickness on the ground.

The night was cold, and the town had quietened down, though I didn't want to think about what was going on behind all them closed doors.

Georgia opened the rear door of the livery stable and we crept inside. The barn was packed with horses, and I recognized Johnny Blue's buckskin and my own pony among them.

The buckboard was parked in the middle of the aisle between the stalls and Georgia told me to hitch up the team. She pointed to two huge Percherons that were pawing the ground and snorting, upset by our sudden entrance.

Boys, I don't know if you've ever been around Percherons much, but they're a mighty peculiar hoss. They're as slow as molasses in January, yet they'll run all day an' then some, pulling any kind of load you want to give 'em.

I got the team hitched in record time, because them big horses was real gentle and obedient, kinda like some big men I know.

"You remember what you have to do?" Georgia asked as I climbed up on the seat of the buckboard.

"I ain't likely to forget it," I said.

"The Major's men are mostly drunk and some of them will be in bed right now," she said. "It will take them a while to get organized and saddled up, so you'll have a good head start."

"I don't much care how many are drunk," I said. "How many are sober?"

"Enough," Georgia said. "So keep your head down."

Georgia walked to the front of the stable and opened the doors wide.

"Go, cowboy!" she yelled. "And good luck."

I yelled, "Yeehaw!" and slapped the reins across the

backs of the Percherons, which leaped forward at a surprising speed.

Pulling the Colt, I kept the reins bunched in my left hand and those horses shot through the open door.

Me, I was a fair way to hunting a heap of trouble, and I knew it was about to come hunting me.

TWENTY-ONE

The Percherons charged through the doors, their huge hooves pounding, and I swung the team in a sharp left, feeling the wagon tilt crazily as the wheels left the road.

Off to my right a man shouted, "What the hell!" and cut loose with his revolver. The wagon righted itself and I just kept on going.

I glanced over my shoulder and saw that I'd caused a considerable commotion. The street looked like a stirred hornet's nest as men ran here and there, yelling and firing guns.

The Percherons were going at a steady lope, but I slapped the reins across their rumps and they stretched out into a full gallop.

We charged down the center of Alpine's main street and I heard the report of rifles in the darkness behind me.

"Remember the Alamo!" I hollered, giving them big cart horses some encouragement.

A man came running out of a house on my left, pulling up his britches. He had a Winchester in his hands and he let his pants fall around his ankles while he levered a round into the chamber and fired.

The stabbing orange flame from the rifle was blinding bright in the darkness, but I ignored it and kept going.

Their necks stretched straight out, the Percherons was enjoying themselves, seeing as how they was full of oats and had been cooped up in the barn for a long spell.

In fact, them horses was galloping so hard, we was fast running out of town. Through a break in the clouds I saw the steep grade that led out of Alpine and up into the hills.

Slapping the lines again, I cheered on the horses. They had the wind under their tails and they was tearing hell for leather.

Ahead of me, another man ran into the street, waving his arms and yelling something. I leveled Canton's Colt and thumbed back the hammer—and the damn gun went off all by itself.

The bullet nicked the ear of the Percheron in the left trace, and he screamed then jumped wildly and crashed into the other horse, which reared and brought the wagon to a skidding stop. The quick halt dragged the screeching rear wheels around so fast the feller who had been running at me had to jump for his life as the wagon swung at him.

Me, I almost fell out of the seat and had to grab on the handrails to save myself from pitching headlong into the street. The Colt fell to the boards between my feet. I reached down to grab it just as the man jumped up in the seat beside me.

"You dern fool!" the man yelled.

The Colt was in my hand as I straightened. I

thumbed back the hammer again ready to shoot—and looked into the angry face of Johnny Blue.

"Yore gonna get us all killed!" he yelled. "Why did you go an' shoot your hoss?"

"I don't know. I was trying to shoot you, an' I don't want to talk about it," I said.

A bullet sang viciously between our heads. "I suggest we get out of here right quick," Johnny Blue said. "Unless of course you plan to do some more hoss huntin'."

I slapped the Percherons into a run, gingerly holding on to that treacherous Colt, which still had the hammer cocked back.

Hearing shouting and a commotion behind us, I looked around and saw men leading horses out of the livery stable. I stuck the long barrel of the Colt under my left arm and just touched the trigger. The big gun went off.

"Jeez," I said, "this thing has a hair trigger."

"Don't shoot again," Johnny Blue said. "We can't afford to lose any more horses."

The Percherons were running flat out again when they hit the grade, but it didn't slow them down in the least. The wagon rolled and bucked up and down. Me and Johnny Blue held on for dear life as we reached the top of the grade and thundered on to the wagon trail at a dead run.

Looking behind me, I saw no sign of pursuit, and I figgered Pink and his boys, most of them drunk, was taking their own sweet time to get organized.

Flogging the team mercilessly along the trail, I yelled and hollered and slapped the reins across their big rumps. The big animals responded, their ears flattened back, their huge hooves throwing up great splattering gobs of freezing mud, which soon covered me and Johnny Blue.

Behind us a rifle barked, then another.

The snow had stopped and the night was so dark, you couldn't find your nose with both hands. But every now and then the scudding black clouds parted and the moon shone brightly for a few moments, lighting up the trail ahead of us.

We passed the bear stone at a crazed gallop and I had to battle the team to a halt and then back them up about two hundred yards before we could leave the trail at the rock and head north into what was rough, hilly country.

Somewhere behind us, Amos Pinkney's voice yelled out. A rifle crashed again, followed by the pounding of hooves that slowly faded into the distance.

We rolled over the crests of a succession of shallow hills, and I let the horses pick their own way through the gulleys between them, filled as they were with piles of brush, fallen trees and scrub pine.

"Me, I don't think they're following us," I said.

"Maybe," Johnny Blue said. "Maybe not."

"Did fate make you a pessimist, Johnny Blue, or was you borned that way?" I asked.

"Noise you're making jawing, they're gonna find us soon enough," he said.

"I swear, you'd complain if they was gonna hang you with a new rope," I told him.

We rolled on in silence for a while, then the hills gave way to a flat, grassy area bounded to our right by a thick stand of Douglas fir.

This struck me as desolate and lonely country, where a man could get lost and never find his way again.

"Look there," Johnny Blue said, pointing to the western end of the pine belt.

"I can't see a thing," I said.

"During that last break in the clouds I thought I caught sight of a cabin," Johnny Blue said. "Mosey on over there."

I turned the team and we rolled to where Johnny Blue had pointed. Sure enough, as we got closer I saw a large cabin tucked just inside the woods, hidden from all but the sharpest eyes.

"That's the miner's shack," I said.

"You sound like you knew it was gonna be here."

"Miss Georgia told me it would be here," I said.

"Maybe you'd better tell me what's going on," Johnny Blue said.

As we rolled toward the shack I quickly outlined what had happened in town, missing out none of the details where my own courage and daring was involved.

"Then you jumped in the wagon, an' you know the rest," I said.

"Yeah," Johnny Blue said, "that was right after you shot your hoss and nearly done for me with the wagon."

"What was you doing there, anyhow?" I asked.

"Tryin' to save your dern fool hide, that's what. There warn't anyone else to do it. Doc and the Mauler took off after they saw Pink hang that old geezer. And Doc, he claimed he saw you through his spyglass being dragged off to the hoosegow, but I don't know about that. At any rate, we all reckoned you was a goner."

"Well, I want to thank you for trying to save me, Johnny Blue," I said. I had a lump in my throat as big as a hen's egg. "That's the true measure of a pardner."

"Hell," Johnny Blue said, "it weren't nothing. Besides, I reckoned if'n it turned out I couldn't save your butt, I could always stick around and watch the skinnin'."

"That's a kicker, ain't it," I said, ignoring his last remark. "I mean about Miss Georgia bein' ol' Pink's daughter an' all."

"Strange ol' world. Stop the wagon."

Johnny Blue jumped down, looked quickly around him, then vanished into the gloom.

I waited, glancing now and then over my shoulder into the darkness behind me. An icy breeze stirred the tops of the Douglas firs, setting them to whispering and sighing. I shivered. The night seemed to be full of eyes, and all of them looking right at me.

Two or three minutes passed, and Johnny Blue didn't return.

I waited a couple of minutes more, then kicked on the buckboard's brake and wrapped the lines around the handle.

Stepping down onto the grass, I pulled the Colt and walked warily in the direction of the shack. My leg was still troubling me some where ol' Pink's bullet had grazed it, so I favored it, which slowed me some.

"Johnny Blue," I whispered. "Are you there?"

No answer came back.

I walked on a few yards, then said again, "Johnny Blue?"

From somewhere deep in the woods, an owl asked: "Whooo? Whooo?"

My mouth was scared dry and I drew little comfort from the Colt in my fist, unreliable as it was.

Somewhere along the way, I'd lost direction and ended up at the tree line. I made my way to my left, figgering the shack had to be close. If it wasn't, I was lost.

I expected at any minute to see Pink and his boys come thundering over the hills, guns blazing. And that thought didn't exactly comfort me either.

After a walk that seemed endless, I reached the end of the timber belt and I peered through the gloom, trying to catch sight of the cabin. But I'm as blind as a snubbin' post in the dark, so I could see nothing.

I cat-footed on—and walked right into the east wall of the cabin. I hit my shin on something hard, and cussed a blue streak as the pain shot all the way up my leg to my wounded thigh.

On a hunch, I groped my way to my right, and came to the open doorway of the cabin. I limped inside, and even my eyes could see that the entire back wall of the shack was gone, torn down by some great wind, I figured.

Georgia had been right about this place. Even in broad daylight a rider could pass close by and never guess that a wagon was stashed inside.

I heard footsteps in the woods and swung the Colt in that direction.

"Come on in real slow," I said aloud. "I got a gun and I can plug you real quick."

"Shut up, you churnhead," Johnny Blue whispered.

"You done roused the whole territory already with your cussin' and fussin'."

"Where have you been?" I asked. "I thought you was a goner for sure."

"While you was tromping around and making more noise than a calf cryin' for momma, I was trying to find us a way out of here," Johnny Blue said. "We can't go back on the trail while Pink and his boys are searching for us."

"I didn't make any noise. I walk like a Indian," I said. "Plenty of folks have told me that."

"A cigar store Indian, maybe."

"What did you find out while you was in the woods anyhow, Dan'l Boone?"

"There's a path through the trees, looks like an old Indian hunting trail, and it's wide enough for a man on a horse to pass through. I'm pretty sure it heads west for a ways. We can take that trail till we're well out of Pink's reach, then cut back on to the wagon road."

Well, all this made good sense to me and I readily agreed to it. Now all we had to do was get the wagon into the shack, which was easier said than done.

For some reason the Percherons balked at walking into the shack, and we had to unhitch them and man-handle the buckboard inside ourselves.

It took the best part of an hour to get the wagon hidden, and by the time it was over, both our tails were dragging in the dirt.

"How much money you say is in there?" Johnny Blue asked.

I told him.

He opened up a sack and looked inside and whistled. "There's enough here to keep a man, or two men, in luxury for the rest of their lives."

"It ain't ours to keep," I said. "It belongs to them folks back in Alpine. I reckoned they've suffered enough without having their money stole again."

"Who said anything about stealing?"

"I know what you're thinking, Johnny Blue."

"You don't know what I'm thinking. You've no idea what I'm thinking. When I find my little sister I couldn't look her in the eye, knowing I was a thief."

"Gold can tempt a man," I said.

"Not this man," Johnny Blue said. "How about you?"

I shook my head at him. "I ain't got much, but what I do have, I come by honest and square. I ain't about to change that."

"So be it," Johnny Blue said.

He began to free the Percherons from their traces, then turned to me and said: "Know something? Sometimes I think we're a couple of derned fools."

A few minutes later, as penniless as before, we mounted the broad backs of the Percherons and rode into the woods.

TWENTY-TWO

Johnny Blue had been right about the hunting trail. It headed due west and I figgered it ran parallel to the freight road, about three miles to the north of it.

We stuck to that trail for three days, letting the Percherons graze where they could along the way.

There was plenty of water in the hollows of the forest floor, which we drank, and on the second day I caught a fat raccoon that fought like a tiger and bit and scratched me all over. We skinned that 'coon then half-cooked it over a fire I could've covered with the palm of my hand.

We had no salt and the 'coon was greasy and tough, but by then we was so hungry it was a feast to remember.

By nightfall on the third day the trail petered out, and we headed south back to the freight trail—and stumbled right into Doc and the Mauler's camp.

Doc had pulled his wagon well away from the road, and he and the Mauler were huddled around a tiny, damp fire, its slender plume of smoke tying knots in the still cold air.

Me and Johnny Blue reined in the Percherons, and I hollered: "Hello the camp!"

Doc jumped up like a startled rabbit. "Go away!" he yelled. "There's a dozen federal marshals here, heavily armed, and we wish to be left alone!"

I kicked my horse forward. "Doc," I said, "it's me. And I got Johnny Blue with me."

Doc peered through the gloom and I guess when he saw me and Johnny Blue emerge from the trees, frost and snow on our hats and the shoulders of our mackinaws, riding those huge gray horses, he really got spooked.

"The runt and Johnny Blue are dead!" Doc hollered. He raised his hands in the air and yelled, "Back, back foul fiends! I hereby banish you hellish specters from roaming the earth and turning the night into a gibbering horror. Oh, something wicked this way comes. Up guards and at 'em! A drum, a drum, Macbeth doth come!"

"Doc," I said, "we ain't ghosts."

"Are you sure?" Doc asked, a little calmer now. "I took ye fer goblins."

"Nah," Johnny Blue said, sliding off his horse, "we ain't ghosts, on account of how we're only half dead."

The Mauler, that big-hearted creature, ran up to each of us in turn and threw his arms around our necks, sobbing on our shoulders, telling us how glad he was to see us alive.

"I thought you were both dead for sure," he said, after he'd recovered enough to talk.

"We almost was, Mauler," I said. "It was close."

"Where did you get those enormous nags?" Doc asked.

"It's a long story," I said.

"Do you have any grub?" Johnny Blue asked.

"Nah," said Doc. "But hunker down by the fire and tell us what happened back there in Alpine. I sure thought both of you were goners."

Me and Johnny Blue sat by the thin firelight and I gave Doc a rundown on our adventures. When it was over, he let his chin drop to his chest.

"I am a cowardly cur," he said. "I deserted you in your time of need, as false Casca fled the side of Caesar ere the envious daggers pierced the breast of the noblest Roman of all. In short, I am undone. Bartholomew, my dear friend, kill me. I am too cowardly and miserable a creature to live."

The Mauler rose, his face puzzled. "How do you want me to do it, Doc?"

Doc, who had waited expectantly, but without much success, for someone to jump up and stop the Mauler, waved a hand. "Not right now, Bartholomew. Later, later. Now, my young friends, what are your plans for the future?"

"We don't have none," Johnny Blue said. "I got a feeling this shindig is over with."

"What Johnny Blue is trying to say," I added, "is that we just can't buck the kind of odds we're facing." I gazed into our miserable fire. "Doc, we tried to play Pink's game an' all that happened is we got plucked cleaner than a Sunday chicken. He won. We lost. That's all there is to it."

"What you gonna do now, young feller?" asked the Mauler.

"I dunno," I said. "Head back to Montana and try to stay out of Pink's way. Maybe we'll find work. Who knows?"

"There ain't no work," Johnny Blue said. "You

know that. I know that. Even Doc here knows that. The cows are all gone an' they ain't never coming back."

Boys, what all four of us done then was to gaze into the fire and, if'n we'd had a mind to, we could've produced enough tears to float an anvil.

Then Doc broke the silence. "Ah yes, this is a scene of sweet melancholy, to be sure. But never let it be said that Doc Fortune deserted his friends twice. He has learned his lesson.

"You two cowboys may be poor as lizard-eating cats, but you can travel with me and Bartholomew and hold your heads high. We will journey south and fleece the flock as we go, leaving ne'er a highway or byway unexplored in our search for the green around the gills, the glum and the gullible. In short, we will peddle snake oil and live off our ill-gotten gains."

I shook my head at Doc. "Thank you most kindly," I said, "but we couldn't be beholdin' to you that way. Me and Johnny Blue, we have to find our own way."

Johnny Blue opened his mouth to speak, but whatever he was about to say is lost to posterity, because just then we heard a pounding of hooves on the trail. Seconds later there was a loud, crashing thump followed by the cry of a woman "in extremis," as Doc would say.

I jumped up and ran to the road. A roan horse lay there, his neck twisted at an odd angle, and beside him sprawled the still form of Miss Georgia Morgan.

"Oh my God, is she dead?" Doc asked from beside me.

Cradling Georgia's head in my arms, I saw that she'd been savagely beaten. Both her eyes were swollen shut and her face was covered in cuts and bruises. She looked even worse than Johnny Blue did after the Mauler got through with him.

Doc ran back to the wagon and returned with a bottle of his elixir. He kneeled beside Georgia and chaffed her hand.

"My dear lady," he said, "please open those nectar lips and utter my name."

"Doc," Georgia gasped, "you lowdown skunk."

"Glory be, she's alive!" Doc said, and put the bottle to Georgia's lips. "Here, drink this, my precious."

Georgia took the bottle from Doc's hand, tilted back her head and drained it.

"I needed that," she said. "How's my horse?"

"Dead," Johnny Blue said. "His neck's broke."

"I saw your smoke," Georgia told us, "and pulled up my horse. But he was already all played out an' . . . an' he just went down."

"There, there, snookums," Doc said. "It's all over now."

Georgia tried to rise, but she winced and flopped back into my arms. "I think I've got some busted ribs," she groaned.

"We've got to get her off the road," Doc said.

"How?" Johnny Blue asked, which drew him a hard look from me.

"I'll do it," the Mauler said.

He bent down and lifted that huge woman as easily and gently as you or me would pick up a baby. The rest of us followed as the Mauler carried Georgia into the woods and laid her by the fire.

"Bartholomew," Doc said, "you'd better get that dead horse out of sight."

"Sure, Doc," the Mauler replied, and he headed back to the trail.

Doc took Georgia's hand again. "My dear one, when I saw you lying there on the road so deathly still, I thought I'd lost you forever."

Georgia painfully raised herself on one elbow. "Did you really, Doc? Did you fear for me?"

"My precious," Doc said, "my thoughts went back to the many times we've shared the bed of pleasure, our two panting souls cojoined as one, and I feared those times had come to an end. My love. My inamorata."

"But, Doc," Georgia said, "every time we done the thing together, you paid for it."

"Ah yes, my precious. Like everything else in this world, the path of true love cannot be traveled on the cheap."

"I hate to break this up," Johnny Blue said, "but who beat you up so bad, Georgia?"

"The Major," Georgia said. She pulled a scrap of lace handkerchief from her sleeve and dabbed at her bruised eyes.

"But why?" I asked.

"He found out about the wagon," Georgia said. "He beat me to make me tell him where it was, but I wouldn't. Then he said he was going to hang me. I'm not brave like you, cowboy. You saved the town of Alpine all by yourself. But I'm just a frail female and I didn't want to hang, so I told the Major everything he wanted to know.

"Then the Major said he was going to hang me anyway. So I stole a horse and hightailed it out of town."

"Yeah," Johnny Blue said, "I noticed before that you got a tolerable liking for other people's ponies."

I gave him another hard look, and said, "You took a terrible risk, Georgia. Frank Canton knew you'd drugged him."

"I thought Canton would figure he got drunk and that you'd escaped. The stuff I put in his whiskey can do things to a man's memory, and I figgered he wouldn't even recollect who gave it to him. But he remembered alright, and he told the Major."

Georgia giggled. "Frank was real mad anyhow when he woke up with that pie in his mouth. It took him all day to comb the crumbs out of his mustache, and he had to cut a good piece of it off. He was very proud of that mustache, and now he says it's ruined."

The Mauler came back to the fire, huge and sweating. "I drug that dead horse into the brush," he said. "Nobody's gonna find it, leastways till it starts to stink."

"Georgia," I asked, "where's the Major now?"

"I reckon he's on the trail, maybe a day behind me. Maybe less."

"Doc," I said, "we gotta douse that fire. We don't want Pink smellin' our smoke."

Doc then kicked out the feeble fire and all of us stared into the cooling ashes. "Sure is gonna be cold tonight," Johnny Blue said at last. "We could all freeze to death without a fire."

"We can huddle together in the wagon," Doc said. "Our own body heat will keep us warm."

"Well, now that's settled, where do we go from here?" Johnny Blue asked no one in particular.

"I . . . I've got a secret," Georgia said.

"What kind of secret?" Johnny Blue asked.

"I can't tell," Georgia said.

"Then why the hell did you bring it up, woman?" Johnny Blue asked angrily.

"It's . . . it's about the Major," Georgia whispered.

"Georgia," I said, "I know that Pink and you are kin, an' blood's thicker than water, even though he planned on hanging you. But if'n you got something to tell us about the Major that might help save our skins, you'd better speak up."

"Georgia, my buttercup," Doc said, taking that large lady's hand, "our lives are presently in terrible danger. If we know where the Major's heading, we can take a different path and thus avoid him and his baleful band of bandits. The life you save, precious heart, could be Doc's."

"Doc, he's planning things. Terrible things."

"Is he gonna raid another town?" I asked.

"Worse than that, much worse."

"Tell us, my dear," Doc urged. "Do."

As you boys know, there just ain't no hurrying a lady, so we sat there in silence, studying Georgia's cruelly battered face while she composed herself and made up her mind whether to tell us.

"Well . . . I . . ." Georgia began.

"Yes, dear heart, go on," Doc said.

"He . . . the Major . . ."

Georgia buried her face in her hands.

"I can't! I can't betray my own daddy."

Johnny Blue stood and ground out his cigarette butt under his heel. "Girl, you're trying my patience. You got two choices as I see it. Either you speak your piece an' tell us what the hell's going on with Pink, or we just haul on out of here an' leave you."

"Doc," Georgia wailed. "Would you let him do that?"

"Dear heart," Doc said, which warn't a yes and warn't exactly a no either.

I guess sweet Georgia saw the writing on the wall, because she made up her mind pretty quick.

"I'll tell you the whole story," she said.

She then spun a tale so plumb amazing and frightening, I wouldn't have believed it if'n I hadn't heard it with my own two ears.

"Come the first thaw of spring, the Major and his Texans are taking the train to Missouri to meet Frank James," she said. "Do any of you boys know Frank James?"

"We all heard of him," I said.

"I knew him a couple of years back," Georgia said. "He's bad news, that one. He's mean and dour and he's got the coldest blue eyes this side of hell. He's a killer.

"And he's bitter that the South lost the war and just plumb bitter at life in general. That's why he sucks those damned peppermints all the time. The bitterness will sometimes well up in him and burn like acid in his throat."

"What's ol' Pink gonna do with Frank? Rob another bank?" I asked.

Georgia shook her head. "No, unless they rob one for funds along the way. Frank's job is to recruit men in Missouri and Tennessee and elsewhere, all of them former Confederates, including what's left of Bloody Bill's Raiders. I heard the Major mention John Jarrette and George Maddox, and there are many others. The Major robbed the Alpine bank to buy guns and horses for these men."

"So the Major's got men and guns and horses, but he ain't robbing any banks," I said. "What's he plan to do with those hombres?"

"He plans to march on Washington," Georgia said.

"He what?"

"I heard him say his men will ride into the city two by two and three by three, then, when the time is right, they'll storm the White House and take President Cleveland hostage," said Georgia.

"Ol' Pink," Johnny Blue said, "he's planning to do something the whole Reb army tried to pull off and couldn't. He's crazy."

"But is he, though?" Doc asked. "The bulk of our army is in the West, keeping guard on our benighted aboriginal brethren. If Pink can take Washington and other parts East, he can stop supplies reaching the army and it will just wither away after a spell."

"Doc, that's a long shot an' you know it."

"Maybe so, but we're dealing with a reckless and ruthless man, my young friend. You saw what he did in Alpine. Wilder schemes than this one have come to pass."

Georgia grabbed Doc's arm. "The Major says that as soon as the Rebel battle flag flies above the White House, Southerners will flock to his cause in droves, because they know our government is conspiring against them. I heard him tell Jericho Gentle, 'I will have fifty thousand determined men under arms in half a month.' He says by the time our army responds, his own Rebel army will be ready and waiting.

"The Major, he says that once all the federal government's conspiracies are revealed, the entire South will rise in rebellion, and this time it will win the new Civil War. The darkies will be back in the cotton fields before Christmas, the Major says."

Georgia fell back and waved a hand in front of her face.

"Oh, now I'm all hot an' bothered," she said. "Doc, let me have some more medicine."

"Right away, my precious."

Doc ran to get another bottle of his snake oil, and Johnny Blue hollered after him, "Make that two, Doc. I feel like a drink myself."

When Doc returned, he said, "Friends, this nefarious plot of Amos Pinkney's has shaken me to the core. But our future course is clear. We must proceed on our way with all possible dispatch and lay what we know before the legal authorities in Helena."

Johnny Blue took the snake oil bottle from his lips and laughed.

"Yeah, right Doc. Look at us. We got us a bawdy house madam who was run out of Texas and a broken down pug with a shaved head an' a face that looks like it was whupped with an ugly stick.

"And we got you, Doc, a shifty-eyed little cuss who looks like he was born to be hanged. No offense, you understand?"

"None taken, my truthful friend."

"Then there's me," Johnny Blue said. "A black man that folks around these parts are just barely willing to tolerate. And you got him"—he pointed the neck of his bottle at me—"a scrawny little half-starved feller who has to stand up twice to cast a shadow, and both of us so worn down and ragged, you can see the wrinkles in our socks through our boots."

"What's your point, Johnny Blue?" I asked.

"My point is, if you was a lawman, would you believe folks like us if we told you a crazy man was planning to meet up with Frank James, kidnap the President and start a new Civil War?"

I considered that carefully.

"No," I said finally. "I don't guess I would."

"The law might believe us when we tell them how Pink robbed the bank in Alpine," Doc said.

"The law in Helena don't give a hoot in hell about what happens in the Idaho Territory," Johnny Blue replied. "An' even if they did, they wouldn't send a posse out after Pink when it's startin' in to winter. And come spring, it will be too late."

"So we can't go to the law," I said. "But it just don't set right with me to do nothing."

"Oh we can do something, alright," Johnny Blue said. "We can go after Amos Pinkney and make sure he never gets to meet Frank James come spring."

"Look at us, boy," Doc waved a hand around our assembled company. "You said it yourself, there's never been a more played out, washed up bunch of losers as ever hitched their wagon to a falling star. What can we do against Pinkney and his hired gunmen?"

Johnny Blue looked at each of us then. Me, the Mauler, Georgia and Doc.

"We can fight," Johnny Blue said.

"With what?" Doc asked.

Johnny Blue said: "With our bare hands if we have to." Then he nodded at me. "My compadre there has a Colt, though the only thing he can shoot with it is his horse."

"And I have this," Georgia said, pulling her Derringer out of her bosom.

"See, Doc, we have two guns," Johnny Blue said. "It's a start."

Boys, I was feeling pretty lowdown just about then. I knew our hopeless, ragtag bunch couldn't go up against the most dangerous outlaw in the West and his professional gunslingers, to say nothing of Jacob Pike and his wolves in wolves' clothing. So I stood and said plain what was on my mind.

"Johnny Blue, we ain't got a prayer."

"Are you in or out?" asked that rangy roper.

I felt an icy knife twisting in my gut and I wanted to throw up. "You can count me out of this one," I said.

TWENTY-THREE

That Johnny Blue, boys, you know how everything he thinks or feels shows on his face. He can't keep nothing secret.

Well, now he looked like I'd hauled off and socked him. He just stood there for a few moments, looking at me. Then he pushed up the sleeve of his mackinaw and showed me the scar on his forearm that Nat Love had put there with his knife.

"Let me see it," he said.

I done as he told me and showed him my scar, a twin to his own.

"We got a blood bond between us, me and you," Johnny Blue said. "Are you telling me it's broken?"

I stood there, shuffling my feet in the mud and I couldn't say nothing. I couldn't even think straight.

"Tell me it's broken and I'll cut this thing right out of my arm," Johnny Blue said.

"Let me tell you something, cowboy. My daddy was one of them darkies that Pink says will be back in the cotton fields by Christmas. My daddy died in the fields because his back was broke from a lifetime of slavery. My little sister was sold down the river and the day it happened my momma turned her face to the wall and died. A summer cold, the overseer said. But everybody knew she died of grief.

"I ain't ever gonna let that happen again as long as there's breath in my body and strength in my back."

I looked up then, into those black eyes of his. I tried, but couldn't find anger there. Just a sadness maybe, and a sense of loss.

At last I found my voice. "Shit, Johnny Blue," I said, "we're brothers. You're headin' straight into hell, but I'll come with you."

I stuck my hand out and Johnny Blue took it.

"Ah," Doc said, "this is indeed a poignant scene, culled from the very pages of history. Thus did Romulus and Remus, those valorous sons of Mars, stand before the gates of Rome and pledge their brotherhood amid the lofty standards of the legions. Such a display of brotherly love has moved me to do mighty deeds, up to and including, I might add, the tracking of the nefarious Pinkney to his evil lair. In short—count me in too."

"Mauler," Johnny Blue asked, "how do you feel about this?"

"I'm with Doc," quoth that steadfast pugilist.

"Georgia?"

The large lady laid her hand on Doc's leg and looked up at him with doe eyes. "I'm seeing a side to Doc Fortune that I never knew was there before. Where my man goes, there go I."

"Then it's settled," Johnny Blue said.

"Do you have a plan?" I asked.

"I thought you was the one with all the plans," Johnny Blue replied.

"Well . . ." I said, "I reckon we lay low till ol' Pink

passes this way. Then we follow and pick off his men one by one."

"That's the ticket," Doc said. "Whittle them down a piece at a time."

Johnny Blue made a face. "It ain't much of a plan, even from you."

"It's all we got," I told him.

Later, we all agreed to pull the wagon and the Percherons farther into the trees and to keep watch on the freight trail till Pinkney and his boys passed, which they did just after dawn the next morning.

They kept the same formation as before as they rode past, except now the buckboard and a team of four had replaced the travois.

Ol' Pink rode in the lead, neither looking left nor right, as erect and proud as Lucifer. Cottontail rode beside him, wrapped in a beautiful coat of white mink, a mink hat of the same color on her pretty head. Pink's standard bearer had rolled up the flag and he now carried it encased in a canvas tube.

I saw Frank Canton riding Johnny Blue's pony with Jericho Gentle next to him, the rest of the heavily armed Texas gunfighters in columns of twos behind them. Even from where I hid in the brush, I saw that ol' Frank's face was black with fury and about half of his mustache was missing.

Boys, I guess Frank Canton wanted a piece of me mighty bad just about then.

And he'd get his chance real soon.

We remained hidden in the brush after that arrogant caravan passed, for fear that it might return. But after the best part of an hour we five hearts of oak stepped into the clear and discussed our next move.

The first thing we did was send the Percherons back on the road to Alpine. We couldn't feed them, since each et as much as three cow ponies. But they was tough, smart animals and I reckoned they'd find their way home alright.

Doc then took inventory of his remaining stock of snake oil, which he kept in a secret compartment hidden under the floorboards of the wagon. He and the Mauler counted nigh on two hunnerd bottles, and Doc declared it enough.

"Enough for what?" I asked.

"We need supplies, boy, unless you want us all to starve to death," he said. "There's a trading post on the other side of Mullin's Pass, owned by a tall German feller named Oskar Gruber. I figure to trade him my elixir for some bacon, beans and coffee. It's a sight better than the rotgut he sells as whiskey."

"What's in that stuff of your's anyhow, Doc?" I asked.

"Oh, it's mostly redeye from my own still. Then there's camphor for the chest, alfalfa and valeriana for sleep, some sugar for taste and a little coal oil for kick."

"Doc, don't ever give that witch's piss to me if I'm took sick sudden," I said.

Our journey back to Montana was uneventful, though it snowed just about every day and the nights were freezing cold. We all huddled in Doc's wagon to keep each other warm and catch what sleep we could, and in the day we caught what chuck we could along the trail. I won't tell you what it was, because we warn't too fussy, but if it walked, crawled or flew, we et it.

On the second week of our travel, we left the freight road that led into Helena and took the trail that forked to the south toward Butte.

Georgia said the trail cut close to Pink's cabin, which was in a sheltered valley in the Rockies southeast of Butte, and that she'd been there once or twice with Cottontail.

Now the weather was really closing in. The sky was the color of a pewter plate, so low it touched the peaks of the mountains. The snow fell ceaselessly and when any of us spoke, which was seldom, our breath clouded in the air. I was cold and miserable and hungry and I guess everyone else felt the same. Once I saw a starving wolf trot parallel to the wagon for a ways. He was interested but wary, and kept out of sight most of the time. But after a while he turned tail and left.

That ol' lobo probably figgered: "There ain't nothing but slim pickin's in that outfit."

Early one afternoon Doc broke the habitual silence that we'd all fallen into.

"By my reckoning, Gruber's post is right ahead," he said. "It sets beside a creek among some birch trees, a pretty enough place in the summer."

We rolled along in silence for a spell, then Doc pulled up the team.

"There's the post over yonder," he said. "And it seems we got company, and if I'm not mistaken, they're riding you boys' horses."

TWENTY-FOUR

Three cow ponies was tied up to a hitching post sheltered by a swaybacked awning that jutted out from the roof of the cabin. Sure enough, one was Johnny Blue's buckskin, one of the others was my paint.

Johnny Blue was at my shoulder. "We got big trouble," he said. "You know who was riding my buckskin."

"Yeah," I said. "Frank Canton."

"Well, this is a pretty kettle o' fish," Doc said. "Do you want I should turn around and we can hide out until they leave?"

Boys, I thought about that hard. But it didn't set right with me to turn tail and run. We'd come this far to stop ol' Pink, and now seemed as good a time as any to start.

"You want to hide, or go get our ponies back?" I asked Johnny Blue.

"I gave you the answer to that back in Idaho," he replied.

Georgia gave Johnny Blue her Derringer and a kiss on the cheek, and I loaded up Canton's Colt, filling all six chambers.

"Now you be careful with that thing," Johnny Blue said. "Don't pull the hammer back unless you have to, and if you do, point it well away from me. And the horses."

"Good luck," Doc said, as we dropped from the wagon into the snow and made our way toward the trading post.

The snow crunched under my boots, freezing my toes, and the wind pushed icy, teasing fingers under my mackinaw like a cold-hearted dance hall girl on a Saturday night. The birch trees stood like watchful sentinels, silent and uncaring, as we walked between them.

The door to the post was closed against the weather, and Johnny Blue whispered: "Do we kick that door in and charge inside?"

"Nah," I said. "We walk in with our guns out, cool as you please."

"Let's do it!" Johnny Blue said.

He strode to the door, pushed it open and walked inside. I came in right after him, then moved a little to his left.

The room was long and narrow with a low ceiling, its shelves stacked with cooking ware, blankets, pants and boxes of shoes.

Three men stood at the counter drinking. One was Frank Canton, the other two I didn't know. All were unshaven and mud spattered from travel.

"Afternoon, Frank," I said.

Frank spun around to face me and I saw the shock of recognition in his eyes. "You!" he said.

"Yup." I smiled at him, my gun on him square. "Me."

Canton wore a long black coat with a fur collar that made his own gun unhandy. I could see from the wild look in his eye that he knew it, and he knew that I knew it.

The other two were Texans, each of them wearing hip-length sheepskin coats. One was a teenager who had a bold, reckless look, the other an older, maybe wiser man with a long black beard streaked with gray.

"Afternoon, boys," I said sociably to the other two. "Me and him, we ain't hunting trouble, but there seems to have been a mixup about horses here."

Canton and the other two fanned back from the counter.

"Go to hell, you damned waddie!" Canton sneered. "You got the drop on me, but if you ever give me an even break I'll show you some work."

"Jest keep your hands away from those guns, gents," Johnny Blue said gently.

After he said that, I recollect wishing he'd had something more convincing in his hands than that itsy-bitsy Derringer.

The man behind the counter, who was the tallest man I'd ever seen in my life, and he must have gone seven feet and more, said, "Cowboy, I don't want no trouble here. This is a respectable place."

"No trouble, Mister Gruber," I said. "We ain't on the prod. We just want to take back what's our'n."

I could see in the teenager Texan's eyes that he was itching to draw real bad.

"I know what you're thinking," I told him. "And I wouldn't."

The kid relaxed some, but I knew I'd have to watch my back with him. He was a wild one.

The older man was wary. He didn't seem scared, but he didn't seem inclined to draw, either.

"I should have killed you back in Alpine," Canton seethed. He fingered his mutilated mustache.

I nodded. "You had your chance, Frank."

Johnny Blue stepped up beside me. "How you gonna play this?" he asked. There was an edge to his voice that I took as tolerable anxiety.

"Here's how," I said. I motioned to Canton. "Frank, my compadre here is gonna go outside and cut out our ponies. I'm gonna follow him in a spell, an' after that I'll shoot the first man who steps through the door after me. Do you savvy?"

"You savvy this," Frank said. "Someday I'm gonna blow your head clean off your scrawny little shoulders. God curse me if I don't."

Boys, things might have gone as I planned. Me and Johnny Blue might have gotten to our ponies and just rode on out of there.

But you know me, I got this mischievous streak, a little devil that sits on my shoulder and tells me to say and do things. I tried hard to resist him that day, but he was way too strong for me. I had to say it.

"Enjoy your pie, Frank?"

And then all hell broke loose.

Canton roared an obscenity and he and the teenager dove for their guns.

I jerked back the hammer of my Colt—and it went off by itself again. The young Texan fell with a bullet in his leg.

I thumbed the hammer a second time and the hammer fell back immediately onto the next round. The gun roared, twisting violently in my hand as it fired—and I shot ol' Frank in the right ear.

The way I heard it later from Johnny Blue, Canton's draw was real fast, but his gun got caught up in that long coat of his. He got all tangled up and couldn't bring it level.

"Then, when you shot the top of his ear off, I had the Derringer on him and he kinda lost interest all of a sudden," Johnny Blue said.

My ears were ringing and the room was full of greasy gray smoke. The older Texan had backed off against the wall with his hands up. The kid was on the floor, chewing the boards and squealing like a baby pig caught under a gate. He didn't look so tough now.

Canton's hand was clapped to his bleeding ear and he was cussing a blue streak.

Boys, there were a lot of pictures made of Frank Canton in later years, after he became a famous lawman an' all. But in every one of them he wears his hat pulled way down over his right ear.

Oskar Gruber ran at me from behind his counter.

For a minute I thought he was going to blame me for what had happened, but he took my hand and pumped it up and down, grinning like a possum and nodding his head.

"Boy, I seen the best," he said. "I was in Sulphur Springs the day Pony Deal killed Johnny-Behind-the-Deuce, and right here in this room I seen Tube Wilson get shot by Sheriff Toad George. But I never in my life seen revolver fighting like I seen today. I gotta tell you, you're the fastest man with the Colt's gun I've ever had the honor of meetin'."

"It wern't nothing," I said modestly, which drew me a look from Johnny Blue.

"Boy, I'm gonna break the habit of a lifetime an' buy you a drink," Gruber said.

Follering Gruber to the bar, I stepped over the young Texan, and kept my eyes on Canton. He'd dropped his gun when I shot him, and he stood there, his hand clapped to his wounded ear, his eyes full of murder.

"Get their guns, Johnny Blue," I said as I lifted Gruber's green whiskey to my lips and gratefully drained the glass.

"Next one'll cost you twenty-five cents," Gruber said.

The door swung open and Georgia rushed inside, Doc at her heels. She took stock of the situation immediately and lowered her enormous bulk to the floor beside the wounded youngster.

She was a warm and gentle lady, that Georgia Morgan, truly a whore with a heart of gold, an' that's about as rare as a tear at a Boot Hill buryin'.

"He done shot my leg off," the kid whined, tears running down his cheeks.

"Doc," Georgia ordered, "take a look at this kid's leg."

TWENTY-FIVE

Doc bent over the young Texan's leg and cut a rip in his pants and drawers and started in to examine it.

Ol' Frank, he was standin' in a corner, still favoring that ear of his, and grinding and gnashing his teeth something horrible. He kept growling over and over again: "Kill . . . gonna kill . . . scrawny neck . . . kill good . . ."

But there was no fight left in him for that day, so I turned to the older Texan.

"You," I said.

"Yessir," the old gunfighter replied.

I pointed to the Winchester rifles and the Henry that was ranged along the bar. "Is one of them yours?"

"Yessir," he said.

"Then take it and ride on out of here, less'n your thinking of dealin' yourself a hand in this here fight."

"Not me, sir," the Texan said. "I'm through buckin' the tiger this trip."

"Where's Pinkney?" I asked him.

"He's gone on ahead to his cabin. Us three, we figgered on stopping here for a drink on the way."

"Bad mistake," I said.

Boys, I was talking like one of them desperados in the dime novels, and I was enjoying the hell out of it.

"Get on your pony an' ride," I said. "And, if'n I was you, I wouldn't stop till I reached the Brazos."

That ol' boy was looking at my hawgleg like I was holdin' a rattlesnake with its buzzer goin'.

Well, that Texan skedaddled out the door like a scalded cat, and I never saw him again.

"This lad will live," Doc said from the floor. "Your bullet went clean through his leg an' missed the bone. He ain't gonna be forking a bronc for a spell, though."

Doc and Georgia helped the boy to his feet, then Georgia went over to Canton to take a look at his ear, but he cursed her and waved her away.

"Gather up all them guns, then get these two outside," I said.

"Sure thing, general," Johnny Blue said.

We prodded Canton and the kid outside. It was snowing steadily and the range was white as far as the eye could see.

"Frank," I said, "Helena is thataway. I reckon you can make it afore the winter sets in too bad."

"I kin barely walk," the kid wailed. "You ain't leavin' us afoot, are you?"

"That's what you done to us, kid," I said.

"This is lowdown," the kid said. "You can't treat us like this."

"Tell that to the folks in Alpine," Johnny Blue said.

Frank Canton caught the kid by the arm.

"You shut your trap," he growled. "You can walk— the cold will numb that leg wound."

He turned to me.

"Cowboy," he said, "our path is gonna cross again. I don't know where and I don't know when, but it will. I may be wearing a badge. I may not. I may be drinking in a saloon. I may be riding on the trail. I may be eating supper. I may be layin' a-bed with a woman. Hell, I might even be singing in the church choir. But I'm gonna see you. And when I do, I ain't gonna say 'Hi' and I ain't even gonna call your name. I'm just gonna come at you a-shootin' right from the start. Depend on it."

Boys, I got to admit, that speech made me a mite uneasy, because Frank Canton was a mean ornery no-account man. But I just grinned, braving it out.

"Frank, Frank, Frank," I said, "pretty soon you'll forget all about this unpleasantness. Years from now, me an' you, we'll set down an' drink coffee and laugh about this. Hell, we might even share a piece of pie."

Ol' Frank's face was grim and the murder was back in his eyes. "I'll see you in hell first," he said.

He took the kid's arm and put it around his shoulder, then they began to walk away.

Me, I shucked the shells out of Frank's Colt and went after him.

"Frank, this is your'n," I said. "A man should have the gun that somebody done shot him with."

Frank took the Colt and stuck it into his coat pocket. "I'll save this for you," he said.

Doc was at my shoulder and together we watched the Texans struggle through the snow, which was about as high as their boot tops.

"You made a bad enemy there, son," Doc said. "An enemy that wears a badge."

"Doc," I said, "he's got no more right to that deputy

marshal's badge than you have, an' if he had any right to it, he lost it in Alpine." I put my arm around Doc's shoulder. "As for enemies, I got plenty of those already, an' mighty few friends."

Doc later traded half of his remaining stock of snake oil to Gruber for flour, coffee, dried beef and beans. He got a tiny bottle of parfum for Georgia, which she dabbed behind her ears and declared it was "direct from Paree, sure enough." But I suspect the closest that bottle got to France was Butte.

As for me and Johnny Blue, we was once again well mounted and armed. I had a Winchester .40–.40, and Johnny Blue had his Henry back. I'd taken Frank Canton's gunbelt, and his replacement Colt was shorter in the barrel and, to Johnny Blue's considerable relief, it had a regular trigger. Johnny Blue wore the kid's belt, which had a Smith and Wesson Schofield .45 in its scabbard. Some say it's a better gun than the Colt, but I've never much held to that belief.

We now had food, horses and arms, and I felt better than I had in many a long month.

But, as we rode out of Gruber's post that afternoon, little did I know that in a few short days, we'd again be as poor and destitute as ever.

TWENTY-SIX

As we once again picked up the trail to the south, the snow held off for the next two days, though the wind continued to blow cold off the mountains. But by the morning of the third day the snow started again, and I figured the mercury must be nudging the freezing mark.

Johnny Blue was huddled in his mackinaw, a woolen scarf he'd borrowed from Doc pulled over his hat and around his ears, tied in an untidy knot under his chin.

Then he said something that must have been sticking in his craw since Gruber's post. I guess he figgered now was the time to spit it out.

"You was lucky back there," he said.

"How come?"

"Because the kid was too slow and Frank's gun got caught up in his coat. If Frank had cleared leather clean, you were dead. He's the fastest I ever saw."

"Maybe so, but Frank doesn't know I was lucky."

We rode on in silence for the best part of an hour, Doc close behind with the wagon. Johnny Blue rode with his head down, and I figgered he was asleep in the saddle.

Then it happened.

They came out of the trees to the left of the trail like ghosts, maybe twenty of them, well armed and mounted on tough little spotted ponies.

"Injuns!" I yelled.

"This is it," Johnny Blue said. "The end of the trail. We're dead."

Doc left the wagon and walked up to my pony.

"Are they hostile?" he asked.

"What's it look like to you?" I said.

Doc studied the Indians, who were sitting silently on their ponies, watching us.

"They ain't painted for war, but they don't look none too friendly, either," he said.

"Downright surly," I told him. "But you can never tell with an Injun."

For a long time we all just sat there, watching each other. Nobody—white, black or red—said a word.

My hand inched down to my holstered Colt, more for the comfort it brought me than anything else. But one of the braves saw me. He yelled a warning and threw his rifle to his shoulder and I took my hand away from my gun like it was red hot.

Johnny Blue turned in his saddle and whispered: "Yup, that did it, we're scalped and dead. All of us."

One of the Indians, wrapped in a gray army blanket, kneed his horse close to mine. It's hard to guess with Indians sometimes, but I figgered this brave was somewhere in his early fifties and looked to be a chief of some kind. Like the rest of his men, he was ragged and half-starved, kinda like me and Johnny Blue, in fact.

The Chief carried a Winchester and he just sat his horse, saying nothing, staring at me.

Boys, I got nothing against Indians.

Like us cowboys, they was once wild and free and could go anywhere and do anything they wanted. Then the wire came an' penned us up, an' the army came an' penned up the Indians. The poor cowboy was told he wasn't free anymore and to stay inside the wire an' let the farmers raise hogs on what was once open range.

But what they done to the Indians was much worse.

Men who sat behind a desk for a living herded the braves onto reservations, then took hands that had never held nothing but the lance and the bow, an' tried to break their fingers around a plow handle.

No wonder many of the braves decided that dying in battle was a better way to go than face a living death as a farmer.

I recollect thinking that maybe the Indian who was looking at me felt that way.

"Is he lookin' at your hair?" Johnny Blue whispered out of the corner of his mouth.

"I dunno," I replied.

The Chief pointed at me and drew his hand across his throat in a slashing motion. He then turned to the rest of his braves and said something and they laughed and whooped and pumped their rifles in the air.

Johnny Blue, forever the peacemaker, joined in the laughter, even though he didn't know a word the Chief had said.

"I think it's gonna be alright," I told him. "They're

Blackfeet an' I speak the lingo. An' if they're laughin' they ain't scalpin'."

I raised my right hand, palm out, and said, "Hail great chief of the Blackfeet tribe. Me come in peace. Smoke úm peace pipe."

"I thought you could speak the lingo?" Johnny Blue said. His face looked real alarmed, like he'd just tipped over the outhouse by mistake.

"This is the lingo," I said. "Charlie Russell taught it to me."

"Oh, Jesus," Johnny Blue said. "We're all dead."

Meantime the Chief listened to all this, then he kneed his horse alongside mine. He looked me right in the eye.

"Are you trying to be funny?" he asked.

Boys, I was surprised as a pup that's just caught his first porcupine.

"You speak American!" I said.

The Chief spat over the side of his horse. "White man, if you'd been through what we've been through for the past twenty years, you'd have learned to speak American pretty damn quick yourself."

"Well, you got nothing to fear from us, Chief," I said. "We're only poor cowboys an' we come in peace."

"Yeah," the Chief said, "that's why you were going for your gun. I heard about you. You're that slick revolver fighter that killed two men back at Gruber's trading post."

"Honest, I was just trying to move my gun," I said. "It was chafing on me something sore." Then it dawned on me what the Chief had just said. "How did you hear about what happened at Gruber's store?" I asked.

"In this territory, word gets around fast," the Chief said.

"You heard the story all wrong, Chief," I said. "I'll tell you how it really happened. Me and him, we—"

But the Chief ignored me and turned to Johnny Blue.

"You, buffalo man, what are you to this white man?"

"I dunno," Johnny Blue said loyally.

"Every white man I've ever known was a snake and not to be trusted," the Chief said.

"That," said Johnny Blue, "has also been my experience, pretty much."

The Chief yelled something to his braves and a couple of them hustled Georgia and the Mauler out of the wagon.

"Johnny Blue," I whispered, "remind me to thank you, first chance I get."

Johnny Blue shrugged. "It seems he's all-fired mad at you white men, not us poor darkies."

"That there," the Chief said, looking appreciatively at Georgia, "is a fine-looking woman."

Georgia put the tip of her forefinger under her chin and did one of them right pretty little curtsey things womenfolk do.

The Chief turned to Johnny Blue.

"Is she yours?"

"Nah," Johnny Blue said. He jerked a thumb at Doc. "His."

The Chief shook his head in amazement.

"Nah, it can't be. What's he got that I can't see from here?"

"Beats me," Johnny Blue said.

"If you don't mind, I can speak for myself," Doc said. He looked up at the Chief.

"Listen, my florid and feathered friend, it's not the size of a man's weapon that counts, it's how often he hits the target. And I hit the target every time I shoot."

I guess the Chief liked this speech, because he translated this for the other braves and then pumped his rifle in the air, letting loose with a war whoop. The rest of the Indians followed suit.

"That wasn't bad, for a white man," the Chief said.

"They call me Doc," said Doc by way of introductions.

"I could tell you my name, but it would mean nothing to you," the Chief said.

Next the Mauler came under close scrutiny on account of his size, and the Chief said he'd make a good slave because he could do the work of ten women without tiring.

The Mauler flexed his muscles and said, "Hell, Chief, make that twenty women."

But then, to my grief, the discussion got back around to me.

"You, the one with desire to shoot down Indians, what did you call us back then when you first saw us?" the Chief asked.

"I dunno," I said. Then I grabbed at a moment of inspiration and added hopefully, "Friends."

"We're not your friends," the Chief said. He studied me closely again. "Think, what did you call us?"

I thought for a spell, then it dawned on me. "Blackfeet," I said.

The Chief nodded. "Right. You said we were Blackfeet." He turned to his braves. "Look at those ponies, what's on them?"

"Injuns?" I said.

The Chief took the muzzle of his Winchester and none too gently pushed my cheek around so I was looking at the ponies again. "On the rumps of the ponies," he said.

"Spots," I replied, and I kinda figgered my life was on the line with that answer.

The Chief nodded. "You have spoken truly. All of our ponies have spots."

He took a bag from the tall, rawhide-covered horn of his wooden saddle and shoved it into my hands. "Look at that. It's a cornhusk bag. To the Sioux and the Cheyenne, that bag is worth a war horse in trade. Look how fine a weave it is. The Blackfoot woman has not yet been born who can make a bag like that."

"You're right, Chief," I said. "It's real good. Bueno."

"Then I will ask you again," the Chief said, grabbing the bag from my hands. "What manner of people are we?"

I shifted uncomfortably in my saddle and looked to Johnny Blue for inspiration, but he was staring straight ahead, and he wouldn't turn.

"Chief," I said, "you mean you don't know?"

I heard Johnny Blue groan.

The Chief shot me an exasperated look. "We're Nez Perce, among the last of our nation, though we once were as many as the stars in the night sky."

"Of course," I said. "I knew that all the time. A bit off your range, Chief, ain't you?"

"No, white man," the Chief said. "It's you who are way off yours."

The Chief kneed his pony beside Johnny Blue. "We have no quarrel with you, buffalo man," he said. "You and the fat woman are welcome to join us. We don't have much left to us anymore, but what little we do have, you are welcome to share."

Johnny Blue shook his head. "Thank you kindly," he said. "But these people are my friends. I can't leave them."

"Does that go for the woman, too?" the Chief asked.

Georgia spoke up. "I stay with my man."

"Suit yourself," the Chief told her. "That decision is yours to make."

Then suddenly he was all business.

"You two," he snapped, "climb off your ponies."

Me and Johnny Blue did as he said, and a couple of braves led our horses away. Then the Indians stripped us of our gunbelts.

A couple more climbed into Doc's wagon, and the wagon took the same route as our departing ponies.

Before he left, the Chief reined up his pony in front of me. "Gunfighter—I believe that is what the white man calls such as you—today you are lucky," he said. "You're lucky to be alive because right at this moment I'm inclined to shoot you like you were going to shoot us."

I opened my mouth to protest, but the Chief cut me off.

"You have been saved by the two buffalo people,

because they say they are your friends, and they are a tribe which has also suffered much at the hands of the white man. But the next time we meet, your luck might run out. That's something you should think about by and by. And remember."

Then, with a wild whoop, the Chief turned his horse and followed the others.

After the Indians were gone, Doc said to me. "Son, you got a real knack for making some powerful enemies. And if that wasn't bad enough, it seems the whole territory is determined to keep you afoot."

"Seems like," I said mildly.

"Strange about them Nez Perce, though," Doc said. "I seem to recollect that since ol' Joseph was took at Snake Creek back in '77, they've been at peace with the white man."

"Army would reckon they didn't break any treaties here today, Doc," I said. "Just that they was maybe a mite careless about whose hoss they saddled."

Johnny Blue kicked at the snow. "Damn!"

Then he turned to me.

"You spoke the lingo, alright! You didn't even know what kind of redskins they was!"

"How was I to know they was Nez Perce?" I asked. "I'd never met a Nez Perce Injun before. Charlie Russell, he taught me about the Blackfeet, and them's the only Injuns I know."

"That much was obvious, my young friend," Doc said. "That chief was real sore about being took for a Blackfoot. I guess the Nez Perce and the Blackfeet don't care for each other too much. You were lucky he didn't lift your scalp."

Georgia was sobbing into the Mauler's shoulder.

"We're miles from anywhere, without a wagon or a scrap of food," she wailed. "We can die out here."

"That, my precious, is closer to the truth than you know," Doc said, which made Georgia wail all the more.

TWENTY-SEVEN

"I should have gone with the Indians," Johnny Blue said. "I knowed I was making a big mistake."

The trail at this point cut through a wide valley, hemmed in by tall, snow-covered peaks. The timber grew thick on the foothills, except in the draws where the snow was already as tall as a man, then thinned out as the trees climbed to the mountains. This was cold, inhospitable country and if a man died here, his body wouldn't be discovered till spring.

I heard a long, lonely howl in the distant trees.

I shivered, the cold and damp seeping into my cracked and worn boots.

Boys, I suddenly felt lonely and forelorn and discouraged and I was fast running out of heart.

Johnny Blue stepped up beside me.

"What we gonna do?" he asked.

I shook my head at him. "I dunno," I said. "Try an' make it back to Gruber's, I guess."

"We're four, five days from Gruber's by foot," Johnny Blue said. "That is if the wind don't kick up even more and we find ourselves in a blizzard." He jerked a thumb over his shoulder. "Look behind you. Look at those people."

I did as he said. The Mauler stood with his arms wrapped around himself, shivering. Doc, tiny and wizened, had his arm around Georgia's thick waist and both of them were looking at me like I was Moses about to lead them to the promised land.

"The Mauler will make it," Johnny Blue said, "that is if the blizzard don't blow and it don't freeze too hard at night. Doc won't. And neither will Georgia. Me and you, we've been through this before, and maybe we can live through it again."

"What are you saying?" I asked.

"I'm saying, if we want to get back to Gruber's store, we gotta leave Doc and Georgia behind. They'll slow us up too much if we take 'em along."

I looked at Doc and Georgia again, treacherous thoughts turning in my head that I really didn't want to give a mind to.

The fat lady's dress was wet from snow and her bonnet sat askew on her head. She shivered even worse than the Mauler and she hugged close to Doc for his meager warmth. Despite her great size, she looked like a little frightened girl lost in the woods.

"Well?" Johnny Blue asked.

There was no other way. I could see that. I had to tell them the plain truth and get it over with.

"Doc," I said, "an' Georgia. Circumstances here has changed for the worst, an' me and Johnny Blue here got to thinking an' . . ."

Georgia's eyes were still swollen bad, and she was crying, which only made them worse. Doc, his face set and grim, was looking right at me, like he was daring me to say what was on my mind.

But they both knew what was coming. They knew I

was getting ready to condemn them to death, and that I'd set myself up as their judge, jury and executioner.

I couldn't look them in the eye. I turned away and started in again. "Like I say, me an' him, we got to thinking an' . . . an' . . ."

There was no way I could do this. We'd come this far together and we'd live or die together. Me, I didn't have any other option, and now I knew it.

". . . an' we decided we all got to keep movin' or we'll freeze to death, on account of how it seems we've landed in hell with the furnace off."

Doc's face cleared and I saw a glimmer of hope in his eyes.

"Then speak up, where are we bound, dear boy? Gruber's post?"

"No, Doc," I said. "With night comin' on an' the mercury droppin', we'd never make it."

"Then what's your plan?"

"We're goin' after them Injuns and stealin' our stuff back," I said. "We need our ponies an' food an' we need the wagon for shelter."

"You're crazy!" Johnny Blue said. "There's at least twenty of them."

"Right," I said, "an' their strength is their weakness. They figger they got nothing to fear from us, so I reckon they'll make camp for the night real soon. When they're asleep, we just walk right in there an' take back our horses an' guns."

"It won't work," Johnny Blue said. "They'll have guards posted."

"We'll take care of the guards."

"It still ain't gonna work."

"It's the only plan I got, Johnny Blue," I said. "Take it or leave it."

Johnny Blue chewed on that for a while.

"Ah, the hell with it," he said finally. "Let's do it. We're all gonna die out here anyway."

Later I took Johnny Blue aside. "Tell me something," I whispered. "Would you really have left Doc and Georgia behind?"

"Would you?" Johnny Blue asked. There was a faint smile tugging at the corners of his lips under his mustache.

"You knew all the time, didn't you?" I said. "Johnny Blue Dupree, you are a one."

I gathered Doc, Georgia and the Mauler together and told them my plan. They was none too eager, but they knew we'd little choice.

"Them Injuns left a trail a blind man could foller," I said. "If'n it don't snow, we can track 'em real easy."

Ten minutes later, it began to snow.

TWENTY-EIGHT

We walked with our heads bent against the driving white, following the route the Indians had taken through the trees. It was heavy going, since the snow was now two feet deep, and deeper in some of the gullies that ran down the hillside.

To me, it seemed like I'd been born in snow, wet and cold and endless.

Georgia had the worst time of it by far, burdened as she was by her weight and her long dress and corsets, but she kept plodding forward, uncomplaining, and I found myself gaining new respect for that lady.

As darkness fell, the mercury plunged.

Georgia was panting now, her breath coming in short, wheezy gasps. The Mauler was holding up well, as I had expected, but Doc's face was ashen gray and he kept clutching at his skinny chest as the bitter cold air froze up his tubes.

Johnny Blue looked behind him at Doc and Georgia struggling.

"We're in big trouble," he said. "They ain't gonna make it. They can't keep going like this."

An outcropping of rock, about twice as tall as a man and shaped like the horn of a saddle, rose from the hillside and there was room for all of us to huddle behind it.

The rock was scant protection, but it cut the force of the wind and swirled the heavy snowflakes around and away from us.

Georgia began to breathe a little easier and even in the gloom I could see some color return to Doc's white cheeks.

"I declare," Georgia said, "it's cold enough to freeze ducks to a pond."

"It's gonna get colder," I said, thinking it would be foolish to spare her the bad news.

"Maybe we could make a fire," Doc said. "We're sheltered here."

"Maybe we could, Doc," I said, "if we could find our way around in the dark to pick up wood that wasn't wet."

Doc nodded. "Yes, I see, that was a foolish suggestion."

I put my hand on his shoulder. "Doc, any suggestion is welcome, situation we're in."

"Boy," Doc said, "I'm not a stupid man. I know what's happening here. Georgia and I, we're only slowing you up. I think you and Bartholomew and Johnny Blue should go on without us."

I shook my head at him. "We're in this together, Doc. We'll come through it together."

Doc opened his mouth to protest, but a shout from Johnny Blue stopped him.

"What is it?" I asked him.

"Over there, to the left, for a minute I thought I saw a light. But I can't see it anymore. I guess I was just seeing things."

I looked and couldn't make out anything.

"Maybe you saw a wolf," I said. "Their eyes can shine in the dark sometimes."

Johnny Blue shook his head. "It looked more like a fire. Look, there it is again!"

I looked where Johnny Blue's finger was pointing, and sure enough I saw a pinprick of flickering light through the trees.

"It's a fire, alright," I said. "A campfire."

"Then it's got to be them Indians," Johnny Blue said.

We left Doc and Georgia in the shelter of the rock, then me, the Mauler and Johnny Blue set out across the snow to find the source of that light.

As it turned out, it was a lot closer than it looked, and we reached the Indian encampment in just a few minutes.

The Nez Perce had camped by a rocky bluff that looked to have been made by a landslip a long time ago. The bluff wasn't high, about as tall as a man on a horse, but it was crowned with a stand of scrub pine and gave protection from the worst of the wind and snow. The Indian ponies and Doc's wagon lay at its base.

The three of us lay on our bellies and studied the camp.

There were Indians sprawled everywhere around the two small fires they'd built. As we watched, one brave, chanting and prancing around with a bottle in his hand, staggered straight toward us until he too fell on his face and lay still.

After that, nothing moved.

"Some party," Johnny Blue said.

"How the hell—" I began.

"They must have found Doc's snake oil in the wagon," the Mauler said.

"Are they alive?" I asked.

The Mauler nodded. "Oh sure. But that stuff of Doc's, it first gets you drunk, then it puts you to sleep."

"Tell me about it," Johnny Blue said, rolling his eyes.

"Well," I said, "let's walk right in there an' take back what's our'n."

We rose and walked into the Indian camp. I picked up a Springfield carbine that was lying handy, but I'd no need of it. Them Nez Perces were as dead drunk as hoedown fiddlers.

Me and Johnny Blue and the Mauler, we searched the camp almost at our leisure and soon recovered our guns and another couple of Winchesters besides.

The Mauler hitched the team to the wagon and Johnny Blue saddled our ponies.

"The snake oil's mostly gone, but all the supplies are still in the wagon," the Mauler said. "Them Injuns was more interested in drinking than eating."

Johnny Blue handed me the reins of my pony.

"Let's get out of here and make tracks," he said. "We want to put distance between us and these Indians before they wake up."

"Wait a spell," I said.

I poked through the sleeping Indians until I found the Chief and then I called the Mauler over.

"Throw the Chief here in the back of the wagon, an' use the rope off'n my saddle to hogtie him good."

"Why are you doing that?" Johnny Blue asked.

"He's our insurance policy," I said. "Just in case the rest of them come after us."

Johnny Blue considered that closely for a spell.

"Makes sense," he said finally.

"Damn right it does," I said.

But I had one more thing to do.

Me and Johnny Blue set the Indian ponies loose, and them broncs tossed their heads and kicked up their heels and took off running in every which direction.

Come daylight, them Indians was gonna wake with an almighty hangover. Then they'd have to run around all morning trying to chase down and catch their ponies.

We cut through the trees and back onto the trail, figuring the going would be easier. The snow had stopped again, but now a bitter frost was settling in for the night and I knew it would be with us till the sun came up. If it came up at all.

Johnny Blue and his horse were steaming from the mouth and nostrils like a yard engine as we rode back toward the rock and Doc and Georgia, and I guess my paint and me were doing the same.

Johnny Blue rode on ahead and brought Doc and Georgia down onto the trail. They were both exhausted and Doc was blue from cold. They lost no time bundling into the back of the wagon.

When Georgia saw the Chief, she yelled: "Mother of God, what's he doing here?" But I told her he was our insurance policy and she calmed down right quick, seeing the sense to it.

Now we was mounted again, I asked her the question I'd been meaning to ask just before the Indians hit. "How far to ol' Pink's cabin?"

Georgia considered that for a spell. "I'd say two days, no more than that. Of course, I always traveled this way in summer."

I didn't know it then, but she was way off in her estimate, as we was all too soon to learn to our cost.

My hat was pulled down over my ears to meet the collar of my mackinaw and my face was stiff with cold. I beat my frozen fingers against my thighs and tried to get my tired brain to work.

We would meet up with Pink and his hired guns in just forty-eight hours, and I needed a plan. Unfortunately nothing came to mind right then, and I felt more than a mite uneasy as I turned my horse and led the wagon along the trail to the south.

One thing was certain. I had to come up with a plan real soon. And it had to be a good one. Our lives depended on it.

The snow made for slow going on the trail, and even though the wheels on Doc's wagon were small and wide, made for the mud of cow towns, they kept plunging into foot-deep creeks and gullies cut across the trail by the summer rains. It seemed like me and Johnny Blue had to dismount a hundred times to help the Mauler push the wagon back onto solid ground. We were numb with cold and bone tired, but we knew with the Indians on our back trail and Pink on up ahead this was no time to stop and rest.

When we wasn't pushing, which wasn't often, me and Johnny Blue rode in silence, each wrapped in our own thoughts and misery, and each of us dreading what the next few days would bring.

It was shading into daylight when Johnny Blue rode ahead to find a spot to camp. We were all plumb tuckered out and I for one needed time to rest and think.

I slowed my pony and let the wagon catch up. Inside, the Chief was coming to and he was groaning softly.

"How is he?" I asked Doc.

"He's got a hangover that could kill an elephant. Apart from that, he'll live."

"We'll camp soon," I said.

Doc nodded. "I could sure use some hot coffee."

Johnny Blue rode up about an hour later and said he'd found a clearing in the timber where the ground was level and there was a sheltered spot near a frozen creek bed.

"Near as I can figger, the snow in there's only about a foot on the level," he said. "We can clear it enough to make camp."

We rode into the clearing an hour later and found it just as Johnny Blue had described. The sheltered area was a small, horseshoe-shaped swath cut in the trees to the north of the clearing, its entrance only about as long as Doc's wagon and then some.

It was a lonely, out-of-the-way place, an ideal spot for a camp, and not bad for defense.

To the south of the cut ran the creek bed, and beyond that the clearing opened out into a wide, flat expanse of virgin snow. I reckoned if a rider came at us across that white flatland, we could have him in our rifle sights when he was still a mile away or more.

Boys, the way I had it figgered, we were real close to Pink's cabin, so we would stay all of that day and night in the cut, then head out the next morning. I reckoned if we rode all the next day and most of the night, we could launch one of them surprise dawn attacks on Pink and his men like he'd done at Alpine.

But how we was gonna do that with just five of us, one of us a woman, with any hope of success, I had no idea. So I figgered I'd keep my thoughts to myself for the time being, until I could work out the details.

Of course, as it turned out later, matters was to be taken right out of my hands.

Twenty-nine

Doc blocked the entrance to the cut with the wagon, then we cleared away some of the snow and got a fire started with some deadwood we found close by.

The wood was damp, but Doc had a way with fires, and he soon had coffee boiling, which cheered all of us considerably.

Me and Johnny Blue fed the horses each a handful of oats from a sack we'd got from Gruber's store. They wanted more, but we had to hold on to what was left. Them ponies might be facing even leaner times later.

"I been watching you," Johnny Blue said out of earshot of the others. "Your face is kinda blank, and you got that dumb expression that makes you look like a mule. That tells me you don't have a plan of any kind in your head, don't it?"

"That's a plain fact," I said. "You got anything in mind?"

"No I don't. You're supposed to be the brains of this outfit."

I chuckled, but there was no humor in it.

"Don't worry," I said, "I'll come up with something."

"It had better be soon," Johnny Blue said. "We don't have much time."

I walked to the wagon and checked on the Chief.

He struggled into a sitting position, and he didn't look none too good. "How do you feel, Chief?" I asked.

"I just sang my death song, does that tell you anything?" he replied. "Where am I, and what are you doing in the place where I am, wherever it is?"

"You're in Doc's wagon," I said.

The Chief looked at the ropes that hogtied him. "Why am I bound up like this?"

"I captured you," I said. "You're our ace in the hole should your friends come lookin' for you."

"They'll come for me. Depend on it."

The Chief lay back against the wagon. "My head aches," he groaned.

"That was ol' Doc's firewater, done that to you."

The Chief looked at me, puzzled. Then he said: "Ahh . . . now I remember. The little green bottles."

"You gotta watch your drinking," I said.

"Go to hell," the Chief said.

I walked back to the fire and Doc handed me a cup of coffee.

"Wood's running low," he said. "I've pretty much used every last twig that's lying around here."

Johnny Blue rose and picked up his Henry.

"I'll scout the timber over there to the right," he said. "I reckon there's gotta be dry wood in there somewhere."

Doc shaded his eyes with his hand and watched Johnny Blue disappear into the trees.

"He's been quiet of late, that one."

"He's kinda worried, Doc," I said, "like we all are. But he's a good man, Johnny Blue is, an' he'll be right at your shoulder when you need him."

"I never doubted it," Doc said. He eyed me like he was trying to read my mind. Then he picked up the coffee pot and swirled it around. "Empty," he said. He stuffed snow into the pot and put it back on the fire. "When that boils I'll throw in what's left of the Arbuckle," he said.

"You're frettin' on something, Doc, " I said. "What's eatin' you?"

"You don't think we've got a hope in hell against Pink and his men, do you, boy?"

"There's always hope, Doc."

"We could just walk away from it," Doc said. "Turn the wagon around, go back. Let somebody else handle it."

"There ain't nobody else, Doc. Just us."

Doc lifted the lid of the pot and studied the melting snow. He talked without raising his eyes. "This thing with Pink. You reckon it's worth dying for?"

I pulled my knees up under my chin and stared into our tiny fire.

"Doc," I said, "the way I see it, the choice we all got is livin' or dyin'. Sometimes a man has to choose, and if'n he really believes in something, it makes the dyin' part easier if it happens that way. I believe Pink has to be stopped before he meets up with Frank James and tears this nation of ours apart again. That's what I believe, an' I guess I'm willing to die for it. So is Johnny Blue."

Doc just studied the pot. "Water's getting to boil," he said.

"Doc," I said, "dyin's a terrible thing, an' I won't blame any man who chooses to live. Just say if'n you want to ride on out of here."

Doc looked right at me then. "Boy," he said, "that's a helluva question to ask me. Me and Georgia and Bartholomew, we talked this thing through on the trail last night. We're in it to the end, whatever that end might be."

"So be it," I said. "Now pour me some of that horse liniment you call coffee."

"Company coming in," Georgia said.

I glanced up and saw her looking out across the clearing.

The sun was full up, glaring on the snow, and I couldn't make the riders out real good. But there was a dozen of them, spread out in a line across the clearing.

Their horses was lifting their legs high because of the snow, and even at this distance I could see these men wern't punchers. There wasn't a remuda in the West, or even in Mexico, that had thoroughbred horses like they rode.

They was either Pink and his boys, or a posse hunting Pink and his boys, and I knew where I was putting my money.

"Doc," I said, "take a Winchester and cover one side of the wagon. Mauler, do the same on the other side."

"What about me?" Georgia asked.

"Can you shoot a long gun?" I asked.

Georgia laughed. "A Texas Ranger taught me to shoot. Is that good enough?"

"Good enough for me," I said. "Get over beside the Mauler."

"My love," Doc hollered out. "Be careful."

I cradled my Winchester in my arms and stepped out in front of the wagon. I hoped Johnny Blue was seeing the same thing we was. I looked around, but there was no sign of that reclusive rider.

I stopped and waited and watched the riders come.

Mostly they were tall men riding upright and alert, like the soldiers some of them had been. They were all well mounted and well armed, and I knew when the chips were down, they'd turn out to be first class fighting men.

The riders pulled up about a hundred yards from the cut, then one of them in a huge fur coat spurred his horse toward me.

There was no mistaking that massive figure. It was Jacob Pike.

I looked around and saw no sign of Johnny Blue, and I prayed he hadn't gone gallivanting off somewheres, which, as you boys know, he's prone to do at times of crisis.

"Better get back to the wagon, Doc," I said. "Looks to me like they're gettin' themselves primed for a charge."

I walked back to the wagon with Doc and stood beside him. Georgia and the Mauler were looking out across the snow and their faces were set and grim, and I knew I had no worries on that score.

The Texans' rifles came flashing out of their scabbards and they kicked their horses into a loose line abreast.

"Get ready, Doc," I said.

"Son, I spent my whole life gettin' ready," Doc said.

"Me, I was just standin' here thinkin'," I told him. "Winter's a time when a cowboy, if'n he ain't ridin' the grub line, holes up in a holler log somewheres an' catches up on his sleep. When this is over, I'm gonna pull the blanket over my head an' I ain't plannin' to wake up till spring."

"To sleep, perchance to dream, there's the rub, boy."

"What's that mean?"

"It means nobody's gonna be sleeping around here, because here they come!"

The Texans came on like Texans always do, straight at you.

The wolfers were in the middle, Pike in the lead, firing as they came and I heard their bullets crash through the trees behind us.

"Hold off a shade," I yelled. "Let 'em get closer."

The snow was maybe a foot and a half on the level out there, and it slowed their charge considerably. The big thoroughbreds, southern raised and unused to snow country, were floundering, throwing up powdery white fountains from their plunging hooves.

I drew a bead on a man in a white hat on a beautiful bay and fired. And missed. He raised his rifle to his shoulder and fired at the wagon and I heard his bullet *ping!* close to Doc's head. The man swung his horse to the left, crossing in front of the other riders and I aimed, this time leading him by a foot. I fired, the Winchester slamming hard against my shoulder. The man gave a terrible cry then threw up his hands and toppled from the saddle.

I recognized the long beard on the Texan I'd just shot. He was the man with the tobacco-stained beard who'd carried off that little gal back in Alpine, and I was glad I'd settled his hash for him.

Georgia drew a bead on a wolfer who was a mite bolder than the rest. He'd ridden far ahead of the others and was firing his rifle only thirty yards from the wagon. Georgia fired. Her bullet drilled the wolfer plumb center and he screamed as he was blasted off the back of his horse.

Pike yelled at his men to split up and attack us from each side of the wagon, and his Texans broke into two parties, coming at us from both directions.

I held my Winchester at the hip and loaded and fired as fast I could crank the lever. Beside me, Doc was firing steadily, his gun to his shoulder.

The leading Texan, a huge man on a gray horse, had forsaken his rifle and was shooting at us with his Colt. I swung my rifle toward him and fired. One of the Texan's bullets kicked up snow at my feet as I fired again. The big man suddenly yelped and doubled over his saddle horn, clutching at his belly. He turned his horse and galloped out of the fight and I let him go.

The Texans behind the big man had been unable to fire because their leader was in the way. Me an' Doc, we poured lead hot and steady into them at close range and I guess they decided to think this thing over because they turned and spurred after their wounded compadre.

I heard Georgia scream and turned just in time to see the Mauler go down, a wide fan of blood blossoming up from his belt, just to the left of the buckle. The wolfer who'd shot him was right in the middle of camp. He swung his horse and with a wild oath aimed his rifle at Georgia.

Cranking my rifle, I squeezed the trigger, only to hear the hammer click on an empty chamber.

The wolfer, a man in a fur hat with an eagle feather slanting across the front of it, saw the dire straits I was in and ignored Georgia, turning his rifle on me.

"I got ye now, ye whelp!" he said.

I heard the loud report of a rifle from the trees, and the wolfer screamed and went down, taking his horse with him.

The hidden rifle fired again, and a Texan who'd been riding close behind the dead wolfer threw his Winchester in a spinning arc high in the air, dying instantly as his head exploded in a shower of blood.

Johnny Blue ran toward the camp, firing his Henry from the hip just as fast as he could lever shells into the chamber. The remaining Texans shot at him, but because of the noise and confusion and the smell of blood, their horses was spooked, and they couldn't shoot straight and control their plunging mounts at the same time.

I heard a man in a blond mustache holler: "Back, boys! Regroup! Regroup!"

That man was obviously cavalry, and I figgered he'd once rode under Bloody Bill's black flag like Pink and the rest.

The Texans turned and rode out of rifle range. I watched them gather around Jacob Pike, and there was some serious chin wagging going on over there.

My hands were shaking like a hound dog passing a

peach pit as I thumbed shells into my Winchester, and I took my fear and nervousness out on Johnny Blue: "What the hell took you so long?" I yelled.

"Me, I was bird watching," he said sarcastically.

"That sounds just like you," I said.

"Well," Johnny Blue said, "you was the one as wanted wood. I walked for miles and couldn't find any that was dry enough to burn. When I heard the shootin' I come running."

"Be quiet, you two," Doc said. "Bartholomew's hit bad."

Kneeling beside the Mauler, I saw that the shirt under his jacket was bright crimson with blood. The big pugilist's face was ghostly pale and I knew he was in pain real bad. But he looked up and managed a smile.

"This is what comes of being such a big target," he said.

Georgia was holding the Mauler's head, and her eyes were filled with tears. "He's just like a son to me," she sobbed. "A big, bald-headed bruiser of a son."

"He's gonna be alright, Georgia," I told her. "We're all gonna make it through this thing."

I stood and looked out across the snow. I counted that Pike had lost four dead and one wounded. The big wolfer had underestimated us, and he'd paid for it dearly.

He would have done better if he'd dismounted and come at us through the trees. But his men were horseback fighters, and them as wasn't in the Civil War had been taught by them as was, and they had been learned the way of the mounted guerilla. Ol' Pink now, being smart, knew guerillas need the element of surprise, like they'd had at Alpine. But ol' Pike, being stupid, never learned that lesson.

He had lost the Battle of the Clearing and Amos Pinkney would surely kill him for it.

THIRTY

I looked out at Pike and his boys. Between us, the snow that had lain smooth and unwrinkled like the white sheet on a Virginia City hotel room bed, was now all plowed up by the Texans' horses.

Counting himself, Ol' Pike was down to eight men. Though the man I'd shot was still sitting his horse, doubled over, I reckoned he was out of the fight.

That left seven against our four rifles.

Boys, make no mistake, we'd been lucky. Them Texans were hell for leather fighting men, but they'd been badly led.

They still outnumbered us, and if Pike decided to play it smart, I still didn't give a busted poker chip for our chances.

We were also low on shells, maybe three or four to a rifle, and I had real doubts we could stop another determined charge.

Johnny Blue was at my shoulder.

"Reckon they'll hit us again?" I asked.

Johnny Blue nodded. "Texans generally do." He jerked a thumb back toward the wagon. "It ain't any of my business, on account of how he's your prisoner, but—"

"Oh my God," I said. "The Chief!"

"Yeah," Johnny Blue said. "Him."

I ran to the wagon. The canvas cover was peppered with bullet holes and one of the bows had been hit and was lying at a crazy angle.

I looked inside.

The Chief was sitting upright and was unharmed.

"What's going on?" he asked.

"There's men trying to kill us," I said. "Us, we was defending ourselves."

"Pretty big damn fight," the Chief said. "Heap much bang-bang, as you would say."

Then I had one of my brilliant ideas, which by now you boys know I get from time to time.

"Chief," I said, "one of our men is down, hurt bad. Will you take his rifle and join in the battle?"

The Chief turned away and spat. "This is a white man's war. It's got nothing to do with me."

"Those are the worst kind of white men out there," I said. "If'n they break through and kill us, they'll kill you too, depend on it. Them men, they don't cotton to redskins much. Think on it."

I turned to walk away, but the Chief stopped me.

"Hold it," he said. "Untie me. I'll fight in your damn white man's war. I don't want to be shot down like a dog with my hands tied behind my back."

"Wise move, Chief," I said.

"Don't patronize me, white man," the Chief grunted. "Now cut these ropes off of me."

As I began to untie him, I asked a question that had been bothering me some. "Chief, I swear, at times you talk just like Doc or one of them college perfessers. Where in the hell did you get your eddication?"

The Chief groaned and stretched his arms. "On the field of battle, then on the reservation," he said. "Custer, Gibbon, Bearcoat Miles and the rest, they taught us real well."

The Chief climbed out of the wagon and I handed him the Mauler's rifle.

"Do you think this is wise?" Doc asked me. "That aborigine is dangerous and he's after your hair."

"Doc," I said, "he's an experienced fighting man. He might jest help save all our hairs."

The Chief looked around the camp at the dead men and those just beyond the wagon.

"Have these dead been touched?" he asked. "Has anyone laid a hand on them?"

"No," I said. "How come you asked?"

The Chief's only reply was to pump his rifle in the air and let out with a terrible shriek.

He then ran to each of the four dead men and touched them with the muzzle of his rifle, yipping and dancing around all the while like . . . well, an Injun.

When he came back to the camp he was breathing hard, but he'd calmed down some and I asked him what the hell was going on.

"I was counting coup," he said. "I was the first here to touch a slain enemy. It's a great honor for a warrior, but it's just something else you wouldn't understand."

"No, Chief," I said. "I guess I wouldn't."

"Well, here's something you'll understand. Ol' Pike and them Texans is getting primed to charge again," Johnny Blue said.

I looked out across the snow. Pike's men had extended themselves in a line again. But this time they was coming in at a walk.

"What are they doin', Johnny Blue?" I asked.

"Beats me."

The Texans drew rein about three hundred yards away. Then they sat their horses and opened up on us with their long guns.

Bullets crashed and whined through the camp, and we ran for cover, except for the Chief who stood in the open singing some kind of Nez Perce war chant, I guess.

Those Texans were expert riflemen, and even at long range, they were making their shots tell.

Johnny Blue, Doc and Georgia opened up on them, but at this distance they didn't have a hope in hell of hitting anybody. Besides, they were using up our few remaining shells real fast, and I yelled at them to stop firing.

A bullet whanged off the stock of my Winchester, shattering it near the breech, and my hands stung like they'd been burned. The gun was ruined so I tossed it away and pulled my Colt, useless at any more than a dozen yards.

I saw Johnny Blue raise up to fire, but blood suddenly spurted from the side of his head and he fell back in a heap. I ran to his side. He wasn't moving and the whole side of his head was covered in blood.

"He's done for!" Doc yelled. "Get back to your position."

Boys, I was numb. I guess I went a little mad from

shock and grief. I leveled my Colt at Pike and his men, thumbed the hammer and yanked the trigger as fast as I could.

Of course I didn't hit nothing, but at least I felt like I was doing something for Johnny Blue.

Pike and the Texans had found the range, and now about all we could do was keep our heads down as bullets split the air above us, and I started in to panic like a schoolmarm that just tipped over the outhouse.

"Georgia, my dear, I love you!" Doc yelled. "My last thoughts are of you, my precious."

The large lady smiled and, though she didn't speak, her mouth formed the words "I love you" right back at him.

Those two, they was saying their last farewells, and me, I didn't have nobody left to say farewell to, less'n you count the Chief, and I don't reckon he cared much.

But it was the Chief who saved our lives.

So far, he hadn't fired his Winchester. Now he kneeled behind the wagon and cranked out the shells from the chamber in his hand, four of them. These he studied closely.

"You." He pointed to Georgia. "Give me the shells from your rifle."

Georgia was puzzled, and the Chief yelled, "Quick, woman!"

Georgia cranked out three rounds, which the Chief took and laid on the pile of shells at his feet. He now had seven of them.

The Chief picked up the shells one by one and examined them closely once more. I guess he found one he liked because he grunted and stuck it, lead end first, in his ear.

"You, Doc," he yelled. "Give me your shells!"

Now Doc didn't like this one bit, you could see, but I nodded at him and told him to go ahead.

Doc ran to the Chief's side, bullets kicking up snow around his feet, and cranked two rounds into the Indian's waiting hands.

The Chief examined them both, threw one away and kept the other one. "Now I'm ready," he said.

"Chief," I wailed, "you just threw away one of the last shells we got."

"We won't need it," he said.

But before he could throw away the rest, I grabbed the shells at his feet and split them between Georgia and Doc. I reloaded my Colt and holstered it, and picked up Johnny Blue's Henry rifle.

Taking a second to look down at my fallen friend, I whispered, "Johnny Blue, when this is over, I'll find our little sister if'n it takes me a lifetime. I swear it."

Then, my eyes stinging, I ran back to the wagon.

The Chief thumbed both of his shells, including the one from his ear, into his Winchester.

Then he did something real strange, I mean besides ignoring the bullets that was flying all around him.

Boys, do you recollect that feller with the short leg and the glass eye that played the piana in Jim Shelton's saloon in Utica for a spell? Remember, he always wore them three pairs o' long johns, even in summer, on account of how he said he was troubled real bad by the rheumatisms?

Well, that feller—I kinda recollect his name was Charles O' Donnell, though most folks jest called him Polecat Charlie—well ol' Charlie had this thing he done before he played. He sort of laced his fingers together then stretched his arms out in front of him so his knuckles cracked. Then he'd shake his hands an' shrug his shoulders up an' down before he played a note.

Well, that's what the Chief done, except of course he wasn't playin' no piana. Now, I don't even know if'n he ever saw Polecat Charlie play, but maybe he did. Who knows?

Well, after the Chief done all that with his fingers, he then took up his rifle.

He stood in full view of Pike and his boys, and triggered off a shot.

I saw the Texan on Pike's left throw up his hands and fall off his horse. Pike turned and looked at his fallen compadre, then began shooting again.

The Chief, cool as you please, fired a second time.

As before, his bullet was true, and the wolfer on ol' Pike's right was blown right out of the saddle.

The Chief's deadly shooting threw Pike and the Texans into confusion. Their ranks broke as men tried to get away from that terrible rifle fire.

"Pour it into them!" I yelled, and me and Doc and Georgia opened up and shot away all the shells we had left.

I saw ol' Pike reel, and I knew he was hit.

Two of the Texans, realizing the game was up, split for the south, heading toward Pink's cabin with the bad news.

Pike opened his mouth and yelled something at their retreating backs. He pulled his Colt and thumbed off a couple of fast shots at the fleeing men, but missed both times. Cursing, Pike led his remaining men into the trees to his left, except for the wounded Texan who just sat on his patient horse out there, doubled over. Only later did we find out he was dead.

Despite the fact that Johnny Blue was gone and the Mauler lay dying, I couldn't help myself and I laughed and slapped the Chief on the back and told him he'd done good.

"That was the purtiest shootin' I've ever seen, and this war ain't even over yet, Chief," I said. "I'd surely be honored if'n you'd join us an' see it through to the end."

But that bad-tempered brave was still on the prod. "The war is over for me, white man," he said. He threw his Winchester down at my feet. "This changes nothing between us, and now we have another score to settle, on account of how you took me prisoner and treated me like I was lowdown."

I opened my mouth to protest, but with a wild whoop, the Chief leaped on a horse that had belonged to one of the dead wolfers and galloped away.

Now I know he'd saved my life an' all, but boys, let me tell you, that was one strange Indian.

"You better get over here," Doc said.

He was kneeling beside Johnny Blue, cradling that fallen rider's bloody head in his hands.

I walked over and Doc said, "He's alive. The bullet only creased his skull and stunned him."

"Johnny Blue, can you hear me?" I asked as I kneeled down at his side.

His eyes fluttered open.

"He's alive, alright," I told Doc.

"What happened?" Johnny Blue whispered weakly.

"A bullet liked to blow your brains out," I said. "But on account of how it wasn't any part of your body you use reg'lar, no harm was done."

Johnny Blue reached up to his head with his hand and his fingers came away bloody. He studied them for a while, then said, "That was close."

"Too close, son," Doc said. "We thought you was a goner for sure."

"Hey you in the camp!"

It was ol' Pike's voice, hollerin' from the woods.

"Take care of Johnny Blue, Doc," I said.

I rose to my feet and pulled my Colt. Then I walked in front of the wagon and yelled, "Is that you, Jacob?"

"Is me."

"What do you want? There's still desperate men here, an' we have Winchesters."

"I'm finished, cowboy," Pike hollered. Then in a softer voice he muttered, "This hoedown is over."

"I don't believe you, Jacob," I hollered. "You're a bad man and lowdown."

"We're all shot to pieces here, for crissakes," Pike yelled. "And I'm done for through and through."

Doc came up and stood beside me. "How's Johnny Blue?" I asked.

"He's gonna be fine."

"The Mauler?"

"He ain't gonna be fine."

I thought for a few moments, then said, "Doc, get Johnny Blue's Schofield, then come stand beside me."

Doc did as he was told and when he came back, I hailed Jacob Pike again.

"Jacob," I said, "come out of them woods on foot, leading your horses. And no funny stuff, do you hear?"

"I hear you," Pike said.

A few minutes passed, then Pike stepped into the clearing, leading his horse. The two remaining Texans walked behind him. One favored his left shoulder, the other was limping and I could see blood on his pants.

"That's far enough, Jacob," I told him when Pike was twenty-five yards from the wagon.

"We ain't huntin' trouble," Pike growled. "Us, we want to get back to Helena an' find a doctor."

"You ain't hurt so bad," I said.

Pike opened his bearskin coat. I saw blood just above his belt and another wound on his chest.

"Damn you," he snarled. "You shot two holes in me."

"That was all your doing, Jacob, not mine," I said.

There was a shriek from out in the clearing and I saw the Flathead women out there on paint ponies. One had dismounted and was kneeling beside a fallen wolfer. She was already hacking at her long black hair with a knife and wailing, a sound as lonely and forelorn as the winter wind around the walls of a mountain line cabin.

"Our women," Pike said.

"I reckon," I said.

"You're calling the shots, cowboy," Pike told me. "Now what?"

Suddenly I was sick of it, all the shooting and the killing. And I felt deathly tired.

"Just go," I said. "Pack your dead and take your women and go."

"That's all? No Johnny law?"

"The rope will catch up with you soon enough, Jacob Pike," I said. "Now get the hell outta here."

THIRTY-ONE

We slept the night in the clearing and prepared to move out early next morning. I felt better when I woke, but I was stiff and sore from the cold. And wouldn't you boys know it, it was snowing again.

We'd built a fire with what wood we could find and had laid the Mauler close to it in a sheltered spot in the cut, his shoulders propped up on a Texas saddle.

"We can't take him with us," Doc said. "Traveling in the wagon would kill him sure enough."

I told the Mauler what Doc had said, and he grinned up at me. "You got a job to do," he said. "Go do it. A dying man would only slow you down."

"You're not dying, Bartholomew," Georgia whispered. "The cold has stopped the bleeding. You're going to be just fine."

"He's gut shot," Johnny Blue said. "I knew a feller over on the Judith was gut shot one time."

"And he lived, didn't he?" Georgia said.

"Nah," Johnny Blue said. "He died."

"You got a way, Johnny Blue, of jest naturally cheerin' folks up, don't you?" I told him.

Johnny Blue had a fat bandage around his head,

torn from one of Georgia's petticoats, and his hat was just balancing on the top of his head.

"I'll go see if I can find more wood for the Mauler's fire," he said.

After we saddled the horses and hitched the team, we all stood around the Mauler, each of us not wanting to be the one to make the first move to leave him there.

We'd found coffee in the Texans' saddlebags, as well as plenty of ammunition, and soon a full pot of Arbuckle bubbled on the fire by the Mauler's side.

Johnny Blue kneeled beside the Mauler and handed him a Colt he'd taken from one of the bodies.

"Mauler," he said, "there's six shells in there. If'n you're attacked by wild Indians or a grizzly or wolves an' sich, make a fight with five of them, then blow your brains out with the sixth. Them's words of wisdom."

Now, the Mauler was so much taken by this display of Johnny Blue's kindness and thoughtfulness, that he burst into tears. He was about to say something, but Johnny Blue stopped him.

"Mauler," he said, "there's one thing else I want to tell you. I been thinking about what you done to me back there in Great Falls, an' I've decided I ain't gonna shoot you anytime real soon. I jest thought you'd like to know that an hear it from my own two lips."

Boys, my own tears is staining the paper as I write this and recollect what happened next. The Mauler, he was so overcome by this further token of Johnny Blue's affection, that he grabbed that warm-hearted puncher's hand and vowed his eternal love and brotherhood.

"'For old lang syne, my friend, for old lang syne,'" quoth the Mauler, "'we'll take a cup of kindness yet, for the sake of old lang's syne.'"

It was a scene so wrenching it would have brought water from a stone, and I could see Doc and Georgia were much affected by it.

Doc, he led us all in singing "Nearer My God to Thee," what we could recollect of it anyhow, and the words of that grand old hymn bolstered all of our spirits. Us, because we was about to depart for ol' Pink's lair and its many perils, and the Mauler because he was, well . . . about to depart.

"This is indeed a bittersweet tableau," Doc said. "I have watched acts of kindness here today that I thought had long vanished from the human condition. The Mauler lies low, yes, but his dusky brother here, whose forebears hailed from Africa's wild shores, has played the white man's part and brought him great comfort in his final hours. Thus, surely, must the armored paladins of the great Charlemagne have once stood around the fallen hero Roland in the snowy pass of Roncesvalles and delivered unto him solace in the moments of his final agony. In short— Bartholomew may be a goner, but he's departing from us in style."

"Oh, Doc, that's so beautiful," Georgia sobbed, her handkerchief to her eyes.

"Thank you, my love," Doc said. "And I meant every last word of it."

"Doc," the Mauler said, "I never thought anybody would say words over me as pretty as that. You're a true friend and you've been a larrupin' good manager."

"Think nothing of it, my boy," Doc said. "Water under the bridge."

Even Johnny Blue was overcome, though he later told me he didn't quite get the bit about him playin' the white man. He took the Mauler's hand, and on behalf of all of us, bade him a last farewell.

We rode out of camp a few minutes later with many a loud cheer and hearty Huzzah! for the Mauler, and that bravehearted soul weakly raised his hand and waved us on our way.

As we took to the trail, Georgia was still very overwrought, sobbing into her scrap of lace as she sat beside Doc. I sought to comfort her.

"I knowed this feller once in Dodge," I said, "little feller by the name of Squint Bodene, on account of how both his eyes looked into the bridge of his nose. He also had a kinda hump on his back and a gamy left arm, but that's neither here nor there."

"What happened to him?" Georgia asked, sniffing and dabbing at her nose with the lace.

"Well, ol' Squint, he got into an argument one night in the Long Branch with this gambler who went by the name of Ford Wilcox over a sportin' gal by the name of Squirrel Tooth Alice."

Johnny Blue, riding on the other side of the wagon groaned. "I swear, your stories never have any point, and they don't never end."

"This one has a point," I said. "Trust me."

"Recount on, my tattered troubador," Doc said.

"Well, one word follered another, an' Squint an' Ford pulled their hawglegs and commenced in to shootin'. Now, Squint, being cockeyed as he was, saw double of everythin' when he was sober. But he was drunk that night, and he later said he was seein' four of everythin'. Ol' Ford, he was drunk, but he warn't cockeyed, so he was only seein' double of everythin'."

"I swear," Johnny Blue said, "I'm gonna shoot you right out of that there saddle if'n you don't come to the point."

"He's getting there," Georgia said. "Ain't you, honey?"

"Sure am," I said. "See, Squint an' Ford was chasin' each other around the pool table, blazing away. But they didn't hit nothin' except a drummer who was standin' at the bar an' a poor cowboy who come inside to see what the commotion was."

"Oh, those poor men," Georgia said.

"Yeah," I said. "It were a downright shame. Well anyway, ol' Squint had to stop an' reload an' he run behind the stove. But when he looked down at his gun hand he seen four Colts, an' he didn't know which one of 'em to put the bullets in."

Johnny Blue groaned and looked surly, but I went right on with my story.

"Well, Ol' Ford Wilcox, on account of how he was only seein' double from the whiskey, got loaded up first and ran behind the stove an' opened up on poor Squint from only three feet away. He fired six times but only managed to hit Squint once, drilled him right through the belly button. Ol' Squint, he yells, 'I'm gut shot an' I'm dyin'. Give me air.' Then he fell, wallowing in his blood."

"Oh, that's horrible," Georgia said.

"Yeah," Johnny Blue said. "The whole story is horrible. Now what's your point?"

"I was gettin' to that," I said. "See, Squint was married to a widder women with sixteen kids, so they carried him home an' laid him in bed. Then the doctor came an' said, 'This man is gut shot an' he won't be alive come morning,' which caused the widder woman a tolerable amount of grief, on account of how them kids could eat their weight in groceries an' ol' Squint, he was the only breadwinner."

"I still don't see what you're driving at," Johnny Blue said.

"Well, the point I'm makin' is that ol' Squint didn't die. Oh sure, he chewed up the bedsheets and begged for water for a couple of months, but in the end he got up out of bed an' was as right as rain."

I took off my hat and brushed off the snow that was laying on it. "What I'm sayin', Georgia, is the Mauler is gut shot, but he's big an' strong an' he might live. Jest like ol' Squint Bodene."

"Oh, thank you," Georgia said. "You've made me feel much better."

"You've given us hope, boy," Doc said. "Hope that Bartholomew might pull through."

Johnny Blue glanced over at me and he looked kinda comical with his hat stuck on top of the fat bandage around his head.

"Couldn't you have just said, 'I knowed a feller once who was gut shot an' lived,' without going into that whole rigmarole?" he asked testily.

"No. I thought it would comfort Georgia some to hear the full story."

"Which it did, sure enough," Georgia said.

"I suppose you're gonna tell us next you was the poor cowboy that got shot," Johnny Blue said.

"Nah," I said. "That was an ol' boy by the name of Tooter Mapes. Rode for the Running M a while back. Ol' Toot had a bad ticker, turned him blue by times, an' he was missin' three fingers. He got shot in the leg that day in the Long Branch, an' he always did say that limb pained him tolerably bad in wet weather ever since."

We rode in silence for a while after that, each of us wrapped in our own thoughts. I heard an owl hoot from the timber on the hill to our left, then I heard another answer to our right.

I didn't pay it any mind at the time. But I should have.

Of course, right then I was too busy trying to put a plan together to concern myself with owls.

Boys, like I said before, we'd been lucky so far, mainly on account of how Jacob Pike was so stupid. But Amos Pinkney was a different breed of hoss entirely.

We was about to go up against the most feared gunman in the West, on his own ground, and he still had two of his Texans left, both of them desperate and skilled fighting men.

And Pink was smart. He wouldn't make any stupid moves like Pike had done. When he made his play it would be fast and deadly, and he'd shoot to kill.

There was four of us, counting Georgia, going after him. And I seriously doubted that there would be one of us left standing to mount up and ride away after it was all over.

THIRTY-TWO

We kept to the trail the rest of that day and huddled together in the wagon at night, moving on again at first light.

I reckoned this was the day we'd meet up with Amos Pinkney and I still had no plan of action. What little food we had was gone, and cold and hunger was making me foggy-brained so I couldn't think straight.

Me, I also had a premonition of danger that I couldn't shake, and it worrried me considerable.

Thus it was that I was weighted down with gloomy thoughts and premonitions, giving no mind to the trail, which in any event seemed to run smoother here, when Johnny Blue said, "Rider ahead. An' he's comin' in."

Peering through the veil of falling snow, I saw an Indian setting his pony at a walk toward us, pulling a pack horse behind him. But as the rider grew closer I could see a gray beard spilling over the front of his buckskins and a low-crowned, plainsman's hat on his head.

He was a white man. I took him for a mountain man, one of them fellers who prefers the high lonesome of the Rockies, trapping and panning a little gold, making a living any way they can. Like the cowboy, mountain men were a fast vanishing breed, and I reckoned this ol' feller was among the last of them.

The mountain man reined in his pony, letting us come up to him. He had a Henry rifle across his saddle horn and a Remington revolver in a rawhide shoulder holster under his left arm. I rode ahead a ways to meet him.

"Howdy, sonny," he said. "Seen your wagon coming for quite a piece off, though I reckon you didn't see me until late."

"I was thinkin'," I said. "I wasn't payin' much attention to the trail."

"Thinkin' man should get himself a dog. Good dog'll tell him what's ahead soon enough."

"I'll keep that in mind," I said. "What brings you out here, old timer?"

"Me, I'm headed for Helena. Got me a mess o' pelts and some dust and I figger to sleep in a soft bed all winter long. Gettin' too old to stay up in them mountains after the first snows. Was a day I would, but no more after I was took bad with the rheumatisms few years back."

The old mountain man studied me closely for a while. Then he ran his eyes over the wagon and the others when they come up behind me. I could tell he didn't think we amounted to much.

"Where are you folks headed?" he asked.

"Us, we're headed south of here," I said. "We're lookin' for a cabin owned by a friend of our'n, name of Amos Pinkney. Ever heard of him?"

The mountain man shook his head, his long hair blowing in the wind. "Never heard of him. 'Course, that ain't surprising. I'm a man who's spent nigh on his whole life up there." He waved a hand toward the high peaks. "Came out here in the spring o' '46, been here ever since. Had a Cheyenne woman then, but she died in '74. Did see a cabin though, sets in a valley two or three days to the south. Seems a cozy enough place."

The old man kicked his pony forward. "Well, sonny, it's been nice chin waggin' with you, but I got to be moving on. You best find that cabin of your'n soon. It's blowing up to be a bear of a winter. An' don't forget what I said about gettin' a dog."

Riding up close beside me, the mountain man reined in his pony and dropped his voice to a whisper. "I didn't want to alarm the young lady none, but I thought I'd warn you. I seen Indian sign in the hills. Looks like they've been follering you for a fair piece, but now they're ahead of you, back there somewheres." He jerked a thumb over his shoulder.

I nodded. "I reckon I know them Indians. They're Nez Perce."

The old man looked surprised. "You tell me so! A shade far north for Nez Perce. This here is Flathead country."

"Maybe so, but they're Nez Perce."

"Them's bad Injuns to tangle with, sonny. You best be on guard an' stop your thinkin' for a spell. Do more watchin'."

Johnny Blue rode up beside us and he listened to the old man intently.

"Seen other sign just south of here," the mountain man said. "These was white men, three of them.

Night riders by the look of their tracks. They're still up there in the hills, keepin' out of sight."

"I reckon I also know who they may be," I said.

"The hell you say! Sonny, way I see it, I reckon there's a passel of folks after your hair, white and Injun, an' that's your business. But if'n I was you, I'd keep my eyes on the trail from now on. 'Course, that's your business too."

The mountain man kneed his pony past me, pulling the pack horse after him.

"Well, good day to ye," he said. And he rode into the falling curtain of the snow.

"You reckon them night riders is Pink and his boys?" Johnny Blue asked me.

"You reckon they're anybody else?"

I told Doc and Georgia what the old trapper had said and warned them to keep their Winchesters handy. We now had a good supply of ammunition we'd taken from Pike and his Texans, and I had a feeling we were gonna need every last round of it.

Telling Johnny Blue to ride ahead a piece, I dropped back and trailed the wagon by a good hunnerd yards, my eyes everywhere on the trail and the surrounding hills.

This was a time when a man could get mighty discouraged and depressed, but my gloom had lifted and I was determined to see this through to the end. After I told them what the mountain man had said, I hadn't heard a single word of complaint from the others, so I knew they felt the same way. They reckoned the fate of our Republic rested on their shoulders and they had accepted the risks. I figgered I could do no less.

Then, just as day was shading into night, Amos Pinkney and his Texans hit us fast and hard.

They came out of the timber to our left at a fast gallop, hollerin' and screaming the Rebel yell.

Pink had both his Remingtons in his fists, blazing away, and behind him his Texans cut loose with their Winchesters.

They came between the wagon and Johnny Blue and I saw Doc stand and raise his rifle to his shoulder.

Yelling at Doc to get down, I set spurs to my pony, firing as I came, and I saw Doc raise up on tiptoe as a bullet hit him and he toppled out of the wagon onto the snow.

Georgia fired once, then twice, then she threw down her rifle and jumped out of the wagon and kneeled beside the stricken Doc.

Pink saw me coming and he turned in his saddle and cut loose with both Remingtons.

Gouts of orange flame shot from his guns in the gathering dusk and I felt a blow like a sledgehammer hit my left shoulder. I grabbed on to the saddle horn to stay in the leather, my Winchester spinning away from me.

Johnny Blue was riding toward us fast, shooting as he came. The Texans pumped a few shots in his direction, then they rode after Pink into the timber to the right of the trail and were gone.

It had been a sudden, slashing, guerilla attack. And it had hurt us real bad.

"How's Doc?" I asked Georgia after I threw myself off my pony and came to her side.

"I don't know," she sobbed. "I think maybe he's dying."

Johnny Blue was still mounted, his rifle to his shoulder, scanning the timber where Pink and his boys had disappeared.

"Let me take a look," I said.

Doc's coat was covered in blood, but I couldn't see any chest or belly wounds.

"Can you hear me, Doc?" I said. "Where are you hit?"

Doc's eyes fluttered open and he pointed to his neck. "It's there. Up there somewhere."

Then I saw it. The .40–.40 ball had torn away a chunk of flesh just where Doc's right shoulder met his neck, and it had broken the collar bone.

"How bad is it?" Doc asked.

"Bullet went clean through, but it broke bone on the way. You ain't gonna be using a rifle again anytime soon."

Me and Georgia got Doc to a sitting position, though his head was lying on his right shoulder.

"Can you straighten your head, Doc?" I asked.

He tried, but gasped in pain. "No, I can't, dear boy," he said. "It hurts too much."

"You gonna walk around like that, with your head on your shoulder?" I asked.

"I don't believe I have any other option, for the time being," quoth that suffering stalwart. "However, it will give me a new aspect on things, seeing the world at a forty-five-degree angle."

"Then I guess maybe we're gonna have to bind you up that way," I said. I turned to Georgia. "Do you have any petticoat left?"

"A lady of breeding always has plenty of petticoat," Georgia said testily, and she hitched up her dress and tore another strip off her tattered undergarments.

"In the wagon, boy," Doc said. "Get a bottle of elixir and pour it on the wound. It will cleanse it before mortification can get started."

I did as Doc said, and Georgia opened the bottle and poured the elixir directly onto his bloody flesh. Ol' Doc, he let out a beller and jumped like a bullfrog caught under a bucket.

"Damn that hurt!" Doc yelled. "Felt hotter'n a June bride in a feather bed."

"And how would you know what a June bride feels like?" asked Georgia.

"Hearsay, my love," Doc gasped. "All hearsay."

As Georgia bound up Doc's neck I felt a sudden wave of pain and nausea and I leaned my head against the wagon wheel.

"Why, you're wounded too," Georgia exclaimed.

"It's my shoulder," I said. "An' I reckon the bullet's still in there."

Georgia finished with Doc, then turned to me. "Let's take a look."

"Hey, you down there in the wagon!"

The voice came from the timber to the right of the trail.

I eased Georgia away from me and stood, pulling my Colt.

"Major wants to talk to you!" the voice said again.

There was a pause of maybe a minute, then I heard Pink's voice loud and clear from the darkness.

"Ye scum!" he yelled. "That was just a taste o' what's waiting for ye!"

I heard a man's laugh from somewhere in the gloom, followed by the Rebel yell, and a man hollered, "You tell 'em, Major!"

It was Jericho Gentle's voice.

"Go back," Pink screamed again. "Go back or I'll send all of you to hell's fire. I'll skin you alive and stretch your mangy hides on my cabin wall, every last one of ye. God curse me if I don't."

Pink's voice died away among the hills and there was quiet again.

Somewhere, way up in the high country, I heard the distant howl of a hunting wolf pack, a wail of ancient and eternal hunger that made the skin of my back crawl.

"Spooky, ain't it," Johnny Blue said, looking down at me from his pony.

"The wolves or ol' Pink?" I asked.

"I ain't talkin' about the wolves," Johnny Blue said, and he chuckled. But there was no humor in it.

"Why the hell don't he get it over with?" I said.

"Now we're ready an' waitin', he won't risk our rifles," Johnny Blue said. "That is, not unless he has to. He knows what happened at the Battle of the Clearing, an' that's made him wary. But if'n he sees no other way, he'll come a-shootin', alright."

"Ye scum!"

It was Pink again.

"I want to speak to my darlin' daughter. I want to speak to Georgia." There was a pause, then he yelled, "Georgia, come to me. Come to your papa. Let me take you in my arms and hold you close, my little darlin'."

I heard a muffled laugh, which ended in a man's choking cough.

Georgia walked up beside me, her face betraying nothing.

"Georgia, I—" I began, but she waved me into silence.

She stood there for a long time, just staring into the darkness, then she turned on her heel and picked up her Winchester. Georgia threw the rifle to her shoulder, but I reached out and lowered the barrel.

"You won't hit nothing in the dark," I said. "All you'll do is give away our position."

Georgia stood stock still, the rifle clenched in her hands. I guess she reckoned what I'd said made sense, because she suddenly threw down the Winchester and went back to Doc's side.

A couple of minutes passed, and I began to think that Pink had left. But then he hollered at us again.

"So be it, Georgia," he said. "You'll die with the rest, ye ungrateful slave whelp."

There was quiet again, and this time it stretched out for such a long time it was swallowed by the night.

"Me, I'm gonna taken my Henry and scout over there," Johnny Blue said. "Make sure they're gone."

"Be careful," I said. "Them's night riders. They could be laying low in the timber jest waitin' and watchin'."

"They ain't gonna see a black man in the dark," Johnny Blue said.

He climbed off his pony, waved his hat at Georgia and vanished into the darkness.

"Now you," Georgia said, "Let me see that shoulder."

Sitting down beside Doc, my back to the wagon wheel, I let Georgia help me off with my mackinaw. She opened my shirt, which was red with blood, and unbuttoned the top of my long johns and took a looksee at my shoulder.

"Ball didn't go through, sure enough," she said, "Though how a skinny, half-starved little feller like you could stop a .44 ball without it going all the way through you is beyond my understanding. Why didn't you tell Johnny Blue you were wounded?"

"Didn't want to add to his problems," I said. "Can you see the ball?"

"No, I'm gonna have to go digging for it." She stretched out a hand to Doc. "Give me that pig sticker of yours."

Doc handed over his Arkansas toothpick and said: "Be careful, my love, don't cut yourself."

Georgia hefted the knife in her hand. "Could use something less, cowboy, but a bowie will get the job done quicker than anything else. Cuts faster."

"Has you done this before?" I asked. "Recent?"

Georgia laughed. "Hell, boy, in my time I taken more bullets out of more waddies than you've had hot dinners."

"Way we've been eatin' lately, that's not too many," I said.

"My love," Doc said, "might it not be wise to wait until our sable companion, who is presently as one with the night, returns and renders assistance? In short, Johnny Blue can hold this cowboy down when the cuttin' starts."

"I don't need nobody to hold me down," I said.

"Bravely spoken," said Doc. "But with the knife my young friend, one slip and—"

Doc drew his finger across his throat.

"Doc, don't scare the boy," Georgia said. "But you're right, we should wait for Johnny Blue's help."

THIRTY-THREE

Me, I'd lost a lot of blood and I drifted in and out of consciousness and when I was out of it, them was the good times, because when I was awake my shoulder hurt like hell.

It was going on to midnight when Doc shook me awake.

"How you feeling, boy?" he asked.

"I'm some down in the mouth, Doc," I said. I looked around. "Where's Johnny Blue?"

Doc began to hum and haw, and I said: "Don't talk around it, Doc. Where is he?"

"He never came back," Doc said. "I fear he's been taken. Or worse."

I started up, but Doc pushed me against the wagon wheel. "You ain't going anywheres, boy, not until Georgia cuts that bullet out of you."

"Then get to cuttin'," I said. "Then I'm gonna take a Winchester gun and find Johnny Blue."

Georgia came at me with the knife. "I'm sorry," she said. "But it's deep."

"Ooh," Doc groaned, "this here's gonna hurt like hell."

"Thanks, Doc," I said. Then I heard a man scream, and a second later realized it was me.

"I'm sorry," I gasped. "That was plumb unmanly."

"That's just fine, boy, let it out," Georgia said. "I'm cutting in there a long ways."

There was another stab of white hot pain in my shoulder and Doc picked up a pine twig that was laying close and jammed it into my mouth. "Bite on that," he said.

Biting down on the wood, the pain kept hitting me in waves as Georgia probed deep, then deeper with the point of the bowie.

I watched her turn to Doc. "I can't find it," she whispered.

"Cut deeper," Doc said. "It's bound to be there."

"His shoulder's broke, and I'm scraping bone already," Georgia said.

Doc's head was laying on one side an' with his bright eyes and beak of a nose he looked like one of them little noisy birds that peck around the door of the cookhouse all summer long.

The thought of that made me laugh and Georgia said: "That's right, boy, laugh. It will help."

But when she cut again, I stopped laughing right quick and stuck that piece of pine back between my clenched teeth.

"I can't find it."

Georgia sat there, the bloody knife in her hand, and her face looked puzzled. Then it cleared and she said: "Listen, boy, do you hurt anywheres else?"

Boys, it seemed to me then that a soft, dark cloud drifted off the mountaintops and it came lower without making a sound and then it was all around me and I just wanted to lay my head on it and sleep forever.

"Stay with us!" Georgia said, and she shook me, none too gently.

Waking up with a start, I looked into her huge dark eyes, dark as any flint.

"Where else does it hurt?" she asked. "Pay attention!" And she shook me again.

"Back," I whispered. "Low on the left."

Georgia leaned me forward, and I felt her hands run down my back. When she touched the lower ribs I felt a quick stab of pain that jolted me fully awake.

"There," I said. "Right there."

"A couple of ribs are broken," Georgia said. "And I can feel the ball. It's stuck right under your bottom rib and I'm gonna have to cut it out of there." She shook me again. "Do you understand? If I leave that ball there it will mortify. I have to cut it free."

"Then cut, dammit," I said. "Cut, an' let me go find Johnny Blue."

"Wait!" Doc said. "I should have thought of this sooner."

He rummaged inside the wagon then returned with two bottles of his elixir. "This is all that's left, but it will do." He put the neck of a bottle to my lips. "Drink, boy. Your stomach's been empty for a spell, so this will paralyze you right quick."

I drank deep. The stuff tasted awful but it felt warm in my belly and my head began to swim.

"More," Doc said. "Get it down."

Draining that bottle, I started on the other and I was halfways to being drunk.

"How you feeling, boy?" Doc asked.

"Fine." I hiccuped. "Jest fine, ol' birdy head Doc."

"Now?" Georgia asked Doc.

"Sure," Doc said. "Me an' this cowboy here, we're gonna sing, ain't we boy?"

"Sing? Why sure we is gonna sing," I said.

" 'Oh, dem golden slippers,' " Doc began in his high tenor voice, " 'Oh, dem golden slippers.' C'mon boy, sing."

" 'Golden slippers I'm gwine to wear . . .' " I whispered.

"That's it, boy. Sing. 'We're marchin' to glory.' "

I saw him nod at Georgia.

" '. . . because they look so neat,' " Doc sang.

I felt the knife cut into my back, a pain like I'd never known in my life. It took everything I had in me to bite back the scream that, all unbidden, sprang to my lips.

"Sing, boy," Doc said. "Sing!"

" 'Oh, dem . . . dem . . . golden slippers,' " I gasped. The knife cut deep and I was screaming through lips that was tight shut.

" 'Oh, dem golden slippers,' " Doc sang. He had both my hands in his'n and he was squeezing them hard.

"Sing it with me, boy," he yelled. " 'Halleujah! Hallelujah! Golden slippers I'm gwine to wear . . .' Sing it!"

" 'To walk . . . to walk . . .' "

" 'Glory! Glory! Glory!' " Doc yelled. "Sing it loud!"

" '. . . to walk de golden streets . . .' " I gasped. "Doc, I'm gonna puke an' I'm gonna pee my pants!"

"Dammit! Sing boy. 'Oh, dem golden slippers—' "

"I got it!" Georgia yelled.

She held high the chewed up revolver ball, then she took me in her arms and I laid my head against her huge bosom and I sobbed like a baby.

Georgia patted my shoulders. "There, there," she crooned, like I was just a hurtin' little 'un.

I guess I passed out then, because when I woke I was leaning against the wagon wheel, covered in my ragged mackinaw, and a bright moon hung in the sky above me.

Looking around, I saw Georgia standing close to the wagon, her Winchester in her hands. Doc stood beside her. He saw me stir.

"I think our patient is awake," he told Georgia, and he kneeled down beside me.

I tried to move my left arm, but it was bound up tight to my chest. I glanced down and saw that a piece of Georgia's petticoat was wrapped around me so snug I could scarcely breathe.

"How you feeling, boy?" Doc asked.

"Terrible," I said. "I reckon that busthead of your'n done for me."

"You've got a bullet hole in you, your shoulder's broke and you've got a pair of busted ribs," Doc said, his head cocked to the side. "Apart from that you're just fine."

"Johnny Blue?"

"He never came in. An' we got other woes. Up there." Doc waved an arm toward the hill above us. I saw the distant flicker of a fire among the trees.

"Injuns?" I asked.

"Seems like," Doc said. "But don't worry none. I can't shoot a rifle with my head this way, but I got your Colt and Georgia's ready."

"When they come, they'll come at first light," I said. "Give me my rifle, Doc."

Doc handed me my Winchester. "When you got hit, it flew out of your hands a considerable piece. Took me a while to find it."

He settled the rifle across my knees and studied me closely, an odd expression on his face like he was sizing me up.

"How long you been riding herd, son?" he asked.

I shook my head. "I don't know. Since I were a younker, I guess. When I was twelve, thirteen maybe. Came up the Goodnight-Loving Trail out of San Antone when I were sixteen."

Doc nodded. "You're a skinny little feller, right enough, but them years has made you tough as an old boot. You should be dead, you know. That wound you got would've killed civilized folks."

"Right now," I said, "I don't feel so tough. Hell, I cried like a baby."

Doc rose to his feet. "Crying don't make a man any less of a man. Better rest up now," he said. "I got a feeling there's gonna be tryin' times ahead."

Cranking a shell into the chamber of the Winchester, a difficult job with one hand, I watched the hillside as Doc went back and stood beside Georgia.

The tall pines cast thin blue shadows on the moonlit snow and the night was so still and quiet a man could hear his heartbeat. There was no sound from the Indian camp, but their fire burned bright through the trees and every now and then I heard one of their ponies snort and thump a hoof on the frozen ground.

Raising up my legs, I laid my chin on my knees. I felt weak as a day-old kittlin and the pain in my shoulder and back was a constant, nagging ache. But just like that Indian fire up there, it was burning hot right where my heart should be.

Johnny Blue had been took, or he was dead, and what was between Amos Pinkney and me was now personal. Before, I'd had a cause. As Doc once said, me and him and Johnny Blue and Georgia was crusaders, riding out to save our nation from the horrors of a second civil war.

But now that was gone. It had died with Johnny Blue.

All that was left in me now was a hatred for Amos Pinkney that was so bitter, it tasted like green bile in my throat.

I made my mind up that night that I was going to kill him. And nothing, not Indians, not my hurtin', not starvation or the winter cold, not even hell itself was going to stop me.

I knew I couldn't sit there like an invalid. I had to get up on my own two feet again. I rose and my head started to swim and I leaned against the wagon for support. Doc came running up to me, but I waved him away.

"Let me be," I said. "Jest leave me be."

The cloth that bound up my shoulder was tied up with a knot, and, despite Georgia's cry of protest, I undone it and let my arm free.

"You can't use that arm," Georgia said. "Your shoulder bone's all shot to pieces."

"Help me get my coat on," I said.

Gritting my teeth against the pain, I struggled into my mackinaw and set my hat on my head.

"Man can't shoot a rifle with one hand," I said.

Georgia's face was shocked. "You won't be able to stand the pain. You'll faint away for sure."

"I'll stand it," I said. "I got a job to do. After it's all over, you can bind me up again."

"Cowboy," Georgia said, "there ain't that much of you left to bind up."

"Then so be it," I replied.

Turning to Doc, I said, "There's maybe three, four hours until first light. I'm confident them Injuns won't attack until then. I'm gonna go look for Johnny Blue, and if'n I ain't back in an hour, get you and Georgia into the wagon and split tail for Gruber's post."

"We'll wait for you," Doc said.

"Doc," I said, "you heard what I tole you."

"I heard." Doc smiled. "And I said we'll wait for you."

They stood there under that hanging moon, little scrawny Doc with his head on one side, and Georgia, huge in her dress and cape, with her Sunday best bonnet askew on her curls and a Winchester rifle in her hands.

I don't know where sand comes from. Maybe it's born in a person, like a gift from God. Or maybe it's a seed that's planted and grows just when it's needed. Maybe there are some folks don't ever have that seed. But wherever it comes from, this unlikely couple had sand in spades.

I turned to go. "Good luck to both of you," I said.

"Wait," Doc said. "I just want to say, we've come a long way together, us and you. It's been a privilege."

I nodded my thanks, then said, "Funny thing is, me an' Johnny Blue, all we ever wanted was a warm place to spend the winter."

Doc smiled. "What happened?"

"Life happened, Doc," I said. "Life has a way of sneakin' up on a man an' spoilin' all his best laid plans."

"Well, take care of yourself," Doc said.

"Yeah, you too."

I took up my rifle in my hands, and crossed the trail and walked up the hill into the trees.

THIRTY-FOUR

Johnny Blue's bootprints was plain in the snow and I had no problem following them. He said he was a black man in the dark, but he didn't reckon on the white petticoat around his head and the bright moon. He was no good at sneakin' up on folks either, though he always said he was, and he wore them California-style jinglebob spurs you could hear coming from a mile away.

I moved through the timber, bent low, but the throbbing pain in my shoulder and lower back made me stop often, gasping against the hurt and leaning against a tree for support.

Johnny Blue's prints climbed the hill, then started back down again at a point maybe three hunnerd yards south of the wagon.

He'd seen something that made him slow up considerable, because here his prints were much closer together like he was moving as quietly as he could.

Despite the freezing cold, my palms were sweaty and I took turns switching the rifle from hand to hand to wipe them on my pants.

Johnny Blue's prints vanished into the trees below me. I followed them, my eyes scanning into every bright, moon-splashed clearing and dark-shadowed ravine.

I saw nothing. And the only sound was my own hard breathing. I stopped, listening.

Then, ahead of me, an owl woke up and ruffled his feathers, sending snow drifting down from his lofty perch high in the timber. I don't know if he saw me or smelled me, but he immediately started to question the darkness, asking who I was.

Keeping to Johnny Blue's prints, I walked on again.

Something moved to my right, higher on the hillside. It was quick, just a flitting shadow that showed dark for a split second across the white surface of the snow, then vanished.

Then I saw another, and another. Furtive shadows trotting swiftly through the trees, noiseless as ghosts.

The timberwolves had smelled the blood on me, and their hunger drove them to be curious, but wary.

As far as I could recollect, wolves had never been known to attack a man, though I'd often seen them hang on the edges of a trailing herd hoping to pull down a sick cow or a straggling calf.

Though I believed I'd nothing to fear from them, the wolf pack made me a mite uneasy as it kept pace with me, keeping maybe twenty-five yards away as I descended the hill and followed Johnny Blue's tracks.

There was an animal trail through the trees and horses had come this way. I saw where Johnny Blue had cut their sign and followed.

The trail led deeper into the timber and it was darker here because the moonlight was filtered through the high canopy of the trees.

Kneeling down on the snow, I caught my breath

and let the waves of pain and nausea from my wounds sweep through me and pass. Then I took stock of my situation.

I reckoned the wagon was maybe half a mile behind me, and given that Johnny Blue had gone after Pinkney and his boys soon after they'd called to us from the timber, it was unlikely they'd ridden much farther than this.

If they'd ambushed Johnny Blue, they'd done it somewhere around here.

Rising, I cast around for a while, looking for signs of a struggle, but saw nothing. The wolves were all around me, standing half in, half out of the deepest shadows. Watching. And waiting with a patience that was nothing human.

Bending down, I scraped together a snowball and threw it with my good arm at a big gray lobo that was skulking around the base of a tree. There wasn't much force in my throw, but my aim was good and I hit the wolf smack on the snout. He yelped, then turned and trotted off, shaking snow from his head, doing his best to hold on to his dignity.

I picked up my rifle again and followed the horse tracks. After a dozen yards I came to a place where the snow was flattened. There were bootprints all over. Something dark stained the snow at my feet and I prodded at it with my toe and saw it was blood.

This is where they'd jumped Johnny Blue. And someone had been hurt in the struggle.

Beyond this area, the horse tracks started again, and there was a single set of bootprints between them, wide spaced, like the man who'd made them was running.

Me, I don't pretend to be a tracker, but it was pretty obvious that someone had roped Johnny Blue and then drug him behind his horse.

He was alive, or at least he'd been at this point, and that gave me a glimmer of hope.

I was about to turn and head back down the hill to the trail when something caught my eye. It looked like a man, standing still in the darkness, watching me. He stood just to the right of the path taken by Pinkney's horses.

My rifle up near to my shoulder, I walked toward the man. He just stood there unmoving, letting me come, making no attempt to pull a gun. As I got closer and my eyes penetrated the gloom, what I'd taken to be a man turned out to be a stunted fir, with a hat jammed on to the top of it. Johnny Blue's hat.

Something white gleamed on the front of the hat, stuck into the band. It was a scrap of paper torn from Johnny Blue's little tally book.

Walking into a bright patch of moonlight, I could just make out the words, written in pencil in block capitals like I'd learned in school:

> SKUM,
> WE GOT THE NEGRO. GO
> AWAY. COME AFTER US
> AND I SKIN HIM ALIVE.

And it was signed: JERICHO GENTLE

I was glad Pinkney planned on keeping Johnny Blue alive. For the time being at least.

I stuck the note in my pocket and took Johnny Blue's hat and walked down the hill to the trail. Behind me the wolves howled among the trees. I guess they wanted me to know they wasn't scared of me, or my snowballs.

When I reached the wagon, Doc and Georgia were still on guard, watching the Indian camp.

That note had given me plenty to think about, though I was so plumb exhausted from my climb through the timber and from the pain that burned like fire in my shoulder and back, that I couldn't seem to get my brain to work.

I handed Doc the note and after he read it, he said: "This is bad, son. There's no way to talk around it."

"Tell me something I don't already know, Doc," I said. "Now all this has become real close to home, and I'm getting madder by the minute. There's personal business waitin' to be settled between me and Amos Pinkney."

"Me and Georgia, we've been talking," Doc said. "We're still in it. We'll stick with it to the end."

"Doc, I wouldn't take it hard if'n you was to ride out of here," I said. "Things being the way they are an' all."

Doc shook his head at me. "Man's got to do what he thinks is right. Woman, too, for that matter."

"Georgia," I said, "this set square with you?"

The large lady nodded. "Doc said it. We'll stick."

"Now, the first thing we do is—" Doc began, but Georgia cut him short.

"First thing this boy does is lie down in the wagon and get a few hours' rest." She took my arm and guided me toward the wagon. "You're dead on your feet and you ain't going to be much use to anybody, including Johnny Blue, unless you get some sleep."

I saw the logic in what Georgia was saying and I lay down in the back of the wagon. I fell into a deep slumber almost immediately.

It seemed that I'd only been asleep for a few minutes when Doc shook me awake. But the night had already become a cold, gray dawn and I reckoned I'd been out for several hours.

"Looks like the Indians are gone," Doc said. "I can't figger it."

Struggling to my feet, I found I could barely move my left arm an inch or two, and my shoulder and back felt numb. The cold had stiffened up my wounds and it would take hours of sun to warm me to life again. If there was any sun.

"Blizzard's coming," Doc said. "I can smell it in the wind."

Gray clouds hung low over the mountains all the way down to the timberline, a sure sign of a coming whiteout. And we'd no place to hide from it.

"If you don't mind me saying so, my boy," Doc continued, "you look like hell. Right about now, I'd say you was the whitest white man I've ever seen."

Me, I hadn't shaved in weeks and my mustache was all tangled up in the beard I'd grown. My mustache was one of them sweeping cavalry models that was popular with Texas and Montana punchers then, and in better times I'd spent a lot of time cultivating it. Now it didn't scarcely seem to matter.

The Indian fire was gone from the hillside, and all I could see among the trees up there was a cold, bleak emptiness.

"Give me back my Colt, Doc," I said. "I'm going up

there to take a look-see. I want to know what those In-juns is up to an' where they've gone."

"Do you think that's wise?" Doc asked. "You ain't in any condition to go climbing that hill."

"If I stay here, I'll freeze up for sure," I said. "I'll never move again."

Toting the Winchester up there was beyond my strength, I knew, but I figgered I could handle the Colt if circumstances called for it. I holstered the gun and said, "Doc, Georgia, if I ain't back in an hour, hightail it."

"Not a chance, cowboy," Georgia said. "We'll wait for you."

I leaned over and kissed her on the cheek, some-thing I'd never done to a woman before, and then I started for the hill.

When I was halfway up toward the place where the Indians had camped, what little strength I had began to give out.

I staggered and fell, got myself to my feet and fell again. Once I tumbled over a low creek bank and landed on my back on the hard ice, which sent a jolt of lightning through my body and made me cry out in pain.

It seemed that every agonizing step I took wrenched a gasp from my lips, and the only thing that kept me going was my hatred of Amos Pinkney. That, and the certain knowledge that I'd kill him. Or die trying.

The Nez Perce couldn't be allowed to interfere with that.

I reached the clearing where the Indians had camped. Their sign was everywhere, and I scouted out to my right beyond the encampment and saw that their ponies had trailed south.

For some reason they hadn't attacked. But they were now ahead of us, and I guessed the Chief would pick the time and the where for an ambush.

Then so be it.

I am not a brave man, nor, most folks who know me would agree, a foolhardy one. But if I had to fight Indians to get to Pinkney, I would.

I doubled back to the camp. Beyond the clearing, about a hundred yards away, rose a massive rocky bluff, an outcrop of ancient rock that stood like a sentinel guarding the cloud-covered peaks.

Something lay on a ledge low on the bluff that I hadn't noticed before. It was long, and wrapped in a red trade blanket, and I knew it could only be a body.

Resisting a sudden, frightened urge to pull my Colt, I struggled through knee-deep snow to the bluff and reached the narrow outcrop where the body lay.

Mostly, if they have the time, Indians will lay their dead in a tree or build a four-legged platform of pine poles for the corpse. But there were no suitable trees around here nor poles for building. So they'd done their best, laying the man on the ledge beyond the reach of the wolves.

Up here the wind blew strong and bitter cold, and it teased a corner of the red blanket, flapping and curling it up and down like it was beckoning me to come closer.

Me, I felt the hair rise on the back of my neck and I wanted to get away from that place and the awful stillness of the Indian corpse. But something, looking back, maybe it was just curiosity, or the urge to see a thing I'd never see again, made me climb up onto the ledge and take a look at the dead man.

It wasn't much of a climb, just six feet or so with plenty of places to put my feet, but it drained what was left of my strength. I sat beside the dead man and leaned my head against the rock, gasping against the torture of my shoulder and back.

The ledge was maybe three feet deep and it had been cleared of snow by the Indians, but frost covered the surface of the rock and whitened the red of the dead warrior's blanket.

Once I'd recovered some, I eased the blanket away from the corpse's face—and looked right into the brave's wide open, staring eyes.

That gave me a start and I jerked back. But the warrior didn't move. And when I looked at him again I saw that he was beyond all movement.

He was old, this Indian. His face was deeply wrinkled, and even in death it was etched with pain and grief and suffering.

The wind caught the thin, gray wisps of his hair and pushed it here and there, and that, along with his open eyes, made it look like he was alive again.

All them eyes was seeing now was eternity, but I reckoned they'd gazed upon sights no man would ever see again. This warrior had been young when buffalo covered the plains in their millions, and his ears had heard the slap of a beaver tail in places where the white man hadn't as yet set foot.

Now the buffalo was all gone and the mountain creeks and pools that had been home to the beaver was empty and deathly quiet.

This old man had seen it all, and then he'd seen it

go. And maybe that explained the pain that must have dwelled inside him for many a long year.

A beaded, cornhusk bag lay on the dead warrior's chest, and I opened it up. The bag held lumps of roasted antelope meat and some slices of dried apple and a few berries. A twenty-dollar double eagle gold piece glinted in a corner.

Boys, it's no small thing to rob the dead, but my duty was to the living.

"Someday I'll come back here and return all the things I took from you," I told that Indian. "If I live."

I sure hope he heard me, because I'd taken his cornhusk bag and eased the thick trade blanket out from under his body. Then I climbed back down off'n the ledge.

Wrapping the blanket around my shoulders, I hunkered down in the snow, cold, weak and mighty discouraged. Now I was driven to robbing corpses, and I wondered how much lower I'd sink before this was all over.

The dead Indian was laying on his side. After my struggle to remove his blanket I didn't have the strength to lay him on his back again. His eyes were still open and he seemed to be looking at me only with pity, not disapproval.

We just stayed there looking at each other, me and him, for a long spell. Me, I was full of hate, a hate all mixed up with anxiety for Johnny Blue and a growing fear for what the future might bring.

And him, all he knew right now was peace and the bounty of the afterlife.

Right then, I would have traded places with him in

a moment and figgered I'd gotten the best of the bargain.

One time Charlie Russell told me the way the Blackfeet thought on life and death. Me, I hadn't paid much heed to him at the time, but now I knowed what he was talking about.

"What is life to an Indian?" Charlie had said. "It is the flash of a firefly in the night. It is the breath of the buffalo in the wintertime. It is the little shadow which runs across the grass and loses itself in the sunset."

Charlie, he'd been whittlin' on a piece of wood, and he gave me what he'd made, a tiny buffalo. "The thing I just tole you is what the Indian thinks, and the wise man knows it's more about living than it is about dying," he said.

I still had that little buffalo. Digging in my mackinaw pocket, I found it and held it in my hand.

Thus it was that I held the buffalo and thought on what Charlie had said. And I sat there for a long time in the snow, having locked myself in a dark and brooding place of my soul.

Then Doc came up the hill, took my arm and led me back to the wagon. He did not chide me.

Later, we shared the food I'd found and I began to feel a little stronger. My arm had enough movement in it now that I believed I could handle a rifle if I was put to it.

The last few oats were given to the horses, then I tied Johnny Blue's buckskin behind the wagon and mounted my paint, riding a hundred yards out in front.

We traveled for the rest of that day, and I didn't see

any sign of Pinkney and his Texans. I was glad of that because, tired and hurting as I was, I felt in no condition for a fight.

The Indians too, stayed out of sight up in the hills, but I could feel their presence and it seemed to me that every tree had a pair of eyes.

Black clouds covered the mountains and had come so low they hung like a thick mist among the pines of the timberline. The sky above us piled cloud on cloud, like heavy rolls of lead.

"She's coming," Doc said after I reined in my pony and let the wagon catch up.

I nodded. "Lookee yonder," I said. "If'n we're gonna ride her out, that looks as good a place as any."

The hill to our right was covered in huge slabs of rock, and a landslip had piled brush and logs between them, piling up a wall maybe twelve feet high. The logs and other debris overhung the rock a good five feet in places, forming a natural cave.

"There's shelter there from the wind," I continued. "Maybe deep under the rocks we can even build a fire. We don't want to be anywhere on that trail when the blizzard hits."

Night was falling fast as Doc drove the wagon under the overhang, which wasn't near as sheltering as it looked from the trail. He unhitched the team, then unsaddled me and Johnny Blue's ponies, figgering when the whiteout struck, they'd be better off fending for themselves.

Then we waited.

THIRTY-FIVE

We found enough wood to make a damp, smoky little fire at the back of the cave that gave no warmth and less light.

In any event, the blizzard struck an hour later with terrible fury, and the few miserable flames quickly guttered out.

The whiteout raged for the next three days.

Midway through the first night, cold drove us from the cave and we huddled in the wagon, the three of us laying close under the dead Indian's blanket.

The wagon shook and creaked as the wind howled its frustration that we'd found even this pitiful shelter, and spitefully sought to cover us in a white shroud of snow.

I don't believe any of us said a single word while the blizzard roared beyond the thin canvas cover of the wagon. Once I fell asleep and woke up with a start, thinking I heard Johnny Blue calling to me.

Grabbing my rifle, I started up, but Georgia saw me and pulled me down beside her. There was no way to talk against the howling wind, but she smiled and shook her head. Then she took me under one massive arm, like a momma hen with a chick, and she lulled me to sleep again.

Then on the third night, the dead Indian came.

I heard my name called over and over, and I knew it was him, standing out there in the storm, his gray hair tossing in the wind, his eyes wide open.

Doc and Georgia were asleep, or unconscious from the cold, I knew not which, so I took up my rifle and I creeped out of the wagon.

The horses were standing in the shelter of the overhang cave, slat thin, their heads down, as cold and miserable as any animals could be. They didn't even move to look at me as I walked past them toward the dead man who was bawling out my name.

He stood there behind the driving curtain of snow, the wind blowing the gray hair across his face, just as I'd imagined it would. Beside him hunched a great lobo wolf, and the Indian had his hand on the wolf's head.

"I know why you've come!" I yelled above the storm. "I et the food. I et all of it, the antelope meat and the apple."

The Indian only smiled, and though he didn't raise his voice, I heard him plain. "It was mine to give."

"I stole it," I hollered. "Stole it plain and simple then et it. And the double eagle, I took that, too. And the red trade blanket. I stole it all."

"I no longer have the need for such things," the Indian said. "Why should I keep a blanket when you are freezing? Why should I hoard food when you are hungry? Why should I keep money when I have nowhere to spend it? This is not the way of the Indian."

"If I live, I'll return everything," I yelled.

The old warrior shook his head. "There is no need.

All these things were mine, and I give them to you freely. This is something I wanted you to know."

"Where will you go?" I said. "There is a terrible storm."

"I will go where you and your people cannot follow," the Indian said. "Where I go, there is buffalo and beaver and the summer grass is as tall as a man on a horse. There are no white men in that place."

"I will go with you," I said. "I'm so cold here. And I'm shot through and through."

But the old Indian shook his head at me. "This is not the time or the season for you." He stroked the snow-covered fur on the lobo wolf's head. "Farewell, and beware of this one," he said. "He is hungry. It is his way. He kills without hate and only to live, and this is a good thing. A thing we could learn perhaps."

I glanced down at the wolf's red eyes in the snowy darkness, and when I looked up the old Indian was gone. The lobo came toward me then, head low and moving slowly from side to side, his teeth drawn back in a snarl.

"God dammit!"

Doc fired my Colt so close to my head my ears rung. I saw snow kick up between the wolf's front paws. The wolf turned and ran into the darkness.

Thumbing back the hammer, Doc fired again, holding the Colt straight out in front of him. But this time he was shooting at shadows.

Georgia was out of the wagon, guiding me back to its thin shelter.

"He was out here all alone talking to a damned wolf!" Doc yelled, the snow in his teeth. "He's gone plumb loco."

Once back in the wagon, Georgia rubbed snow on my forehead. "He's burning up with fever, Doc," I heard her say. "That bullet he took caused a bad wound."

"Will he live?" Doc asked, his head on his shoulder, his eyes wide with concern.

"I don't know," Georgia said. "Today and the next day will tell the story. If the fever breaks, he'll live. If it doesn't, we'll bury him."

I tried to talk, to tell her about the dead Indian. But I felt a darkness descend on me and I gratefully sank into its peaceful nothingness.

I woke to see Georgia's face leaning over me. "You've decided to join us," she said.

"How long have I been out?" I asked. My lips were parched and hunger gnawed at my stomach.

"Two days, more or less," Georgia said. "Blizzard blew itself out yesterday."

I made to get up. "We gotta move," I said.

But Georgia pushed me back. "It's night, cowboy. We're not going anywhere."

She put a cup to my lips. "Melted snow," she said. "It will quench your thirst."

Drinking deeply, I found I was hungrier than ever, and something smelled good. Georgia took up another cup and a spoon and she put the spoon to my lips. "Broth. It will do you good. Give you strength."

"How—?"

"Doc shot a jackrabbit with the Colt's gun. An old, slow jackrabbit, else Doc would have missed it."

Between spoonfuls of the jackrabbit broth, I asked

Georgia to fill me in on what had happened while I was unconscious.

"Nothing much," she said. "You were out of your head with a fever. Doc, he brought you inside night before last. You were out there freezing to death, talking to a big lobo wolf."

"And the Indian," I said.

"Boy, there was no Indian. Nothing could live out there in that storm. Nothing human, that is."

"But that's just it," I said. "He wasn't human, the Indian. He was a ghost or a spirit, an' he come to tell me it was fine by him that I taken his food an' his blanket an' his gold coin."

"You were talking to a wolf, was all," Doc said. "I come out with the Colt when I seen you gone and you was out there talking to the biggest, hungriest lobo I'd ever seen."

The broth was gone and I lay back, staring at the canvas roof of the wagon. "The Indian said the wolf kills without anger an' without hate," I said. "I got so much anger an' hate in me, it's making me sick to my stomach. I wish I could take a knife an' cut it out of me like you cut out a bullet. Then I'd take it an' throw it away."

"Amos Pinkney, he done that to you, boy," Doc said. "He done wrong by you, and yours."

Raising myself up on one elbow, I said, "Doc, I'm gonna kill him. I'm gonna shoot him down like the mad dog he is. Maybe then the hate will go."

"Maybe," Doc said. He still couldn't straighten his head and it lay on his skinny shoulder. "Or maybe killing him won't solve anything and the hate will always claw at your insides, and you'll never get rid of it. And no matter what you do and no matter where you go, you'll never be the same man as you once was."

Me, I lay back again and covered my eyes with my arm.

"This is a thing we could learn, perhaps," Doc continued.

I jerked straight up and looked at him.

Doc, he only smiled.

Come daybreak I rose and took stock of our situation.

First thing I done was to check the bullet hole in my shoulder. The flesh around the wound was less red, less angry and it didn't smell, which I took to be a good sign. I reckoned the cut on my back was the same way. When I tried it, my shoulder felt a lot easier, and I could heft my Winchester pretty good.

The horses had all survived the blizzard, though they was in a sorry state, and I doubted they had more than another day of hard riding in them.

Snow covered the wagon to the top of the cover on the side away from the log cave, and we'd have to abandon it. It would've taken six strong men half a day to dig it out, and we didn't have the men or that kind of time.

A heavy frost had followed the storm, and when I walked down to look at it, the snow on the trail was hard-packed with an icy sheen covering it, but it seemed like it would allow the passage of horses.

Back at the wagon, I saddled my pony and Johnny Blue's buckskin. I reckoned Doc could ride one of the team, though he'd have to do it bareback with only the Indian blanket between him and the horse's sharp bones.

"I'll survive," Doc said. "I've rode worse."

He handed me a scrap of jackrabbit bone with some burned meat sticking to it. "Gnaw on this. It might be all the food you're gonna see for a long time."

I ate what Doc had given me, then rounded off my breakfast with a handful of snow.

Georgia came out of the wagon and slammed her Winchester into the boot of Johnny Blue's saddle. Her once plump cheeks had started to thin out some, and she looked haggard and deathly tired. But she mounted the buckskin limber enough, and waited patiently for Doc to scramble onto the back of the team horse.

Mounting up, I kneed my pony toward the trail, but Doc jumped back off his horse. "Wait up," he said, "I got to get something."

He ran back to the wagon, rummaged inside for a few minutes, then returned with a bulging burlap sack tied at the neck with a string of rawhide.

"What you got there, Doc?" I asked.

"Something we might need," was all Doc said.

He took the sack to Georgia's pony and tied it to the saddle horn. "Take care of this, my love," he told her.

Georgia nodded without speaking.

Like me and Doc, the strain on her was beginning to tell, and like the rest of us she was riding the last reserves of her strength and wanted only to see this thing over and done with.

We took to the trail and, like I'd guessed, the surface of the wagon road was good and firm because of the icy cold. Even the horses, half-starved as they was, began to perk up some, glad to be going somewheres at last.

It had been now six days since Johnny Blue had been taken. Was he still alive? Or had Amos Pinkney reckoned we weren't coming and just shot him out of hand?

As we rode, I asked myself a lot of questions and came up with mighty few answers.

And above all was the biggest question, the one that would make the difference between us living or dying when the shooting started: What was I going to do when we reached Pinkney's cabin?

Me, I didn't have an answer for that one either.

We'd been on the trail for about three hours when I saw Georgia begin to sit up in the saddle and take notice of her surroundings.

I asked her if she recognized the country, but she shook her head at me. "I don't know," she said. "Like I told you, I only came here once or twice with Cottontail and always in the summer. Everything looks different because of the snow."

"Keep lookin', Georgia," I told her. "I got the feelin' we're almighty close."

We saw the Indians about an hour later.

It was Doc who spotted them first. "Lookee," he said. "Up on the hill."

They rode through the timber, keeping pace with us. Not one warrior's head turned to look at us. They kept their eyes straight ahead, but I reckoned they saw everything we were doing.

"Will this come to a fight?" Doc asked.

"I reckon," I said.

"Maybe we should find a place to fort up," Doc suggested. "We can stand them off, maybe."

"I don't see anywhere," I said. "This is rough country, but it's open."

"We can't fight them on the trail."

"No, we can't," I said. "If they come at us down that hill, we'll break to our right an' dismount when we reach the timber. Maybe we can hold them off with the Winchesters from there."

"Son, there's twenty of them," Doc said mildly.

"I know," I said.

THIRTY-SIX

The Indians kept pace with us for the next couple of miles, making no move to attack. Once I spurred my pony toward them, to see what they'd make of it, but they retreated higher into the timber. When I rode back to the trail, they came down and took up their original position.

"Never can tell what an Indian's thinking," Doc said. "You figger you've got them pegged, then they'll do the very opposite of what you thought they'd do."

"That's what makes 'em Injuns, I guess," I said.

Georgia suddenly started up in her saddle. "That rock!" she said. "I remember that rock. The valley cuts off close to here, between a pair of low hills to the right."

A spire of rock jutted tall and slender out of the hillside, looking for all the world like a church's steeple.

"You sure?" I asked.

"For certain sure," Georgia replied. "We'll see the valley in an hour, maybe less."

I looked up at the sky, which was blue and cloudless. The sun was shining bright and I felt it touch my face with warmth. Except for the snow on the ground, it was like the blizzard had never been, and that we'd all three dreamed it.

"We got maybe four, five hours until dark," I said. "You two want we should go ahead an' get the job done?"

"I'm game," Doc said. "It's been too long in coming already."

Georgia nodded. "Let's get it over with," she said.

Doc, his little bird head cocked on his shoulder, said to no one in particular, "I wonder if any of us will see the moon come up tonight?"

I checked the loads in my Colt and cranked a round into the chamber of my Winchester. Then I took it upon myself to reply to Doc for me and Georgia.

"Only God can answer that one, Doc," I said.

But that was a lie.

I could have answered Doc's question easy enough, and the truthful answer was that the moon would spend a long time tonight looking for us on the trail and in the hills among the tall timber, and maybe even in our abandoned wagon. But he wouldn't find us.

We'd be gone from this place.

Boys, I guess right about now you're thinking I was beat before I'd even started. So be it. But that's how I felt in my insides, and I couldn't shake it.

Amos Pinkney's valley was right where Georgia said it would be. It angled off to the southwest between two shallow, brush-covered hills. Beyond these rose higher hills studded with pine, and above all these were the mountains, rising in blue-hazed majesty, their snow-covered peaks touching the sky.

We entered the valley, then cut to our right to put the crest of the hill between us and anyone who might be watching from the cabin.

Turning in my saddle, I saw the Indians knee their ponies in single file down the steep slope to the left of the spire rock. Their rifles were at the ready, and even at this distance I could see both them and their horses was painted for war.

Doc was looking at me, his face concerned. But there was no way to jaw around this. It looked bad. We was about to fight Amos Pinkney and his Texans, and a war party of twenty Indians. Both at the same time.

Now you know how come I said all that stuff about the moon an' all. Boys, sometimes it takes a crazy man to be an optimist.

We rode for a mile or so along the base of the hill, and somewhere along the way the Indians vanished from sight. But they were still there. And so close I could smell them.

Georgia reined in her pony. "The cabin sets midway down the valley," she said. She pointed to the crest of the hill. "I think it's right over there."

She swayed in her saddle and for a moment I thought she'd fall off her pony.

I took her arm and said: "Georgia, are you feelin' all right?"

"I'm fine, I'm fine," she said.

"I thought you was about to faint," I said.

"It's him." Georgia shuddered. "The Major. I can sense his presence. It's like just by riding into this valley he destroyed its beauty and turned it rank and rotten. This place has the stench of death. The Major carries it with him and it rubs off on everything he touches, including me."

"Beloved," Doc said. He rode up beside Georgia

and she laid her head on his good shoulder. He patted her broad back as she sobbed.

Me, I stepped down off my pony and, crouching low, ran to the top of the hill. I covered the last few yards on my belly and looked down into the valley.

And saw Johnny Blue.

This must have been a beautiful enough place in summer. In winter, it was calculated to take a man's breath away.

The cabin, built snug and tight against the cold, nestled nice amid a grove of red cedar. A thin plume of smoke drifted straight up from its roughstone chimney and a smell of burning pine logs hung in the air like incense. The main cabin had two windows facing me, both to the right of the door, and a dog trot separated it from a smaller storeroom with one window and no door to the front. Beyond the cabin was a well-built barn with a corral out front where eight horses stood and enjoyed the pale warmth of the afternoon sun.

Johnny Blue was tied upright in the dog trot, his arms and legs spread-eagled by ropes that angled tight from the corners, binding his wrists and ankles.

His shirt had been stripped from his body and lay over his hips in tatters. He was thus naked from the waist up and his head hung on his chest.

He didn't move.

Me, I guess I went a little crazy.

Getting up on one knee, in full view of the cabin, I fired at the window farthest away from the door. I saw a pane of glass shatter. I cranked the rifle and fired again, and again glass shattered and splashed out of the window frame in a million pieces.

I saw a stab of flame as someone fired at me from the cabin, kicking up snow at my knee. I ignored it, and fired again and once again.

Three rifles was firing at me from the cabin, and the snow was throwing up pretty good all around me.

"Get down, you dern fool, you'll get your head blown off!" Doc yelled. He dove at me and flattened me to the ground. The firing became general, and Doc lay beside Georgia, thumbing and firing my Colt as fast as he could work hammer and trigger.

There was a side door to the cabin I'd failed to see, because two men suddenly burst from it and ran across the dog trot into the storeroom. I sent a wild shot after them, but because of Johnny Blue, I was forced to fire high and wide.

We now came under heavy and accurate fire from the main cabin and the storeroom, which forced us to keep our heads down. Doc still persevered with the Colt, sticking it over the crest of the hill to shoot. But since he couldn't see what he was aiming at, he did no execution.

During a lull in the firing, Doc reloaded the Colt and said, "This is going to get us nowhere."

I nodded. "Nowhere but dead, Doc."

"I have a plan," Doc said. "If you'll agree to let me try."

"Go ahead," I said. "What have we got to lose?"

Doc got up on one knee and cupped his hands around his mouth. "You down there in the cabin!" he yelled.

"What the hell do you want?"

It was Pinkney's voice.

"We have twenty federal marshals here, determined

men and well armed and well mounted," Doc hollered. "Throw down your arms and come out with your hands up an' you'll all live to be hanged."

The only answer was Pinkney's mocking laugh and a flurry of shots that sent Doc diving for the snow.

"It didn't work, dear boy," he said.

"I noticed," I said.

We settled into a hopeless pattern of sniping at the cabin, then ducking back down when Pinkney and his gunmen opened up on us in reply.

One thing was certain: we couldn't go on like this.

Once night fell, the advantages would all be with Pinkney. He and his Texans was night riders who could move like phantoms in the dark, while Doc and me were sorely wounded and slow, and Georgia's great bulk made her an easy target.

A gunfight among these hills at night would be a disaster for us. We would have to pull back, out of the valley, and try again at daybreak tomorrow. Of course, by then the enemy would be expecting us and they'd be prepared.

And Johnny Blue would be dead, if'n he wasn't already.

I bit my bottom lip till it bled, thinking, trying to come up with another way. But there wasn't one. We was beat. We just didn't know it yet.

Then the Indians made their move. And now I knowed it.

They came out of the timber behind us, line abreast, their rifle butts resting on their thighs, ready and painted for war. The Chief rode in the middle of them, a single mottled eagle feather slanting down behind his head.

"Oh, my God," Doc gasped.

Georgia laid her face on the snow and began to sob. We all have our limits, and it seemed that brave lady had just discovered hers.

"Georgia," I said harshly. "Face them Injuns an' have your Winchester ready." I turned to Doc. "You, keep up your fire on the cabin."

I got to hand it to Georgia, she did as I told her, levering a round into her rifle, sobbing and snuffling as she done it.

She was game, that gal. Game as any I've met, man or woman.

Doc thumbed off a shot at the cabin, and the rifles answered. He ducked down behind the crest of the hill, then got up to fire again.

"Get ready, Georgia," I said. "They'll break and run at us any minute."

My breath was coming in short gasps, and fear was twisting at my gut with iron fingers. Despite the cold, my palms were sweaty where they touched the icy metal and wood of my Winchester, and I felt a real bad need to puke and pee at the same time.

The Indians kept coming. Slow. Seemingly in no hurry.

Throwing my rifle to my shoulder, I drew a bead on the Chief. Dammit, if I was going, he was a-coming with me.

To my surprise, the Chief held up his hand and his braves reined in their ponies. He then kneed his horse in my direction, stopping a few feet away. He made no move to level his rifle.

"Howdy, white man," the Chief said.

He was on the other side of the hill from the cabin,

but the bullets kept zipping over his head. He ignored them like they was gnats in the summertime.

"Howdy, Chief," I said. "Long time no see."

I taken my rifle from my shoulder, but I kept it nice and handy.

"I tried to talk them out of it," the Chief said. "But these men"—he waved a hand at the waiting warriors—"also want to fight in the white man's war. They know I counted coup, and they wish very much to do it for themselves."

My face must have shown my puzzlement, because the Chief continued, "This is the only war against the white man they have right now. It's better than nothing."

"You mean, you follered us all this way just to see who we was gonna fight?" I asked,

The Chief shrugged, a strange gesture coming from an Indian. "I figgered you were on the warpath. I didn't know with who, and these braves don't much care. They want in the fight, is all."

The Chief looked around. "I see the buffalo lady. Where is the buffalo man?"

"He's down there, tied to a stake," I said. "I don't know if'n he's alive or dead, but tell your braves when the shootin' starts to be careful."

"They will not harm the buffalo man," the Chief said. "His spirit is good and is one with ours."

Me, I was breathing easier now, and I smiled up at the Chief. "To tell you the plain truth, Chief," I said. "I thought you was gonna massacree us fer sure."

"Why is it, that when the Indian wins a battle, the white men always call it a massacre?" the Chief asked.

"I don't know Chief, an' that's a fact," I said. "But if'n you could help us win this battle, I'd surely appreciate it."

The Chief grunted and rode his pony to the crest of the hill. Now, I don't know what Amos Pinkney and his Texans thought, seeing a war chief of the Nez Perce nation up there looking down on them, but after a few moments of quiet—they was most surprised, I guess—they opened up on him.

Bullets kicked up snow all around him, but again he took no notice of them. When he'd seen all he wanted to see, he grunted again and rode his pony down the hill.

The Chief passed me without speaking, and went back to his braves. He sat his pony in front of them and spoke to them in their own tongue for a while. Then he threw his right arm up in the air, holding his rifle aloft, and them Injuns started in to whoopin' and hollerin' their war cries.

It were a gallant sight, and one I ain't likely to forget anytime soon.

Next thing I knew, them Indians rode past us and swarmed over the hill, shooting at the cabin as they went, and suddenly it sounded like there was a war going on, which I guess there was.

There was no windows to the back of the cabin, and the Indians quickly realized that bullets was useless against them stout log walls. So they all come round the front, charging them swift, thick-necked ponies of theirs up and down in front of the windows, firing their rifles and caterwauling like wildcats.

Me and Doc and Georgia commenced in to firing at the cabin every chance we got when there wasn't an

Injun on a spotted pony in the way, and pretty soon there wasn't an unbroken pane of glass in any of the cabin windows.

The Indians kept this up for a while, then they pulled off and started in to talking. So far we'd all burned up a heap of ammunition, but there had been no casualties on either side, which is how it happens in a gunfight like this sometimes.

"What's them redskins doing now?" Doc asked.

"Palavering," I said.

"This ain't a time for palavering, it's a time for fighting," Doc said.

"Tell them that," I said.

No sooner were the words out of my mouth than the Indians attacked again. It was the same as before, jest riding up and down outside the cabin, hollering and shooting.

But this time the Chief showed all of us his sand.

He rode his pony up to Johnny Blue, jumped off and began to cut the ropes that so cruelly bound that pathetic puncher.

Once Johnny Blue was free, The Chief threw him over the withers of his pony and mounted up behind him. He kicked his pony toward the hill—and all hell broke loose.

A man burst from the door of the storeroom, rapid firing a Colt in each hand. I recognized the tall, gaunt figure of Jericho Gentle. Gentle's face was all twisted up in hate and fury, and even above the din of battle I heard him scream and curse like a madman, which I reckon he was.

"Oh, no you don't, Mary Ann," Gentle hollered at the Chief's retreating back. "That nigger's mine!"

Gentle thumbed off a shot at the Chief, missed and fired again. A young brave came at him then, his pony running fast, the brave shooting and cranking his Winchester. I fired at Gentle and saw my bullet stagger him. Then a shot from the Indian drove him three or four steps backward, but Gentle kept on his feet, working his guns. Gentle's bullet smashed square into the young brave's chest and the Indian screamed and toppled off his pony into the snow.

An instant later I saw another brave fall as a shot from the cabin window cut him down.

Gentle turned to face a brave coming hard at him, a war lance raised high above the Indian's head. Gentle fired at the same time the Indian threw his lance. Gentle's bullet caught the Indian plumb between the eyes and the brave thudded off his horse into the snow just as the broad steel head of the lance buried itself in Gentle's thigh.

Screaming, Gentle dropped to one knee and fired at a brave charging straight toward him. He missed, then triggered the Colt in his left hand. The hammer clicked on a fired round. Gentle thumbed his second Colt, but it too had run dry. Yelling, his lips pulled back from his teeth in a defiant snarl, Gentle threw away his useless Colts and pulled a bowie knife from his boot, waving it straight out in front of him. The charging brave rode past, his Winchester in his left hand, held like a revolver. He fired a bullet into Gentle's head and the Texan fell. Gentle arched his back, his entire body held up by his head and heels, and lifted his knife straight into the air where it glinted in the late afternoon sun. Then he fell back and lay still.

Boys, you know me, I got no liking for Texans. But

if you're gonna fight one bring your lunch, because it's gonna take all day, and when it's over you'll think you've been in a sack with a grizzly.

I guess Jericho Gentle, bad as he was, had just proved that.

THIRTY-SEVEN

The Indians' fight with Gentle takes a long time in the telling, but it actually lasted only a few seconds.

As it was going on, the Chief's pony struggled up the hill, weighed down as it was by the extra load of Johnny Blue. But when he reached the crest of the hill, the Chief charged past us at a fast lope and threw Johnny Blue down beside me without slowing his pace. Then he rode back into the fight.

Johnny Blue lay on his back and I kneeled beside him and cradled his head in my arms.

"Johnny Blue," I said. "Are you alive?"

That reviving rider's eyes fluttered open. He saw me, and he groaned, "Oh, God, it's you again."

"Like who was you maybe expectin'?" I asked. "Lily Langtry?"

Despite his protests, because he was as weak as a kittlin', I eased Johnny Blue into a sitting position. Then I saw his back.

It was crisscrossed with huge, red welts. Most of them oozed blood where the skin was broken, and they stretched from his neck and shoulders to his lower back.

"Jesus, Mary and Joseph," Georgia said, crossing herself. "Who did this to you, boy?"

"Amos Pinkney," Johnny Blue said. "This is what him and his kind do to niggers who won't work. They give them a taste o' the lash."

"But how—" I began.

"He ordered me to fetch and carry for him," Johnny Blue said. "Clean out the barn and the outhouse, stuff he called darkie work. Me, I spit in his eye, so he strung me up in the dog trot and gave me what he said was thirty 'o the best. He counts real good, ol' Pink. He didn't miss nary a one."

Doc had run to his horse. He now returned with the Indian blanket, which he gently draped around Johnny Blue's shoulders.

"Me, I'm gonna kill that son-of-a-bitch," I said.

Johnny Blue shook his head at me. "Ain't you had a bellyful of killing yet? Pinkney lashed me because he wanted me to feel I was less than a man, that I was some kind of black animal bred for work," he said. "Maybe he succeeded, I don't know. Me, I don't even know how I feel. The scars on my back will heal, but I got others I'm carrying inside me and I don't know if'n they're ever gonna get better.

"But if you kill him, you *will* feel a heap less than you was before because Pinkney has a poison in him and it will infect you and rot you from the inside for the rest of your life.

"Best you let him go."

"Let him go?" I yelled. "Are you plumb crazy?"

"Maybe," Johnny Blue said. "Or maybe I'm the only one left around here who's still sane."

I left Johnny Blue then as he sat in the snow, staring

straight ahead, covered by the Indian blanket. Below us the battle still raged. Amos Pinkney was still alive. And I badly wanted him dead.

There were four lifeless Indians sprawled in front of the cabin where Gentle and Pinkney and the other Texan had done their deadly work.

The remaining Indians had drawn off a fair piece and was keeping up a steady fire on the cabin. But, as far as I could see, they were doing no execution among the foemen.

Then we got a stroke of luck.

I guess the Texan in the storehouse got lonely or something, because he burst through the door, his rifle blazing, and crossed the dog trot to the main cabin.

But Pinkney must have barred the cabin door, because the Texan pounded on it and yelled to be let inside, but the door never opened.

Me and Georgia fired at the same time, and we'll never know whose bullet hit him, but the Texan went down. He crawled back to the cabin door and pounded on it, but Pinkney still refused to open it. Then an Indian on a beautiful spotted pony loped casually past the dog trot and fired at the Texan, and this time he went down for good.

Now we had only two enemies left, Pinkney and Cottontail, but it was going to take a long time to shoot them out of that cabin. That is if our ammunition held out, and the blizzards held off. And me, I wasn't sure of either.

The Indians drew off and had another long talk. Then they arranged themselves into twos, and made another run at the cabin.

This time they made no attempt to shoot their rifles, and I wondered what in hell they was up to now. But I soon got my answer.

Two braves loped toward the body of one of their fallen companions, and, swooping low from the backs of their ponies, grabbed him under the arms and rode on, the dead brave hanging limp between them.

Pinkney's lone rifle fired from the cabin, but he didn't hit anything until the last body was being picked up. I saw an Indian who was closest to the cabin jerk as a bullet smashed into him, but he managed to hold on to his dead compadre until he reached the Chief and the others. Then he fell off'n his pony and died.

I counted the Chief had now lost five warriors out of twenty. He had paid a terrible price to fight in this war, but without him, I reckoned we'd all be dead by now.

There was now a lull in the firing as Pinkney settled in for a long siege. The Chief left his warriors, their dead draped across the backs of their ponies, and rode up the lee side of the hill toward me and the others.

He reined in his pony and said, "It was a good fight, but we're going home now."

"I wish you'd stay, Chief," I said. "This war ain't over yet."

"It is for us," the Chief said. "We will fight no more today."

Well, there's no arguing with an Indian, and the Chief had done so much for us, I figgered it was hardly polite. So I thanked him for what he and his men had done.

The Chief didn't answer right away. He jest sat his pony, studying me. Then he said:

"I had a vision during the time of the great snow. And in this vision, an old warrior of the Nez Perce came and spoke to me. He had been brave, this warrior, and had fought with Joseph against Bearcoat Miles and in the olden days he had counted many coup against the Blackfeet and the Crow and others. He told me to forgive the scrawny little white man for his many offenses, because, he said, that white man was as a child and did not know when offense had been given."

The Chief looked at me thoughtfully. "In my vision he said that he'd given you a blanket and food because you were cold and hungry and a gold coin to pay your way. What do you know of these things?"

I felt trapped. I didn't want to tell the Chief I'd seen the same old man when I was out of my mind with fever. I didn't want to tell him I robbed his dead body either. So I jest shrugged and said, "Charlie Russell, he's an artist feller, he tole me a lot about Injuns like that."

The Chief nodded. "As I expected. This is the way of the white man, to answer a question but not answer it at all."

There was another long pause in what was turning out to be a real strange conversation, then the Chief continued, "That old warrior's name, in your tongue, was He Who Rides Two Horses. You would do well to remember him."

"I will, Chief," I said. "I ain't likely to forget him."

The Chief turned and began to ride away, but I called out after him. "I'm right sorry about your dead warriors," I said. "Me, if I could, I would bring 'em all back again."

"Bring them back?" The Chief reined in his pony. "They died bravely in battle, while me and the others who survived must go on living in your world. Think about that, and tell me who are the lucky ones."

Well, there warn't no answer to that one either that I could see, so I bit my tongue and said nothing.

I watched the Chief ride down to join the others of his band. Then they rode out of the valley and I never saw them again.

"You," said Johnny Blue after the Indians had gone, "sure got a knack for getting up people's noses."

"I sure didn't hear you jumpin' in right quick and helpin' me," I said.

Johnny Blue shrugged. "Like I tole you before, them Indians is mad at the white man, not me."

As I cast around in my mind for a right sharp reply, Doc said, "We only got a couple of hours until dark. If we're gonna make our move, we have to do it soon."

"Short of chargin' right at him, I don't see how we're gonna get Pinkney out of there," I said. "Before dark or any other time."

"Hell, he'd kill us all before we even made it halfway to the cabin," Doc said.

"That's a fact, Doc," I said. "But I don't see no other way."

Whatever our next move was going to be, Pinkney's voice from the cabin put it on hold for the time being.

"You up there on the hill!" he hollered. "I want to talk to you."

Edging up to the crest of the hill, I looked down at the cabin and yelled, "What do you want?"

"I know your redskin friends are gone," Pinkney shouted. "Now maybe we can talk. We found the money in the barn in the buckboard. I'll split it with you, fifty-fifty. Come on down here and we'll discuss things."

"Go to hell!" I hollered.

"This is your last chance, and you won't get another one!" Pinkney yelled.

Raising my rifle to my shoulder, I fired into the cabin.

"There's your answer, Pinkney," I said, only loud enough for the others around me to hear.

A fusillade of bullets from the cabin kicked up snow all around me, and I squirmed back down the hill again.

"Where was we?" I asked Doc.

"You was trying to come up with a plan, and ended up empty-handed as usual," Johnny Blue said.

Doc snapped his fingers.

"Wait," he said, "I just thought of something. Is the cabin chimney still smoking?"

"Sure," I said, "more'n ever. Pinkney must have thrown more logs on the fire. Must be cold in there with all them windows shot out."

"Then I got it. Wait right here."

"Doc, we wasn't plannin' on goin' anywheres," I said.

Hot-footing it to the saddle on Georgia's pony, Doc grabbed the burlap sack and brought it back. He opened the sack and pulled out an earthenware jug.

"What's that?" I asked.

"Coal ile," Doc said. "The secret ingredient in my elixir."

"What's your idea, Doc?"

"We need a stouthearted fellow to climb up on the roof of the cabin and pour this stuff down the chimney," Doc said. "If Pinkney's got a blaze going and this ile hits it, the cabin will go up like a bonfire on the Fourth of July."

I thought about that for a spell, then I said: "Doc, it might jest work. When Pinkney comes out of the cabin, we can pick him off easy."

"Damn right," Doc said.

"Only thing is, we're both a mite slow an' there's a lot of open ground to cover. I'm all shot up and your head's laying to the side. I don't even know if we can climb up on the roof."

"Let me try," Georgia said.

"No, beloved," Doc said. "If you'll forgive me for saying so, my love, you're slower than either of us and you're a bigger target." He reached out his hand and took Georgia's.

"Hell," Johnny Blue said, "give me the jug. I'll do it."

"Are you sure?" I asked. "With your back an' all."

"Me, I'm so weak, I can't find the strength to lick my upper lip, but even so, I got to be in better shape than either of you two," Johnny Blue said. "You didn't tell me you was shot."

"Here," I said, pointing to my shoulder. "An' the bullet came out down here."

"You should be pushing up daises," Johnny Blue said. "Wound like that."

"I almost was," I said.

Johnny Blue stood, swaying a little, and let the Indian blanket drop to his feet.

"You sure you can do this?" I asked.

"Can you?"

"No, I guess not," I said.

"Give me the Colt and the jug," Johnny Blue said. Doc handed them to him. "Now, when I make my run across the roof, start blazing away at the cabin. I want Pinkney's head down so he don't have a chance to run outside and plug me."

Johnny Blue started off along the slope of the hill away from the cabin, planning to come up on it from the storeroom side.

Doc didn't have a gun, but me and Georgia inched our way up to the crest of the hill.

I'd been right about the fire, because a goodly amount of smoke was pouring from the roughstone chimney. That coal oil would cause an almighty blaze once it hit them burning logs.

THIRTY-EIGHT

It seemed Johnny Blue was in no hurry, because a good five minutes passed before we seen him pick his way through the red cedars toward the storeroom side of the cabin.

He reached the storeroom and I watched him as he started to look for a way up.

Holding the jug and Colt in one hand, Johnny Blue began to climb the logs that butted out from the corner of the storeroom. He reached the roof, then, with the Colt in his right hand, he carefully made his way along the snow-covered slope of the roof toward the main cabin.

"Now, Georgia!" I yelled, and we opened up on the cabin. Pinkney's rifle barked back, and once again bullets was kicking up snow all around us.

Johnny Blue was halfway across the roof to the chimney, and me and Georgia kept up a fast rate of fire.

Now Pinkney, he must have guessed something underhand was going on, or he heard Johnny Blue's boots on the roof, I know not which. But the front door of the cabin was suddenly kicked wide open and he ran out, a Winchester in his hands.

Pinkney turned and fired up at Johnny Blue. But he aimed too fast and he missed clean. Johnny Blue fired back, and he missed too.

Pinkney steadied himself to shoot again, but me and Georgia's fire was too much for him, and he scampered back inside.

We watched as Johnny Blue poured the coal oil from the jug down the chimney, and for a while after that nothing happened.

Then a sheet of flame shot across the cabin, followed by another, and smoke started to pour out of the windows.

The door swung open again and Pinkney stood there, holding Cottontail in front of him like a shield. He had a Remington in his right hand.

"Shoot at me and you'll kill the woman!" Pinkney hollered.

Me and Doc and Georgia, we stood up and started to walk down the hill, our rifles at the ready.

"Stay right there," Pinkney snarled. "No closer."

Smoke was billowing out of the doorway and Pinkney was forced to move away from it. He knew Johnny Blue was still on the roof, behind a cloud of smoke pouring from the chimney. He turned and fired into the smoke, fast as a striking rattler and Johnny Blue went down, a sudden splash of blood spurting from his right thigh.

I raised up my rifle, but couldn't get a clear shot at Pinkney. Treacherous as she was, I didn't want to kill Cottontail if'n I could avoid it.

"Now you, you sorry cow-nursing son-of-a-bitch!" Pinkney screamed at me. He brought his Remington to eye level to fire, but Johnny Blue shot first from the roof. The .45 bullet hit Pinkney's revolver, smashing it out of his hand, taking two of his fingers with it.

Pinkney screamed, holding up his bloody, mangled hand with its stumps of fingers and Cottontail spun away from him and ran toward Georgia.

That kindhearted soul opened her arms and took Cottontail to her bosom, patting her back while the little blonde sobbed on her shoulder.

Me, I taken my Winchester and walked toward Pinkney, who was looking at me with eyes filled with hate. "Yeah," he said, "go ahead and kill me. Get it over with, you drover scum."

My hands was shaking and my whole body trembled with anger. I wanted to smash this man, pump round after round into him, and after he was dead, kill him again.

There was an urge to murder in me so strong, my belly felt like it was on fire, a sick, burning flame that rapidly spread through my entire body, making me all a-fever like I had some kind of loathsome disease.

Later they told me I was screaming nonsense words like a rabid wild animal, making no sense. They was right. At that moment I guess I was completely insane with hate.

It was Johnny Blue who saved me.

"No!" he yelled. "Let him be!" He slid down off the roof and landed hard, groaning as his wounded leg buckled under him. From the ground, he looked up at me and hollered: "If you kill him, you'll be as bad as him. And that's what he wants. He wants to infect you with his own evil."

And right at that moment, as Pinkney cursed at me,

his face was twisted into an ugly mask and it did look like the devil was standing there in human form.

"Don't kill him!" Johnny Blue screamed.

Me, I stood there looking at Pinkney's contorted face through the sights of my Winchester. My finger tightened on the trigger, and despite the cold, I felt beads of sweat pop out on my forehead.

"Sam'l," Johnny Blue whispered, "don't kill him."

Pinkney and me stood there frozen like two statues for what seemed an eternity. Then I taken my rifle down from my shoulder and I throwed it far away from me. I felt sick, defeated, beaten.

"You scum, all of you!" Pinkney screamed. "I'm not done. I'll be back, you'll see. The South shall rise again and I will lead it to glory."

"You're not the South," Doc said mildly. "And you never were the South. You're just some of the dregs like Frank and Jesse and Bloody Bill and others who used her for their own ends. The real Confederates knew that when the South was beat, they were beat, and they went home. You were never man enough to realize that."

"Liar!" Pinkney screamed. "Liar! I'll be back. I'll meet up with Frank and we'll march on Washington to glory." Suddenly an insane, crafty look stole across his face and he glanced behind him at the burning cabin. "I just realized that you can't kill me. None of you can kill me." He laughed, a mad cackle that chilled me to the bone. Slowly he backed up toward the blazing cabin, pointing a finger at me as he went. "Look, scum, even fire can't touch me." He was still backing toward the cabin, then he stopped and opened his mouth again.

Boys, we'll never know what else Amos Pinkney was gonna say to me, because suddenly a tongue of flame leaped from the cabin and licked the back of his shirt, and a second later his whole upper body was ablaze.

I reckon he must have been right close to that fire when the coal oil hit and it must have drenched his shirt, because he went up as fast as the snap of a bull-whip.

Then he started to scream.

Pinkney shrieked as the fire consumed him. His hair was on fire and I could see the skin of his face blacken and bubble like hot tar. As the fire nourished itself on the fat of his body, Pink's skin turned blacker and blacker until all I could see was the white of his teeth and his staring eyes.

"Look at his eyes!" Doc yelled. "His eyes aren't burning."

Pinkney's shrieks grew louder, shrill and piercing. The man was in mortal agony, but he didn't run. He stood as though rooted to the ground, screaming.

I heard somebody calling my name, but I was so intent on watching Amos Pinkney burn, I didn't turn round. Then Cottontail was standing in front of me, beating me with her fists. "Kill him!" she screamed. "Kill him!"

It took me a while to realize what she was saying. Then, like a man coming out of a trance I looked at her and said: "What? What do you want?"

"Shoot him!" Cottontail yelled. "Put him out of his misery."

Pinkney was still shrieking, though now his legs had buckled and he was on his knees.

"Please," Cottontail pleaded. "Please kill him."

Later I couldn't recall much of what happened in the next few seconds. But Johnny Blue told me that I picked up my rifle and I fired a bullet into Pinkney's head, and suddenly the screaming stopped. I fired again, and again until I'd emptied the rifle into him.

His body didn't fall. It just stayed there on its knees, charred black, blacker than any field slave Pink and his kind had ever owned and mistreated.

The fire was rapidly burning up the cabin, and I tore my eyes from Pinkney and said to Doc: "Let's get all we can out of the storeroom before it burns down."

Pinkney had not stinted on provisions for himself, and as Doc began to carry out sacks of flour and beans and a side or two of bacon, I checked on Johnny Blue.

The bullet had burned across the inside of his leg without hitting bone. He'd be stiff and sore for a spell and a mite uncomfortable in the saddle, but he was in good shape for a man who'd suffered as much as he had.

Helping Johnny Blue to his feet, I got him away from the burning cabin. "That was some shootin', cowboy," I said. "Was you meanin' to kill him?"

Johnny Blue shook his head at me. "I didn't want to kill him. I tole you that."

"Still, you shot the revolver out of his hand. That's impressive shootin' with a Colt's gun. I never took you fer a puncher who could do that."

"He was gonna kill you," Johnny Blue said. "Now, there are them as might say that would be no great loss, but you're the only partner I got. I had to do some serious shooting, and when I shoot serious, I generally hit what I'm aiming at."

"I'm glad you did, Johnny Blue," I said. "I reckon you saved my life."

That reckless rider only shrugged. "Hell, I would've done it for anybody."

Doc came running toward us, yoo-hooing. He was waving a shirt in one hand, carrying what looked like a pile of sheepskin coats in the other.

"Lookee what I found," Doc said. He passed the shirt and a coat to Johnny Blue and handed one of the sheepskins to me.

"You boys are gonna be better dressed than you ever was in your entire life," he said. "Found these in the storeroom an' they're brand new."

Me and Johnny Blue, we didn't need no urging. I threw off my ragged mackinaw and put on that warm coat, and it felt good.

"You look a lot better now you're dressed an' all," I told Johnny Blue. "Guess we look prosperous like we used to look when we was ridin' for the ol' DHS."

"A hunnerd years ago, seems like," Johnny Blue said.

Well, boys, after that we got the buckboard from the barn and the money from the Alpine bank was in it right enough. We hitched up the four-horse team, then we took the thoroughbred horses from the corral.

Then we set the barn afire and burned everything we couldn't carry. The cabin and storeroom burned to the ground, and we left the dead where they lay.

"Bet our hunnerd and thirty-five dollars was in there," Johnny Blue said, as the fire raged through the cabin.

"We got blooded horses to sell," I said. "An' I reckon we'll get us a ree-ward for returning the Alpine bank's money to the sheriff in Helena. Seems to me, Blue boy, we gonna be in clover all winter long."

"Unless something comes along and screws us up, like it always do," Johnny Blue said morosely.

Boys, that Johnny Blue, he could be surly by times. And a heap pessimistic when he wanted to be, which was mostly.

When it come to leave, we still had a good hour of daylight left, and Doc, he said we should get as far from the valley in that time as we could.

A light snow was falling as Doc and Georgia climbed into the driver's seat of the buckboard with Cottontail, while Amos Pinkney's body still kneeled in front of his burned cabin, almost like he was in prayer.

Georgia, she never said a word about her pa. I guess the hurt inside her went too deep for that. Or maybe she just realized she was free of him at last. Either way, she turned her back on him and she never looked at where he was.

And me and Johnny Blue, we jest sat our ponies, studying this man who'd been our deadliest enemy.

Johnny Blue shook his head. "That Pinkney was a mad dog," he said. "He wasn't worth a bullet." He glanced up at the muddy sky, heavy with massive, iron gray clouds, and he shivered. "Blizzard coming up. I can smell it plain."

We turned our ponies and rode after the departing buckboard.

When we caught up, Cottontail was looking behind her at Pinkney's body. "Stop the wagon," she yelled.

"Whaa—?" Doc began.

"I said stop the wagon!"

Doc pulled the wagon to a halt, and Cottontail jumped down off the seat. "I'm going to him," she said. "He needs to be buried decent."

"Don't be a fool," Georgia told her. "You never meant anything to him, and besides, the ground's hard as iron. They'll be no burying here until spring.

"Cottontail, listen to me, honey," Georgia went on. "You've got a bright future ahead of you in the whoring business, maybe even a sporting house of your own one day. You don't have to concern yourself with the likes of Amos Pinkney anymore. He wasn't worth it when he was alive, and he sure as hell ain't worth it now."

Cottontail looked very young and very vulnerable as she climbed back into her seat, settled her shawl around her shoulders and said: "I guess you're right, Georgia. It's over, isn't it?"

Georgia nodded. "It's over, honey. All of it."

Doc clucked the team into motion and the wagon rolled forward.

None of us looked back.

THIRTY-NINE

The blizzard hit later that night. But this time we were well-clothed and we'd plenty of Arbuckle and bacon and beans. We rode it out in good shape camped at the base of a sheltered bluff that curved out of the hillside among the timber.

This time, the whiteout only lasted for the whole of the next day, and we were on the trail again at dawn the day after.

"We have a melancholy task ahead of us," Doc said. "One I wish I did not have to perform."

"You mean buryin' the Mauler?" I asked.

"What else, dear boy?"

"I think maybe he survived," Georgia said. "He's big and strong and he's full of life."

"Not after two blizzards, and him with a belly wound, Georgia," I said. "I don't mean to sound the pessimist, but there ain't no man alive that strong."

Later we picked up the spare horse from Doc's team. He looked to be on his last legs, but we'd brung corn from Pinkney's barn, and after a bucketful of that, he perked up jest fine.

The wagon was so snowed in, there was no saving it. Me, as I stood there looking at its scarred wooden sides and holed canvas, I had the odd fancy that some day, maybe a hunnerd or so years from now, a writer feller would pass this way and see the rotten bones of that wagon and wonder at it, and maybe spin a yarn around it. I sure hope he gets everything right, and sets it down jest the way it all happened.

We had one more stop to make before we reached the Mauler's body.

I taken the red trade blanket and the gold coin and some bacon and beans and I climbed the hill to where the dead Indian lay.

He was covered in snow, and when I brushed it off, he was still on his side, his eyes open. My wounds continued to bother me, and I was real weak, but I managed to lay him on his back and then I spread the blanket tight and snug around him.

Then I gave him the bacon and beans and the gold coin, and then I walked down the hill again.

Later, as we drew close to the clearing where we had fought our great battle, Doc began to sob. His head was still cocked to the side, so his tears wet his shoulder.

"He wouldn't have felt any pain, Doc," I said. "A man freezing to death don't feel the cold after a spell."

"God bless him," Georgia said. "God bless his great heart. Bartholomew was a pugilist to remember."

But when we pulled into the clearing, we saw a tall, stalwart figure standing over a small, smoky fire. Behind him there was a lean-to shelter built against a sturdy tree that looked snug and strong enough to protect a man from the elements.

It was the Mauler. And when he seen us, he raised his hand and gave out with a hearty "Huzzah!"

Doc stopped the wagon and run to him, throwing his arms around the huge man. "You're alive, Bartholomew!" he yelled. "Oh happy, happy day!"

Later, the Mauler told us the sheltering trees in the cut had saved him from the worst of the storm, and that after he built his shelter he'd even been able to keep a fire going most of the time. As for his belly wound, it had began to heal after the bleeding stopped, and even though the bullet was still inside him, it had been stopped by his thick belly fat and it didn't seem to be troubling him none.

We got the fire going brighter and boiled up some Arbuckle and fried some bacon. The Mauler ate heartily and he seemed to be well on the mend. Cottontail sat close to him as we sat around the fire, and they gazed into each other's eyes and shared strips of bacon with each other.

Georgia smiled and whispered into Doc's ear, loud enough for all of us to hear: "Doc, I think the Mauler is falling in love."

The Mauler, he just smiled kinda shy an' all, and from somewhere Cottontail even managed to summon up a blush. It seemed to me that she was all through grieving for Pinkney and had pretty quick found her another man.

"I shot me some jackrabbit," the Mauler said by way of explaining how come he was alive instead of dead. "I got me four of them to be exact, an' I kept the last bullet in the Colt for myself, just as Johnny Blue said."

"Them was words of wisdom," Johnny Blue allowed, nodding. "You did the right thing."

Doc cleared his throat and said, "Boys, I have an announcement to make."

"Announce away, Doc," quoth Johnny Blue through the steam of his cup. "But first, tell me why you haven't straightened up your head. It's been puzzling me some."

"Alas," Doc replied. "I find that no matter how I try, it won't straighten. Which is no never mind. I've took to liking it cocked over this way."

"Suit yourself," Johnny Blue said.

"Now, back to the pressing matter at hand," Doc began. "Georgia Morgan, *Miss* Georgia Morgan I say, has graciously consented to be my wife."

Me and Johnny Blue, the Mauler and Cottontail broke into hearty Huzzahs! but Doc held up his hand for quiet. "Thank you, thank you one and all," he said. "But there is more. Miss Georgia, soon to be Missus Fortune"—here he paused as we cheered again— "has also graciously consented to give up the whoring business and to devote her life to my very own enterprise, in short, the purveying of Doctor Fortune's Elixir of Life."

We let out with further Huzzahs, but again Doc held up his hand.

"Wait, there is but one item more. We have also decided to adopt Bartholomew, sometimes known as The Boston Mauler, as our only son and heir."

This drew the loudest cheers of all, and before all our Huzzahs was spent, my voice was hoarse.

"Look at us, dear friends," Doc said at last, "there was but five of us, all homely as a bunch of buck-toothed buzzards, yet, I say we were fit to stand beside the great Henry, the Fifth of that name, on the plashy field of Agincourt and hear him call us 'we few, we happy few, we band of brothers.' We have met an overwhelming enemy, like those gallant English knights of yore, and defeated him in open battle. And we have survived to tell the tale. In short—I'm glad we made it with our hides more or less intact."

Boys, that was a truly great speech, and after it was over, our Huzzahs began anew. Then we cheered even louder when Johnny Blue, that sentimental rider, leaned over to Doc and Georgia and said, "I want to give this happy couple their first wedding present. I jest want you both to know that I don't plan to plug your son-to-be anymore. At least, not in the foreseeable future."

Thus it seemed to all that our happiness was complete as we loaded the Mauler into the buckboard the next morning, Cottontail by his side, and took to the trail again.

The snow was falling as we rode and the chill penetrated even the stout sheepskin of our coats.

"Winter's taking off hard," Johnny Blue said.

"Seems like," I said. "But I got a feelin' we're gonna be fine. We'll fatten up some then find us a holler log somewheres an' jest crawl inside and stay there till the sun shines."

"I dunno," Johnny Blue said. "Look at me. What do you see?"

"Well," I replied, "like Doc said, for starters you're downright homely."

"I mean, do I seem different to you?"

Me, I knew what he was driving at, and I said, "I don't see no scars on you, if'n that's what you mean."

"But you and me," Johnny Blue said. "Are we still the same as we was, I mean way back when, before all this began?"

"I reckon we're still the same as we was, right enough. Jest two poor cowboys, tryin' to survive the winter."

Johnny Blue thought this over for a spell, then he said: "Scars heal, don't they? I mean them on the inside as well as the out."

"If a man will let them," I said. "They'll heal."

"You reckon?"

"I reckon."

We rode in silence for a while, then I said, "Talkin' about survivin' and healin' an' all, I got me a great plan."

Johnny Blue sighed, and taken out his tally book and pencil that we'd got back from Jericho Gentle's body.

"What's that fer?" I asked.

"Go ahead and talk," Johnny Blue said. "While you're yackin' about that plan of your'n, I'll write down some more of your faults."

"This can't fail," I said. "Do you recollect that feller Bill Cody that came around the DHS one time lookin' for riders an' ropers for his Wild West Show?"

"I recollect him," Johnny Blue said. "Says he's looking for riders and ropers, and all the time he couldn't tell a steer's beller from its butt."

"Well anyhow, when we was ridin' the grub line, I heard tell that ol' Billy winters a spell in Virginia City."

"So?"

"So, we get us a job from him in his show. See, then we kin travel all over lookin' for our little sister at ol' Bill's expense. It's a natural plan."

"The hell it is," Johnny Blue said.

"Once Bill hears we beat Amos Pinkney and his gang, and fought wild Injuns, he'll make us big stars like Annie Oakley an' Buck Taylor an' Sittin' Bull an' them."

"We never fought no Injuns. As I recollect, the Injuns fit for us."

"Well, all ol' Bill has to say is somethin' like, 'Here's the punchers who beat Amos Pinkney an' almost fought wild Injuns.'"

"You're crazy," Johnny Blue said. "I ain't gonna be a freak in a circus show."

It was my turn to sigh. "Well, let's change the subject for the time bein'. How many of my faults have you wrote down?"

"Still got jest the one," Johnny Blue said. "Stupid. Trouble is, it seems to cover all the rest."

"Well, keep tryin'," I said. "I'm sure you'll come up with somethin'."

"Reckon I will," Johnny Blue said.

"Now, back to what I were sayin' about Bill Cody an' his Wild West Show . . ." I said.

I knew it was gonna take a lot of convincing to get Johnny Blue into that circus show.

But I'd talk him into it.

Hell, I always do.

HISTORICAL NOTE

M any of the events and characters in this book are real.

It should be noted, however, that Granville Stuart paid off the DHS hands in the spring of 1887, not the fall.

Charles M. Russell headed into Canada to live with the Blackfeet and their close kin, the Bloods, in the spring of 1888, not the fall of '87 as I have stated in the book.

There is also some confusion about when the Great Falls silver smelter became operational. I have gone with the more popular opinion that it was still under construction in the fall of 1887.

I have not gone into detail about the fate of the Nez Perce Indians. But by the year 1887, their way of life, like the cowboys', was rapidly passing into history.

Miss Georgia Morgan's run-in with Mysterious Dave Mather is documented in the Fort Worth Democrat-Advance of January 27, 1882.

Frank Canton, real name Joe Horner, was born in Texas in 1849, and by age twenty-six he was wanted for bank robbery, rustling, and assault with intent to kill. He murdered a black cavalry trooper in 1874, later surfacing under his new identity in Wyoming as the sheriff of Johnson County. Canton was top gun in the Johnson County War of 1892, and in 1907, was appointed adjutant general of the Oklahoma National Guard.

The heyday of the cowboy began with the Texas trail drives of 1866, and ended twenty years later with the terrible winter of 1886–1887. Of the 30,000 cowboys who rode the trails north during that twenty years, at least one-fifth were African American. Many of them lie in unmarked graves alongside their white compadres on the Goodnight-Loving, Western, Chisholm, Sedalia, Shawnee, Platchers, and Nelson Story trails.